THE CRYING PLACE

DREW DUNMOORE

THE CRYING PLACE

Previously published mystery
titles by Drew Dunmoore:

RENT TO KILL
A HARBOR OF RESENTMENT

Previously published dark fairy tale novella
title by Drew Dunmoore:

THE GLASS-STAINED PATH

Author's Note

While there is a state called California, there is no city in California named Sunshine Beach. There is also no retirement home in California called Shady Sunset, another liberty taken. Shady Sunset is a fictitious place where seniors reside, friendships are made, activities are held, and a murder is solved.

To my dad, who taught me the hand is quicker than the eye. He loved bathroom humor, too… so this one is for him.

This book is also dedicated to all the "Violets" who feel they lost a loved one too soon. There is a light at the end of the tunnel…

Chapter One

The End of the Line

May 14, 2019

Germ coated turnstiles rotated around and around, admitting the park's eager guests. Droves of people from all over the state, country, and world arrived at the same place with the same idea; to have one of the greatest days of their lives. But Maybel Morgan wasn't in a happy place, for she missed her son Jeffrey.

"Another line?!" Maybel asked her former neighbor and much younger friend Celeste Ravenna.

Standing behind dozens of people, Celeste replied, "If you don't like lines, this is going to be a very long day." She watched a fussy toddler's goldfish crackers cascade onto the brick covered ground.

"I'm just saying we already stood in a line to be searched, and they took away my tweezers! Then we stood in a line to ride a golf cart over here, and now we are in another line again to get in!" Maybel's silver hair shined like tinsel hanging from a Christmas tree.

Celeste shook her head. "It wasn't a golf cart, it was… never mind."

"Don't any of these people have jobs they need to be at? And what about all these kids? Don't they need to be in school? You know what else? In my day, they let us park right in front of this place," Maybel explained, pointing behind her.

"It's still your day, especially today since it's your 80th birthday. Should we get you a balloon?" Celeste offered, her dark eyes glistening in the golden hour of California sunshine. Her smile made her eyes look like warm, melted chocolate.

"Then I'd have to carry it around all day like an idiot."

"I'll take that as a no. We'll start having fun once we get inside. I think it is nice Jeffrey wanted to bring you here for your birthday."

"Except that Jeffrey isn't even here yet! It was his idea to come here for my birthday, and I'm standing here all alone without him on my 80th birthday."

"It's not Jeff's fault he had to work overtime. I'm sure he'll be able to leave the firehouse soon, and I'm here with you. Brian had to work overtime on a case late last night, but he said he thinks he can get here around noon," Celeste said, referring to Detective Brian Bahn (pronounced BANE), a man she had been dating after meeting him months earlier when he worked on a case at the condo complex she and Maybel lived in.

Entering the amusement park transported them into another world. A train's whistle blowing signaled its arrival at the station. A park worker standing at the steps to the station dressed in a conductor's outfit tipped his hat to them and said, "You ladies look like you need a train ride!"

Shaking her head, Maybel replied, "Maybe later. We want to explore the park first."

An announcement to walk and not run to your next destination ended and ragtime music tickled the airwaves. Colorful window displays lined the Americana themed street leading into the park. Parents with maps in hand and excited children in tow scattered and scurried all over. Celeste overheard a little boy pleading with his mother. "Mommy, I want to get the genie's sword today!" To which his mother replied, "I'm not buying you a sword. Every time you have a sword in your hand, you hurt your little brother with it." The hope crushing denial rolled away when they hopped aboard the train. Choo Choo!

Another frustrated parent untangled her two fighting children, shouting, "I'll spank both of you if you don't stop!"

Turning to Maybel, who was like a mother to Celeste, she asked, "What shall we do first?"

"How about we get a cup of coffee?"

Walking to the breakfast bakery inside the amusement park revealed a line circling around the building. They skipped their caffeine boost.

"Well, let's see… if we go to the right, we can ride the space rollercoaster," Celeste said.

"I don't follow all those spaceship battles. Jeffrey does. Let's wait until he gets here to go on that one. Brian would probably like that ride, too."

"Good idea. OK, if we walk across the drawbridge there is a merry-go-round on the other side. We could do that," Celeste suggested, hearing the screams of ride goers. Looking up revealed the peak of a snowcapped alp. The thunderous sound of wheels speeding along the metal rollercoaster tracks rang out through the park.

"Oh, that brings back memories! The last time I was here, Jeffrey was a boy. George and I took him on it. But now neither one of them is here with me," Maybel said, reminiscing about her late husband, George. "Let's go on the elephant ride instead."

While walking along, the warm sun kissed their skin, and dewdrops glistened on blooming spring flowers. Furry theme park characters danced around for the children's delight. Iridescent soapy bubbles sprayed out of bubble guns, gently floating through the crowd. Mobile carts popped corn, and park attendants scooped the buttery snack into corrugated boxes.

Later, a bouquet of bromine and cinnamon swirled around the salty pretzel scented air, and Maybel's stomach growled at her. After a few hours of an alternating pattern of waiting in a line, going on an attraction, waiting in line, going on an attraction, waiting in a line, and going on an attraction, Maybel told Celeste, "I'm hungry as a bear."

"Since it's your 80th birthday, let me buy you lunch," Celeste offered. They headed towards an outdoor cafe, ordering mushroom Swiss burgers.

Sitting in a shaded area by a greenish colored river, Maybel nibbled at her burger, setting it down seconds later. She tore open a packet of salt and the grains flew out uncontrollably all over her side dish. "This is the rubberiest cheese I've ever had. These mushrooms taste like dirty gummy bears, and tater tots are supposed to be crispy on the outside and soft on the inside. These are mushy and over salted. I can't believe they charged you $20 for a burger!"

"Not everyone is as good of a cook as you are," Celeste said, smiling. She agreed the burger tasted subpar, but the ambiance at the restaurant compensated for it. The breeze blowing through her long raven colored hair calmed her. Feeling happy not to be at work, she didn't care what the lunch cost.

"That's true, but I don't cook much anymore these days. Now that I live at Shady Sunset Retirement Home, I usually eat in the main dining room so I can socialize with the other residents," Maybel explained.

At a table next to them, a mother tried convincing her son to eat his lunch. "No, you can't have another churro. You need to eat something healthy." Her child shook his head while his father slathered sunscreen on their chubby cheeked fussy baby girl.

"How is the food there?" Celeste wondered.

"A little better than this," Maybel said, tossing a tater tot back onto her plate. "Once in a while I will order groceries to be delivered, and I do a little cooking in my kitchenette, but not very often. I will admit it's nice not to have to cook all the time and wash dishes. It allows me to spend more time making friends and doing crafts and other activities they have there for us. Next week we're supposed to bring a prized possession and talk about it, so it's like an adult show and tell."

Giggling, Celeste replied, "You might want to rephrase that."

"I'm really trying to fit in because I want this place to feel like home, but so far, it's been difficult for me. Since I've moved out of Regal Palms, being at Shady Sunset has been so lonely."

"I know it's been a tough transition for you, Maybel."

"Jeffrey gave me a cat to help keep me company. The staff encourages us to have pets."

"Oh, that's wonderful! You didn't mention you'd gotten a cat. Boy or girl? What did you name it?"

Maybel smiled and said, "A boy… he's a domestic shorthair and mostly white with green eyes, but he has a black patch over his right eye and three black paws. I guess I could have named him Pirate, but I settled on Mr. Piddles after he peed all over my kitchen floor. He's quite a curious, clever little kitty. The other day I found him in my kitchen cupboard, and he clawed into a box of Cheez-Its."

"I hope you two will be very happy together."

"He loves to cuddle when he's not trying to shred my curtains, that is. Jeffrey bought a cat tree with a scratching post for him, and he seems to really like that. I'm still trying to get used to him shedding all over my bedspread, but other than that, Mr. Piddles brings me a lot of joy. Jeffrey even got some of that kitty litter that changes color if they have any health issues. How do you like living in your new place?"

"I love my new loft. I feel so much more at peace there than I did at Regal Palms… but I miss my old neighbors," Celeste said, winking.

"Me too, dear. Me too." Maybel pointed to a salad sitting next to Celeste's plate. "Who is that for?"

"Brian. He texted me about an hour ago and said he's on his way. I ordered him a salad so I wouldn't have to worry about his food getting cold."

"That explains the mystery of the phantom entrée, and speaking of phantoms, did I tell you that some folks living at Shady Sunset think it's haunted?"

Celeste shook her head. Since they were no longer neighbors, they didn't talk as much as they used to. "Why on earth would they think the place is haunted? It's so swanky."

"I'm not entirely sure. Vera said she hears strange noises at night, and Sylvia said her lights flicker sometimes, but you know the only ghost I believe in is the Holy Ghost."

"So, you're not afraid of things that go bump in the night? Does anyone else think it's haunted?"

"Arnie said he saw a strange burst of fog over by the cemetery one night. I told Jeffrey I didn't think it was a good idea to put me in a retirement home right next to a graveyard. The only good thing about being next to it is it would make it easy for me to visit George's grave and take him flowers… which I still haven't done. I just can't seem to muster up the strength."

Celeste frowned. "A strange burst of fog? What could that have been?"

"Fog! Arnie just likes to group text all of us at the retirement home and get everyone riled up. Once he does that, my phone goes off all night! Everyone has to chime in." Maybel sipped her tart lemonade.

"Any other strange goings on?" Celeste leaned in, elbows on the table.

"Violet said one of her necklaces went missing, but she probably just misplaced it, or maybe Vick stole it!"

"You don't really think Vick stole her necklace, do you?"

Maybel ate another mushy tater tot. "No, but he's still just such a jerk and even after I got him the job as the security guard at Shady Sunset. I didn't even mention his injuries to Colleen, the retirement home administrator. You know Vick's man parts got crushed when he had that accident last year."

"I'm not sure that rumor is true. You two have always had such a rivalry going on. I know Vick can be kind of gross with women, but I would have thought now that you don't live at Regal Palms, you two could get along better."

"Dear, this goes further back than Vick. His father Arnie stole the Regal Palms HOA presidency from me! I won the election fair and square. I made sure he couldn't steal the election away from me, but after I got in the office, he did something horrible and blamed it on me. The board believed him and asked *me* to step down!"

"Wait–is Vick's dad Arnie, the same as the group texter Arnie at Shady Sunset who saw the mysterious fog?"

"One and the same." Maybel flung the rest of her tater tots in the trash can next to them.

"But Vick's last name is Arnold," Celeste said, frowning.

"Arnie Arnold. His full name is Arnold Randolph Arnold. I think his parents knew he would be a moron, and they named him accordingly. He's a bigger buffoon than Vick. They're a family of idiots!" Maybel wiped her hands on a napkin and continued, "He moved into Shady Sunset right after I did. I think he did it just to spite me! And now I have to see him and Vick *all* the time."

"Oh boy. Perhaps Arnie moved in because he's retired now and Shady Sunset is one of the highest rated, most exclusive retirement homes in Sunshine Beach, California."

"Well, I'm not so sure that Shady Sunset is exclusive and hard to get into. Apparently, they'll let anyone in because they let Arnie in! And these retirement apartments are supposed to be luxury apartments, but the place has an old creaky staircase in the lobby… and from the outside, Shady Sunset looks like a haunted house," Maybel said.

"I thought you said you don't believe in ghosts."

"I don't, but it still looks like one! I think it's because of the large columns in front, and it's an old building. You saw it for yourself this morning when you picked me up. They converted the old mansion with dozens of bedrooms into one-bedroom apartments, each with a small living room and kitchenette. They installed an elevator for residents that have a hard time with stairs. Most folks use the elevator, but I like to get my exercise, so I use the stairs. There's a beautiful garden area in the back, and they built a dancehall and some additional apartments next to the garden area. Speaking of the dancehall, we're having a talent show soon. I can get tickets for you and Brian."

"That sounds fun. By the way, what did Arnie do years ago that he blamed on you?"

Maybel shook her head. "I can't talk about it, dear. It's too embarrassing. But he never admitted to what he really did. He just told some cock and bull story about me not being fit for the presidency!"

Just then, off duty, Detective Brian Bahn burst through a crowd of hungry park guests walking around the cafe with their trays full of food. From behind his gold-rimmed aviator sunglasses, he scanned the outdoor seating area, looking for Celeste and Maybel. Spotting them, he zigzagged, circumventing all the people, and landed at their table.

"There's the birthday girl! Happy birthday!" He held out his arms, widening his broad shoulders further.

Maybel stood and hugged him. "Thank you, Brian. Please sit down and eat the salad Celeste bought for you." She pointed to the measly sized pile of leafy greens inside a plastic container.

He sat down next to Celeste and kissed her cheek, grumbling in her ear, "*I asked you to get me a corndog!*"

"Your doctor said no fried food for a while because of your high cholesterol," she reminded him.

He popped open the tiny container and poured sour dressing over it. Stabbing at the rabbit food with a two-pronged plastic fork sent a piece of celery flying onto the table. He shoved lettuce and carrots into his disappointed mouth.

"Your fork is going to break if you keep jabbing with it like that," Celeste warned.

He sighed. "I should be so lucky."

Maybel's cellphone binged, and after reading a text, she reported, "Oh good, Jeffrey is leaving the firehouse now, and he's on his way!" Maybel looked around at the scenery, smiling. "Look how pretty that river view is!"

"On my way to this cafe, I passed some canoes. We could do that while we wait for Jeff to get here," Brian suggested.

Maybel laughed. "Great, just what I wanted—to row my own boat on my 80th birthday!"

"I'm sure it won't be that bad." Celeste picked up a piece of carrot from the table and threw it away.

Standing in line, Celeste pointed to the ducks on the dock. They napped with their heads nestled into their feathers.

"Oh, how charming! I've always loved mallards," Maybel cooed.

With paddles in hand, they carefully boarded the canoe decorated with a cheery sun on the side of it. The guide shouted out rehearsed instructions. Sailing down the river, the guide continually called out to everyone to keep paddling. About three minutes in, the muscles in Maybel's arm burned, and she stopped paddling. Another minute after that, Celeste's arm got tired. She stopped paddling, resting her oar idle across the gunwale. She watched Brian's back muscles through his tight t-shirt move in tandem with the powerful strokes of his paddle. Paddling so vigorously, he splashed water on Celeste, sitting behind him. The guide, Brian, and a few others kept the canoe sailing along.

After docking, Brian turned to Celeste. "I noticed you stopped paddling halfway through. I paddled the whole time. You know why I paddled the whole time?"

"Because you follow orders well?" She slid her paddle back into the basket on the dock.

Brian flexed his muscles. "Because I'm a man! We don't give up! I'm like a mighty Viking, and I got us where we needed to go."

Celeste tugged on her wet jeans to pull them away from her cold skin, wondering how much bacteria floated around in that green water. "That's ridiculous. We would have gotten back. I think the canoe is on a track."

Brian laughed and tugged on her ponytail. "It's not on a track! You and Maybel would have been dead in the water without me. I'm an expert canoer!"

Celeste frowned. "You have a piece of lettuce in your teeth, and why do you have to argue about everything I say?"

"I'm not arguing. I'm simply right."

Celeste shook her head and wiped water off her neck and arm. She looked up at the devastatingly handsome man standing in front of her. The sun shined behind Brian's head, and he grinned at her. His smile made her heart beat faster. She breathed in the moment. "I think we should go towards the space ride and meet Jeff there. Maybel said it's his favorite."

While waiting for Jeffrey to arrive, Brian suggested they watch a bird show, but as soon as the show started, he excused himself to go to the bathroom.

"I'll have one corndog please," Brian said to the lady behind the cart. With gusto, he dug into the girthy corn-meal coated dog slathered in condiments, biting the crunchy tip off. *Oh, the mustard!*

He slipped back in under the parrot's wing just in time to hear a tropical tune.

Jeffrey's arrival brought them lots of rides on the faster rollercoasters. "How is single life treating you?" Brian asked while they waited in line.

Jeff's face saddened a bit at the thought of his ex-wife, who was currently in prison. "It's not too bad. I'm dating someone new, but it's not serious yet."

"I guess that's why I haven't met her yet," Maybel huffed.

"I know you get a little dizzy, mom, but this ride is great!" He fastened his seatbelt, blasting off seconds later and his smile shining brighter than the stars.

After going on several more rides and walking more miles, an alfresco dinner topped off their night. "They have a pasta dish with grilled chicken and vegetables," Celeste suggested to Brian moments before Brian ordered a fried chicken platter for himself.

After dinner, Jeffrey took his mom on the merry-go-round, while Brian took Celeste on a moonlit train ride around the park. As the cool May evening went on, a breeze blew through her hair, and when Brian noticed she shivered, he took off his coat, wrapping it around her shoulders. Feeling enamored by the scent of his aftershave on it, she reached for his hand. He held her tiny palm in his. With her head resting on his shoulder, the train chugged along, the motion soothing her and the wind whistling in her ear. He nuzzled her neck, sending another shiver down her spine. Thinking about inviting him back to her place that evening, she heard his phone bing. He let go of her hand to read a text. "I'm going to need to leave as soon as the train pulls into the station,"

"Really? Why?"

"Duty calls." Looking at the saddened expression on her pretty face, he informed her, "I've seen that look before on both of my ex-wives' faces."

"Talk about killing a mood," she said, handing him back his jacket and crossing her arms over her chest.

"I'm sorry, Celeste," he said, putting on his jacket. "There was a possible homicide at Tube Solutions."

"Tube Solutions? The Oil Country Tubular Goods company in Sunshine Beach? Isn't that where that big protest was the other day?"

Brian nodded. "That's the one."

"Who died?"

"All I know so far is there was a minor explosion at the manufacturing plant."

Celeste frowned. "It can't be too minor if someone died. Why do you think it was a murder?"

"Because the person who died in the explosion was one of the protestors. He was the head of that environmental organization called Save Our Planet."

"Michael Turnblast from SOP is dead?" Celeste's face showed her shock. The train pulled into the station, and they stood up.

Brian nodded. "I need to get over there. You know him?"

Departing the train, Celeste said, "I've seen him on the news, and I read a lot about him. His organization recently took a very strong stance against the OCTG companies. They're really against anything involved with oil and gas production."

"That's why this is so suspicious," Brian said, kissing Celeste goodbye.

Maybel, Jeffrey and Celeste stayed to watch a spectacular fireworks show. While popping explosives boomed overhead, flying fairies dazzled the crowd below.

"Mom, I want to buy you something. Pick something out for yourself," Jeffrey offered while they shopped around on the main street of the park.

"My feet are killing me!" Maybel whimpered, hobbling to Celeste's car with a stuffed animal in her hand.

"Well, you only turn 80 once." Celeste smiled as sweet as the confections they bought in the candy shop.

"Thank God for that! Now take me back to my haunted house, and not the one in the park."

A short time later, Celeste pulled into the driveway of Shady Sunset Retirement Home. She had to admit Shady Sunset looked like a haunted mansion. Painted white with immense columns in front, a well-manicured lawn sat in front of it. Celeste rounded the U-shaped driveway, stopping in front of the entrance. Looking out her car window and up at the front windows, she spotted something unusual. A flash of light presented an eerie-looking face. "Maybel, I don't want to scare you, but I think I just saw a ghost."

"Oh, dear. Not you too!"

"In that window up there," Celeste said, pointing. "I saw a face peeking out. It looked weird. I think it was glowing!"

Maybel waved off Celeste's concern. "That's impossible. That room is empty. No one even lives there." She thanked Celeste for a lovely birthday, said goodbye, and went inside Shady Sunset Retirement Home. Closing the large wooden ornate door behind her made a hollow echo call out into the large empty foyer. A crystal chandelier above her glistened in the dim light. She walked past the sign in the lobby that read '*Home is where the heart is*'. My heart isn't here, she thought. Exhausted, Maybel slowly crept up the stairs, the floorboards groaning underneath her.

With Mr. Piddles on her lap, Maybel soaked her throbbing feet in a footbath while they watched late night tv. Her phone binged, and a group text from Arnie Arnold read: **I saw it again! The strange burst of fog over by the Heavenly Souls Cemetery!**

"What a dunce," Maybel said, feeling too tired from her birthday celebration to go to her window and look out. She turned her ringer off so as not to be disturbed by the chain of texts that would surely follow.

Chapter Two

Ghosts of the Past

In the morning, Maybel read the texts from the others. Vera's text read: **I heard strange noises again last night. It sounded like someone dragged something around up in the attic.**

"It was probably just the wind," Maybel said, proceeding to the kitchen to feed Mr. Piddles his breakfast. Scampering behind her, he impatiently waited for it, meowing at her to hurry. She showered, dressed, and went downstairs to the dining room for her breakfast. Walking in, she looked through the windows all around the room that gave a delightful view of the courtyard garden, having a calming effect on her. Sun streamed in, making the glass pitchers of ice water sparkle. The dining room felt at least 10 degrees warmer than the lobby, and Maybel heard muffled conversations from different tables as she made her way to her table. The smell of cooking bacon and sausage wafted from the kitchen. Like she normally did, she sat at a table with Vera, Violet, and Norma.

Maybel ordered orange juice to go with her scrambled eggs. Still tired from the day at the amusement park, she thought a blast of vitamin C would do her some good.

"How was your birthday celebration with your family?" Vera asked, placing her napkin properly on her lap, looking smart in her blue tweed blazer. Despite the grapefruit sitting in front of her, she would wait for everyone to be served before eating. Good manners were essential to her.

Maybel grabbed a tiny pitcher of cream from the lazy Susan in the middle of the table and poured some into her coffee and replied, "Wonderful! Jeffrey didn't show until after lunch, so I felt disappointed about that, but Celeste is such a sweetheart. We had a delightful morning going on rides before he got there. After Jeffrey arrived, we traveled all over the park. At one point, I felt so tired I just plopped down on Thomas Soiler's Island and rested for a while. My feet are still sore today."

Sprinkling a little sugar on her grapefruit, Vera said, "I think you mean Tom Sawyer."

"Isn't that what I said?" Maybel wondered.

"Speaking of feet," Norma leaned in, whispering, "I think I heard someone walking down the hall late last night." A bun perched on top of her head looked like a halo above her sky-blue eyes.

"So?" Maybel asked, sipping her coffee.

Norma blinked. "So? So, when I looked out of my door to see who it was, there was no one there!"

Vera gasped. "Do you think it was a ghost?"

Maybel shook her head. "There is no such thing as ghosts."

"Well, I heard noises up in the attic, and there are always ghosts in an attic!" Vera said, steeping her tea.

"That's just the silly stuff in movies… or Nancy Drew books. Ghosts are not real," Maybel insisted. "The noises you heard were probably just mice or the wind or something."

"Oh, good grief! There better not be mice in the attic above me, not with what I pay to live here," Vera replied. "They'd have to be awfully big mice, too, what with all the creaking and peculiar scraping noises I heard."

Norma said, "It must be a ghost. Why else would I hear footsteps but not see anyone in the hall?"

"Maybe it was the ghost of Beatrice Parkins," Vera replied.

"Who?" Maybel wondered.

Vera cleared her throat. "Beatrice Parkins. She was the original owner of this property from years ago. Rumor has it, shortly after she purchased this property with her inheritance, she got engaged. Well, she insisted on having the wedding ceremony here. She was all dressed up in her wedding gown and when she descended the curved staircase in the lobby, she tripped and fell, tumbling to her death!"

Norma gasped.

Vera continued, "The legend of Shady Sunset says that residents can still hear her walking the halls at night, turning lights on and off and closing and opening doors. Some people have said you can still smell her lavender perfume."

"Oh, my goodness!" Norma clutched her chest.

"And that's not all," Vera went on, "there were reports of a young girl drowning in the pool prior to her wedding."

"That's horrific!" Norma shook her head.

"But I think the strangest story is about the cook," Vera said, pausing to sip her tea. "One night, while he was preparing a roast lamb for Beatrice, he went into the pantry to get some potatoes. The heavy door to the pantry slammed closed on him, cutting him in half! After that, they kept the pantry locked, and no one was allowed to go in there."

"You know what else? I heard that Shady Sunset has secret passageways. They put them in when this place was built back in 1921. They did stuff like that back in wartime… like in case they needed to hide from the enemy. I bet that's where the ghosts live!"

"Where did you hear about these secret passageways?" Maybel asked.

Norma thought for a second before giving a voluble answer. "I don't remember, but someone here told me about a binder in the library room that has all kinds of information about this property, with pictures of what it originally looked like before they remodeled it. I think a while back I looked at it once or twice. It was pretty interesting. Did you know that the fireplace that's in the library was once part of the living room, but when they remodeled the property, they sectioned off that part of the living room and turned it into the library. Then they turned the rest of the living room into the lobby of Shady Sunset. I really like hanging out in the library. People come and go, and I get to chat with everyone. Sometimes I give recommendations on what books to read. I'm very familiar with the selection there because it's not very big, but the room is so cozy. The rocking chairs have the softest cushions. The staff here really does a good job of making us feel at home. Sometimes Morty and I play backgammon. He always wins, but I think that's because he cheats, but I don't care because I like his company. He's a good listener. Arnie is a hoot! One time he showed up at the library wearing his antique smoking jacket. It's really nice red velvet with a black lapel. He looked so dashing! We played checkers and read some Shakespear. Did you know Arnie is into Shakespear?"

Maybel suppressed an eye roll at Arnie's pretentious behavior. "Listen ladies, if any of these ghost stories leading to death were real, it would have had to have been disclosed to the new property owner. Norma, did you see anything about these incidents in the binder?"

Norma shook her head. "I don't think so… not that I remember."

"See, then all of this is just conjecture!" Maybel said.

Violet removed her oxygen mask and spoke, "I still haven't found my missing diamond necklace. It's so upsetting. I've looked everywhere for it. I really think someone stole it." She sat petite in the dining room chair, and sadness stayed with her.

"Well, that would mean someone had to have been in your apartment. Was there any evidence of a break-in? Who all has been in your place?" Maybel asked, fancying herself as an amateur detective. She helped the Sunshine Beach police solve a few murders that took place at Regal Palms (which you can read all about in a book called *Rent to Kill*).

Violet, reluctant to admit to all her visitors, said, "Let's see… my daughter came to visit me a few weeks ago. Obviously, it wasn't her. The cleaning staff, Vick, the maintenance man, and Vera and Norma came over for tea."

"Wait," Maybel asked, "I thought Vick was working the security job here that I got for him. Is he doing maintenance now?"

"I heard he fell asleep on the night shift job, so they let him go as the security guard," Norma answered. "But they needed a maintenance and janitorial man, and he knows so much about plumbing. They moved him to that job."

While the head server of the Shady Sunset dining room served the ladies their breakfasts, Jo Stelliano, the activities director, approached their table. "Hello, hello, hello ladies! I hope you've all been thinking about what you want to do for our talent show!" A clipboard in the pert 30-year-old's hand held the sign-up sheet.

Vera piped up, "I love to play the piano. I was classically trained, you know."

"Oh, wonderful!" Jo scribbled a note on her clipboard. "I'll put you down for that. How about the rest of you?"

A deep male voice from behind Maybel spoke up, "Hey cupcake! I've got a magic act that will knock everyone's socks off!"

Jo made a note while an eye roll escaped Maybel at the sound of Arnie's voice. Maybel noticed the toothpick in Arnie's mouth.

Arnie reached behind Vera's ear, and with sleight of hand, he pulled out a quarter. The ladies, sans Maybel, giggled with impressed delight. Arnie went on, "I can also throw my voice!"

Under hostile breath, Maybel mumbled, "That's not all you throw around."

"Did you say something, Maybel?" Arnie asked, taking the toothpick out of his mouth, having picked his morning sausage from between his yellowing teeth. He tossed the toothpick on the table, and it landed near Maybel's plate.

Maybel picked up her fork and rolled the toothpick away from her, and she never picked up that fork again.

Norma offered, "I can tap dance!"

Jo kept scribbling notes on her sign-up sheet. "And Maybel, what about you?"

"I haven't decided yet," Maybel answered, looking at Arnie's toothpick with disgust.

"OK. Let me know when you decide. Arnie, I take it you'll do your magic act?" Jo wondered.

Arnie smiled proudly, taking out two red sponge balls from his pocket. "Indeed, I will! Norma, will you oblige me?" he asked, handing her one of the red balls. Arnie kept the second red sponge ball in his own hand, waving his free hand around his closed hand and Norma's closed hand holding the sponge ball. "Norma, sweetheart, please open your hand."

When Norma opened her hand, the sponge ball disappeared. Arnie opened his hand and held the two red sponge balls in it. "Oh! What a wonderful trick!" Norma clapped her hands. "How did you do that?"

Arnie put the sponge balls back in his pocket. "A magician never reveals how he does his tricks. But I can tell you, the hand is quicker than the eye." He winked at her.

Maybel's lips curled into a snarl behind her juice glass. "Your tricks are so cliché!"

"Violet, what would you like to do for the show?" Jo asked.

"My daughter says I have a lovely singing voice. But now that I need to use this oxygen tank for several hours a day," she pointed to her tank and went on, "I'm not sure what I can do."

"Don't worry. We'll think of something you can do." Jo excused herself, walking through the sea of silver and gray curly hair in the dining room to talk to some other residents of Shady Sunset.

"Well, my lovely ladies," Arnie began with hands on hips clothed in garishly colored golf pants, "did any of you see the strange burst of fog over by the graveyard last night?"

"I looked out my window when I got your text, but I couldn't see anything," Vera said. "Arnie, why are your pants so shiny? They're shinier than my silk blouse."

Arnie stood up straight. "These slacks are a silk gaberdine blend. They cost me a small fortune. Some of us like to spend money on our clothes so we can look nice."

Maybel replied, "Vera, you didn't see anything because there was nothing to see."

Arnie, face set for a fight, asked, "What was that, Maybel?"

Referring to the thick marine layer, she said, "It was probably just June gloom."

"It's May, Maybel, and June gloom is in the morning," Arnie scoffed.

"Then it was May gray." Maybel set down her empty juice glass.

Arnie insisted, "I know what I saw!"

Maybel warned, "Stop getting everyone riled up! Everyone's imagination is getting the best of them. Norma even thinks she's seeing ghosts now. I don't know how all of you rational adults can think this place is haunted."

"I didn't actually see the ghost, but I heard him… or her," Norma interjected.

Saddened, Violet said, "Well, it's not my imagination that my diamond necklace is missing."

"Speaking of that," Maybel proceeded, looking at Arnie and wiggling her fingers for effect, "Violet said your son Vick was in her place. Perhaps he has some sticky fingers."

Arnie's aged face reddened. "Are you accusing my son of stealing?"

Maybel stood up, but stood too short to go nose to nose, hose to hose with Arnie. She spat out, "If his morals are anything like his father's, then yes!"

With his finger pointed in Maybel's face, Arnie warned, "You better watch it, Maybel!"

Maybel looked up at Arnie, countering, "Are you threatening me? If you're threatening me, I'm going to make you sorry—you washed up shiny-ass president!"

Sheila Anderson, the new age healthcare facilitator, who believed everyone in the universe was connected to each other through a stream of collective consciousness, approached them with a concerned look on her face. She asked in a soothing tone, "Hey, hey… What's going on here?"

Arnie steamed. "Maybel just accused my son, Vick, of theft and insulted my clothing!"

With widened eyes, Sheila looked at Maybel. "Is this true?"

"He started it. Look, Violet thinks her diamond necklace was stolen, and Vick was in her place. Has anyone on the Shady Sunset staff investigated this yet?"

Sheila took a deep breath. "I'll talk to Colleen, and we'll look into it, but in the meantime, Maybel, try to calm yourself. We may have to cleanse your aura again because this isn't good for your chi."

"I don't have that," Maybel insisted.

"I can help you with that, Maybel. I came over to the table to let you all know I'm going to be hosting a fireside chant later. It will be tonight out at the firepit in the garden area. We'll make s'mores too, just like when we were kids! It will be wonderful for your energy. Will you all attend?" Sheila looked around at everyone seated at the table.

Norma and Vera nodded.

Violet said, "I get too cold outside at night. I think I'll pass. Maybel, what about you?"

Maybel reluctantly agreed.

"Wonderful!" Sheila clapped her hands.

"I'll be there too," Arnie said. "I love to tell a good ghost story."

"Oh, no. We won't be telling ghost stories. We'll probably sing and chant and do some deep breathing. It's also good to stare at the flames of the fire. It really connects us to nature," Sheila explained.

Maybel fought the urge to roll her eyes again. "Please excuse me. I'm going to go back to my apartment. Sheila, please don't forget to talk to Colleen about the missing jewelry." She shot an accusatory look at Arnie.

Arnie placed his hands on his hips. "How dare you imply my son would do anything below board! I ought to report *you* to Colleen!"

"Report me for what?! Telling the truth?! You're just trying to silence me with your bullying, Arnie!"

Arnie laughed in Maybel's face. "I'd never try to silence you! I remember your rendition of silent but deadly at that board meeting years ago!"

"You're an idiot!" Maybel turned on her heel and headed out of the dining room.

Arnie called out after her, "This isn't over, Maybel!"

Chapter Three

Thank You for Being a Friend

Back at her apartment, Maybel nestled in on the couch in her tiny living room and Mr. Piddles curled up next to her, purring a soothing sound while Maybel pet his silky fur. A fluffy ball of emerald green yarn sat on her other side. After he dozed off, she picked up her kitting. Knit one, pearl two, knit one, pearl two, knit one, pearl two. Her phone rang.

"Hello, Violet," Maybel greeted. "What's going on?"

"Oh, I just wanted to thank you for standing up for me. No one seems to care that my diamond necklace is missing."

"No problem, Violet. What are friends for?"

"Would you like to come over for tea today?"

Maybel gladly accepted. "Let me do some more work on this scarf I'm knitting, and then I'll come over."

Mr. Piddles swatted the ball of yarn away from Maybel. He jumped on top of it and rolled around, not giving it back. His will proved to be stronger than hers, so Maybel gave up. Before heading over to Violet's apartment, an idea came to her. With a rubber mouse in her hand, she got Mr. Piddles attention. Throwing it across the room proved to be an excellent distraction. Snatching up the abandoned ball of yarn, Maybel put the yarn and the scarf it was attached to back in her sewing basket. An old family picnic basket she repurposed now served as her sewing basket for her knitting. Maybel thought the two-sided lids would keep Mr. Piddles away from her yarn, but he'd quickly figured out how to lift the basket lids. Often, she found him inside the basket. Before leaving, she placed a couple of books on the basket lid to keep him out.

Strolling along to Violet's, Maybel thought about how much she missed living next to Celeste at Regal Palms, but Violet made a nice friend too and seemed so lonely. As a fellow widow, Maybel understood the pain. She knocked on Violet's door, and on a hunch that it was unlocked, she turned the doorknob and let herself in. "Please don't get up," Maybel said to Violet, who had her oxygen mask on. "I'll make us some tea." Violet slowly sunk back down on her velvet settee, and Maybel scooted around Violet's clutter of furniture and went into her kitchenette.

While waiting for water in the teakettle to boil, Maybel took out Violet's silver serving tray from her cupboard and placed two china teacups with saucers on it from her curio cabinet. She admired the beautiful pink country rose pattern on them. Once the water in the teakettle came to a boil, Maybel dipped the tea bags in it, letting them steep for several minutes. Knowing Violet liked a fancy teatime, Maybel also put a few lady fingers on one of Violet's china plates and added that with her sugar bowl to the tray. Before bringing the tray into Violet's living room, Maybel set two lace napkins on it. Unsure if she'd prepared a proper tea service, she shrugged, thinking it was the best she could do.

Sitting on Violet's moss green brocade covered couch across from her yellow settee, Maybel sipped soothing chamomile.

"I'm glad you're here at Shady Sunset, Maybel. I feel comfortable talking with you." Violet smiled.

Maybel drew in a deep breath. "Thank you, Violet. It's nice of you to say that. I'm still struggling to feel at home here. I really miss my old place."

"Sheila says that wherever we are, that is exactly where we are supposed to be." Violet's hand shook slightly as she set her teacup on her saucer.

Maybel chuckled. "That sounds like more of her new age voodoo."

The ladies chatted for quite a while. Inevitably, the subject of their late husbands came up. "I miss John every day," Violet said, looking down at her spotted hands.

"I know," Maybel sympathized. "I think of George all the time. I talk to him too… and I swear sometimes I can hear him answer me back."

"He's buried at Heavenly Souls Cemetery, isn't he?" Violet inquired.

Maybel nodded, feeling the hole in her heart. "I need to take flowers to his grave again. It's been a while."

"I visit John and Tim once a week. I roll my tank along with me, and I walk there. Then I sit on that little cement bench under the great big pine tree, the one with the huge pinecones. I almost tripped over a pinecone once. I must be careful to wheel my oxygen tank around them. The tree is right by their headstones. I know they're not there. I know their souls are in heaven, but I feel connected to them there." Violet wiped a tear from her eye. "Their bones under my feet… it's all I have now.

"It wasn't all happy times. We had tough times too. When John lost his job, we almost ran out of money. That was difficult… but we got back on our feet. And then when I lost my son Tim, that was almost unbearable."

Maybel's eyes widened. "Oh, I didn't know you had a son, Violet. I'm so sorry for your loss."

The deep lines on Violet's pained face mapped the sadness of her life's journey. "He died of a brain aneurism. It happened so suddenly. Sometimes, I still can't believe it. I felt so isolated in my shock, and it's like a part of me is gone. It's a feeling of loss that never stops. I'm not close to my daughter. She is so busy with her own life… and she always accused me of favoring Tim. I feel like there is a wedge between us. Sometimes I feel like God is all I have."

"Well, you know what they say… when God is all you have, you have all you need."

Violet smiled. "I suppose that's true. In one of our counseling sessions, Colleen helped me to see things from a different perspective. She said when there is nowhere else to turn, turn to God. God uses our pain and suffering to draw us near to Him. Despite my suffering, I do feel closer to God through all of this."

Maybel thought of her son, Jeffrey. When she got back to her apartment, she would call him and check in. "So, your son is buried in Heavenly Souls, too?"

"Yes, I have a double plot with John and Tim's is a few rows over from ours. After I pass away, they'll add my name to John's headstone. The graves of our household are all there…"

"I have a double plot with George, too."

"I'm sorry. I don't mean to be such a downer," Violet said and put her oxygen mask back on.

"That's OK. Believe me, I understand," Maybel assured her. "And please know you have all of us here as your friends. I know it's tough to be a widow, but at least we were blessed with long, happy marriages."

Violet took her mask back off to speak. "Yes, but it's just that I have some regrets about my relationship with my son. I wish I could have been wiser about how I raised him when he was young." Violet looked out her window. "I told Colleen this in one of our counseling sessions. I said I wished God would have given me more knowledge about how to raise children. My son had a bad drinking problem, and I always felt so guilty about it. But Colleen pointed out that without wisdom, knowledge is useless."

Maybel frowned. "How so?"

"Well, she said knowledge is just information, but wisdom is knowing how to use and apply that information. I told her that was a wise statement," Violet said, letting a little croaking laugh escape her wrinkled lips.

"Yes, I suppose that's true. What is your daughter's name?"

"Leah… she always thought I loved her less than Tim, but she was just so independent. I never worried about her. I knew she could take care of herself. Leah had so much financial success. But Tim… he couldn't seem to hold a job. I helped him out financially. Leah accused me of having a codependent relationship with him… she even accused me of being a narcissist."

"Oh, that can't be true. Violet, you're such a dear woman."

"I got so angry at her that I wrote her out of my will… decided to leave it all to Tim. He needed it more… but he passed away before me."

"Will everything go to Leah by default?" Violet wheezed a breath. "No. It will go to a charity very near and dear to my heart. If she thinks I'm a narcissist and won't speak to me, then I won't give her a dime!"

"Violet, I know this is none of my business, but I feel compelled to say something to you. You seem angry at your daughter. The Bible commands us to forgive each other. There is even a verse in the book of Matthew that says, '*For if you forgive others their trespasses, your Heavenly Father will also forgive you, but if you do not forgive others their trespasses, neither will your Father forgive your trespasses*'. Forgiveness is such an important thing. You don't want to live in a place of unforgiving anger, and you don't want to make decisions from a place of unforgiving anger, and you certainly don't want to die while in a place of unforgiving anger. It would not be good for you spiritually."

Tears filled Violet's eyes as she thought for a minute. "I guess you're right… I'm sorry I'm crying. I tried to be a good mother to Leah, but I feel like she hates me."

"You don't need to apologize. Tears are good. They're cleansing. I know you love your daughter. Sometimes we get the angriest at the people we love the most."

Violet looked down and nodded. "Colleen said crying is good, too. She said our crying place is where we are the most vulnerable… where you release pain and heal. She said the crying place is where we find our true selves."

"Well, see there, more words of wisdom. Now, let's talk about something more cheerful. Let's come up with something we can do for the talent show."

The ladies went over a few ideas, but none of them seemed feasible because of Violet's limitations. "I'm looking forward to seeing Arnie's magic act," Violet said.

Maybel huffed, "Oh, don't get me started on him! He's such a jackass."

"Why do you dislike him so much?"

"It's a long story, and I won't bore you with the details. Let's just say he betrayed me and undermined my presidency of the board of the Regal Palms homeowner's association."

"That sounds terrible!"

"It was! And his son Vick is just as bad!" Maybel said, nursing her grudge. "And speaking of Vick, I wanted to ask you when exactly was he in your place and what all did he do while he was here?"

Violet pulled her mask off again to speak. "Let's see… about two weeks ago he was here… and at least three days after that, I realized my necklace was missing. The sink in my kitchenette got clogged up, so he came in to fix it. I think he's quite charming and tall… just like Arnie."

Maybel's eyes rolled like marbles dropped on the ground. "Was anyone else in your place between the time Vick was in your place and three days later when you discovered your necklace was missing?"

"Sheila Anderson stopped by to see how I was feeling and did a quick checkup on me. She encouraged me to attend her health and wellness class. She's also going to be teaching a nutrition class soon that sounded rather interesting."

"Anyone else?"

Violet looked down again and shook her head. "Just the house cleaners," she said, omitting a visitor.

"Where was the last place you saw your necklace?" Maybel asked.

"I don't wear it very often. I only wear it on Sundays when I go to the chapel for church service."

"When you take it off after church, where do you leave it?"

"On my nightstand." Violet pointed towards her bedroom.

Maybel stood up. "Do you mind if I go search for it?"

Violet smiled, appreciating the help. "Be my guest."

Maybel went into Violet's bedroom, finding it to be clean, orderly, and simply decorated with a floral duvet cover on her bed. It smelled faintly of pot-pourri. She went over to the nightstand and looked around. She pulled the nightstand out away from the wall and looked behind it. Nothing. She got down on her hands and knees and looked under the bed. Nothing. She went into Violet's bathroom and searched around in there. After finding nothing, she went back to the nightstand and pulled out the little drawer in it, looking thoroughly through the contents of the drawer but finding nothing.

She walked over to Violet's dresser and searched there but still found nothing. Noting Violet's safe sitting on her dresser, Maybel checked, finding it locked. She went back out to the living room and sat down next to Violet. "I'm sorry, but I didn't find anything."

Violet rewarded Maybel with a grateful smile. "I appreciate you looking. Truly, I do."

"I noticed you have a safe. Could you have put the necklace in your safe?"

Violet shook her head. "I checked that. The combination is my birthday, and the necklace isn't there. The only thing I keep in my safe are some old Bearer bonds John bought for us years and years ago. I probably should go cash them in, but I don't need the money, and they are so sentimental to me that I can't bear to part with them… no pun intended."

"I see," Maybel said. "I also noticed you didn't have your front door locked when I got here. Do you normally leave it unlocked?"

"I try to remember to lock it, but I think sometimes I forget. I've been forgetting a lot lately. Colleen thinks I just forgot where I put my necklace. She thinks it will turn up, eventually."

"Speaking of forgetting, isn't today the day of the week you go visit John and Tim?"

"Good heavens! It is!" Violet slowly stood up.

"Would you like for me to go with you?"

"That is so sweet of you to offer, but if you don't mind, I like to go alone. I just sit in peace and cry. I talk to them too. I think a lot about death now, and I remember that Bible verse; *to die is to gain.* I wish I was with them."

Maybel smiled at her friend. "I understand." She excused herself and walked back to her place, thinking along the way of the language of grief and how it is an unspoken language; you don't hear it, you feel it.

Chapter Four

Whoever Smelled It, Dealt It

Mr. Piddles launched a full-blown attack on the ball of yarn Maybel knitted with. His claws dug in, and she tried unsuccessfully to pull it back away from him. "You're being a little jerk, you know that?" Maybel chuckled as he stared back at her through his marbled green eyes with black slits. Maybel gave up the fight and rang Jeffrey.

"Hi mom! How are you feeling today? I know we walked a lot. Did you have fun?"

Maybel laughed. "My feet are sore, but yes, I had a lot of fun! Thank you again for the trip to the amusement park. I know admission isn't cheap!"

"You're welcome. So, what's new?" he asked.

"Oh, you know, there's not much new with me anymore. Same old same old."

"I don't believe that. There has to be something new," Jeffrey said.

"Shady Sunset is going to have a talent show, but I'm not sure what I should do for it."

"Remember when I was a kid, and you gave me something special for Christmas in my Christmas stocking?

And then you taught me some tricks? And dad taught me some tricks?"

"That was many years ago. I'm not sure I could do that now." Maybel gave Jeffrey the date of the talent show and he marked his calendar.

"I'm glad I got to see Celeste and Brian again. Will they be coming to the talent show?" Jeffrey asked.

"Yes, I invited them yesterday when we were eating lunch. There are a lot of other activities coming up, too."

"Like what?"

Maybel listed them, "Like a show and tell, a square dance, an art therapy class, a book club, field trips, bingo, an ice cream social, board games, crafts, a luau, swing dance lessons. I just heard that Sheila Anderson, the new age resident healthcare facilitator, is going to be teaching a class on nutrition. That should be useful."

"That all sounds fun! I'm glad you took my suggestion and moved there. I think it's been good for you." Jeffrey said.

"I guess so, but I'm still trying to fit in, and that Arnie Arnold drives me crazy!"

Jeffrey chuckled. "Just forget about that old coot."

"I can't," Maybel responded. "He always gets in my face. And you know what else? I think Vick might have stolen Violet's diamond necklace."

"Oh, you don't really think that, do you?"

Maybel paused before speaking. "I don't know. I guess not, but he was in her place and then a day or two later, she couldn't find her necklace. I helped search for it today, but I couldn't find it either."

"Well, hopefully it will turn up soon." Jeffrey said.

"Let's hope so, but in case it doesn't, I asked the staff to look into it. We can't have theft here. That just won't be good for anyone's mental health. This place should feel like a safe space in our final days."

"Final days? Mom, you have years, not days."

"Maybe, but who knows what the future holds? I'm clearly at the tail end of my journey."

Changing the subject, Jeffrey asked when the ice cream social was and marked his calendar for that too, since guests were welcome. They chatted a while longer about her fun her birthday celebration before signing off.

Maybel went back to her knitting while Mr. Piddles took a nap in the warm sun gleaming from the windowsill he curled up on. She knew he wasn't asleep because his tail moved around from time to time. She admired how the green yarn looked against the blue yarn. Knit one, pearl two, knit one, pearl two, knit one, pearl two…

Then an unexpected knock hit Maybel's front door.

Celeste smiled back at her, holding the stuffed animal Maybel had picked out for her birthday the day before at the amusement park. "You forgot this in my car yesterday. I was in the area for a doctor's appointment, so I decided to drop it off and give you a little visit." Her cheerful face brightened Maybel's spirits.

"Wonderful! Since it's a stuffed mouse, Mr. Piddles will probably end up with it. Hey, I was just thinking about going down to the dining room for a late lunch. Would you like to join me?"

The ladies strolled down to the dining room arm in arm. Celeste knew this transition was difficult for Maybel, realizing the day before that a visit was long overdue. They sat by themselves at a quiet table in the corner of the dining room that smelled like a school cafeteria. "What's good here?" Celeste asked, looking at the simple one-page menu.

"For lunch, I always get a sandwich. They have a meatloaf sandwich that's pretty darn good."

"It can't possibly be as good as your meatloaf," Celeste said, smiling. The server approached them, and Celeste said, "I'll have the turkey club with salad instead of French fries."

Maybel's face lit up. "That sounds good! I'll have the same and a piece of peach pie for dessert."

"How are you feeling today? I know we walked a lot yesterday. I checked the steps on my phone, and I estimate we walked about six miles." Celeste put her napkin on her lap.

"No wonder my feet are killing me today." Maybel took a sip of water, then shifted gears. "I don't mean to be nosey, but I noticed your body language with Brian is different. You seem much more comfortable with him now."

"We've been on a few more dates, and I've gotten to know him better," Celeste said.

"Oh, that's good. What kind of bed does he have?"

Celeste laughed. "No, stop! I'm not doing this with you."

Arnie walked up with the easy gait of a man half his age. His deep voice bellowed from behind Maybel, "Well, hello! Maybel, who is this lovely lady you're dining with?"

"She's too young for you, Arnie, and she's in a serious, active sexual relationship."

"I never said that!" Celeste protested. She stood and shook Arnie's hand.

Maybel reluctantly introduced the two of them. "Celeste, this is Arnie. He's Vick's dad."

Celeste raised her eyebrows. "Oh, yeah. I know Vick. I used to live at Regal Palms. I lived next door to Maybel."

"Well, then, my condolences to you," Arnie said, still holding Celeste's hand.

Maybel steamed, "Stuff it, Arnie!"

"Will you be attending the talent show?" Arnie asked, not able to take his eyes off of Celeste.

Celeste smiled. "I sure will. I like your yellow sweater, Arnie. Yellow is my favorite color. You look as bright as the sun."

"Or a sour lemon! Arnie, would you leave us alone? We're trying to enjoy lunch." Maybel said.

Arnie retorted, "It's a free country, Maybel. I can do whatever I want."

Maybel snapped, "Don't you have a golf ball you need to *NOT* hit? Or another ridiculous outfit you need to go put together?"

"I'll have you know Maybel, I hit *A HOLE IN ONE* this morning!"

Maybel snickered to Celeste, "Emphasis on the *A HOLE.*"

Arnie waved her off. "Celeste darling, it was a pleasure meeting you. I look forward to seeing you at the talent show. Now, if you'll excuse me, there's an art therapy class starting in about ten minutes."

Maybel snorted. "There's not enough therapy in the world to fix you."

"You're crazy, not me!" Arnie snapped.

Maybel shouted, "If Sigmund Freud were alive today, he'd resign just to keep from having to deal with you!"

"Speaking or resigning, remember when you had to resign from the presidency of the Regal Palms Homeowners Association? Shameful what you did!"

Maybel gasped. "You know that wasn't me!"

Interrupting the verbal jousting, Celeste spoke in a soothing tone. "OK, Arnie, it was nice meeting you. We'll see you later." She sat back down, and when she and Maybel were alone again, she said, "Wow, you're even feistier with Arnie than you are with Vick."

"Dear, if you knew what I know about Arnie, you'd understand." Maybel replied.

"What happened between the two of you?"

"I still can't talk about it. It's too painful," Maybel said, looking down at her hands.

Celeste looked at Maybel like a mother and cared about her wellbeing. She didn't think it was a good idea for Maybel to hold so much animosity towards him, especially when they lived in such close quarters. She prompted her again, "Maybel, I really think you need to talk about it. Please tell me what happened between you two."

After a long thoughtful pause, Maybel began, "As you know, years ago, I served as the president of the board for the Regal Palms Homeowner's Association. I was the best president Regal Palms ever had! I took my position seriously. I always tried to do what was in everyone's best interest while keeping the HOA dues as low as possible. But Arnie thought he could do a better job than me. He kept bad-mouthing me to the board, claiming I was unfit to hold office, and that there was too much frivolous spending. Now, dear, I assure you, any money we spent was necessary. Arnie just wanted the power for himself. He'd show up at the board meetings and heckle everything I said. He really pushed me to my limit.

"Then, one day, he showed up at the meeting like he always did. The meeting hadn't begun yet, and we were all standing around talking. Well, suddenly, an awful pungent smell filled the air. I asked what the heck it was, and Arnie implied that I had passed gas!"

Celeste tried to suppress her laughter.

"Dear, this isn't funny," Maybel said.

"So that is what this is about? Your past political scandal and long-standing rival with Arnie and Vick is because someone broke wind?"

"Dear, I don't think you realize how bad his flatulence was. He really broke through the wind!"

"I think you mean broke wind."

"Isn't that what I said? It smelled like a three-day-old leftover Thanksgiving turkey in a broccoli pie topped with hard-boiled eggs soaked in vinegar. The stench was so disgusting! Norma served on the board back then, and she almost puked in her mouth when she smelled it! Arnie expelled the foulest gas I'd ever encountered… and I know Arnie did it! Then he blamed it on me! And the worst part of all is that the board members believed him. The next meeting, they asked me to step down, stating that if I couldn't control my bodily functions, they didn't think I was fit to hold the office. I was mortified! And it wasn't even me that did it, but it was like the more I protested, the more they thought I did it. Meanwhile, the whole time Arnie knew he did it and just sat there with that smug look on his dumb face! The board asked him to step in and take over for me, which isn't even allowed in the bylaws. I don't know how he got away with that. So, that's how he stole the presidency from me. I couldn't even believe it. I was devastated."

Celeste, still dumbfounded by the story, sipped her water. Finally, she spoke. "Maybel, maybe it's time for some forgiveness."

"Ppppfffft! That barbarian doesn't deserve it!"

"You know, you call Arnie a lot of names, and I know you are a good Christian woman. I don't think Jesus would want you calling him so many names. What's that old saying… what would Jesus do?"

"Dear, I attend a Bible study class here every Thursday and we were just talking about the passage where Jesus called the Pharisees a brood of vipers. So, if Jesus can call people names, so can I." "I don't think that's the spirit of that Bible story lesson."

Maybel folded her arms across her chest. "Sure it is."

"God grants forgiveness to you, therefore you are to forgive others, right?"

Maybel sat silently.

"Just think about what I said. Life is too short to hold grudges," Celeste went on, "and from what you've told me, I think Arnie really likes you."

"What makes you think that?"

"Because he's always coming over to talk to you at Regal Palms and now at Shady Sunset," Celeste answered.

Maybel grunted. "He just likes to gloat, and he's always got his balls in his hand."

Celeste bristled and queried, "Excuse me?"

Maybel waved her hand. "It's one of his dumb magic tricks. He makes red sponge balls disappear. Don't you think Arnie looks like the devil with that stupid pencil mustache of his?"

"I think he looks quite dashing for an older man."

"Oh, don't tell him that! It will go to his head. He already gallivants around here like he's a fox in the henhouse!"

Sheila Anderson approached their table. "Ladies, I didn't mean to eavesdrop, but I thought I heard someone talking about bad gas. That's usually caused by poor nutrition and that leaky gut syndrome. I'm teaching a new class on nutrition, and I'd encourage you both to attend. Guests are always welcome at our activities."

"I didn't have gas," Maybel protested. "Arnie did! He's the one that has bad gas!"

"Oh, I see. Well, I think I'll pay a visit to him and make sure he signs up for my nutrition class, too." Sheila smiled.

"Is that a bird in your hair?" Maybel asked, looking at a shiny clip in Sheila's flouncy reddish hair.

"Yes! Isn't it cute? I know it's not real, but it makes me feel close to nature."

Maybel politely stayed silent.

"Well, I've got to be on my way. Ida asked me to do a tarot card reading for her." Sheila waved goodbye.

With Sheila out of earshot, Maybel leaned in and said to Celeste, "Maybe Sheila took Violet's necklace."

"Why do you think that?"

Keeping her voice low, Maybel replied, "Don't you think Sheila's nose looks strange?"

"What do you mean?"

"It looks like someone molded it out of clay or something. It looks misshapen and pliable."

"What does that have to do with Violet's necklace?"

"Nothing. But Sheila was in Violet's place doing a wellness check-up."

"Perhaps Violet misplaced her necklace," Celeste said.

"I don't think so, and even if she did, when I visited her for tea, I looked everywhere and couldn't find it for her. She's so glum about it."

"You don't like tea."

"But I like gossip. All the ladies like tea in the afternoon, and when I have tea with them, that's how I find out how they're doing and what's really going on around this place. I have to say, I've gotten quite fond of Vera's raspberry tea, even though it's a little bitter. Two sugar cubes take care of that. At Regal Palms, I had my phone tree because I had lived there for so many years, but here I have to start all over."

Celeste smiled. "So, you get them to spill the tea over tea?"

"No one spills their tea, dear. They carefully sip it."

"I didn't mean literally… it's an expression."

"I've gotten quite fond of the spearmint tea Norma serves. Mint can be so overpowering. Spearmint is like mint's less obnoxious cousin. But back to Sheila. I just don't trust that gal. I don't trust a woman that looks rode hard and put away wet."

Celeste almost spit out the water she sipped. "What?!"

"Oh, that's just an old expression. It's about horses, and speaking of horses, doesn't Sheila kind of have a horse mouth?"

"I hadn't noticed."

After a long lunch of catching up and talking about old times, Celeste let Maybel know she needed to get going.

"Veronica invited Brian and I to go on a double date with her and Tom. I think she called it 'bowling, beers and burgers'."

"Oh, George and I used to be in a bowling league years ago! I just loved it. We had so much fun," Maybel reminisced.

"I've only been bowling a few times in my life. I'm pretty good at it, but Brian is already smack talking, saying he's going to beat everyone."

Maybel chuckled. "He's competitive, for sure. George was like that; thought he was better than me at everything."

"It should be a fun night, though. I haven't seen Veronica in a while, and she hinted that they have a big announcement," Celeste said.

"Engaged?"

"Probably so."

"Tonight we're having some sort of fireside chant with Sheila."

"Who is Sheila?"

Maybel pursed her lips before speaking, "The redhead with the silly putty nose. Dear, you just met her. Don't you remember anyone's name? Sheila is the hippy dippy new age health care facilitator here."

"Is she a nurse?" Celeste took her car keys out of her purse.

Maybel shook her head. "I don't think so. We have an onsite nurse, but Sheila is more of a holistic healer or something like that."

Celeste smiled. "That sounds cool!"

"I guess so. She focuses in on our spiritual, mental, and emotional wellbeing."

"That's always a good thing. Before I go, tell me more about this fireside chant."

Maybel chuckled. "I don't really know what that's going to be like. This morning she said we'd sit by the firepit outside in the courtyard garden and make s'mores. I think we're going to chant or tell stories or something."

"I'm sure you'll have a nice time. Will Arnie be there?"

"Yes," Maybel nodded. "I think he's going to try to tell one of his stupid ghost stories."

"You should try to have a good time with him."

"Speaking of a good time, where do you think your relationship with Brian is going?" Maybel asked.

"I don't know… right now we're so busy having all that serious, active sexual relations that I can't figure it out."

"All right, all right. I get it. It's none of my business," Maybel conceded.

Celeste smiled. "If there's something worth telling you, I will tell you. But as of right now, I'm still trying to build trust with him. I really want to trust him."

"Ah, yes. Trust. It's the most important thing in a relationship. When you have it, you take it for granted. When you don't have it, you realize it's everything," Maybel mused.

Celeste nodded. "And I have deep trust issues that I can't just change overnight, and I wonder if I can trust a man that has been divorced twice."

"He's a smart man, dear. My guess is he's learned and grown a lot from the two marriages. I can see how much he cares for you. You don't want to screw this up by pushing him away."

"I think he always puts his work first."

"You should give him a reason to put his work second." Maybel pushed her fork down on some pie crust crumbs on her plate, getting the last of them.

"I have to get going now. We haven't had a Saturday lunch since I moved to my new place. We'll need to do that soon, but I will for sure see you at your talent show. Brian and I are looking forward to it." She stood up and gave Maybel a hug goodbye.

Watching her leave, Maybel wondered if Celeste would ever get to that place of trust she longed for, and she wondered if she could find it in her heart to forgive Arnie.

Chapter Five

Bowled Over

"**I** think I know more about this topic than you do," Brian said while driving to the bowling alley with Celeste for their double date with Veronica and Tom.

"I don't think you do. I know as much about music as you do, and I think you're placing too much importance on it," Celeste responded.

"I'm certainly not. Music is the fabric of our lives," Brian said.

"It's the fabric of *your* life, but not necessarily everyone else's."

"Well, take Sam Cooke, for example. Our first dance was to one of his songs, and now when I hear his music on the oldies station, I think of you. That's how powerful music is. How can you not understand that?"

Celeste frowned. "Are you saying I'm stupid?"

"You're putting words in my mouth. I'm not saying that you're not smart. I'm just saying that I'm smarter," Brian explained.

With the imperious remark taunting her ears, Celeste replied, "I don't know why you think you're smarter than me. I know you know a lot of things, but I know a lot of things too."

"I know you know a lot of things, sweetie. It's just that I know even more things than you do. That's all," he said, laughing.

Celeste shook her head and changed the subject. "Do you know what really happened the other day at Tube Solutions?"

"Not really… we know a small chemical explosion took place. OSHA is looking into that. I questioned the owner as to why Michael Turnblast would have been on site, and he didn't know much. He just said it was probably because of the protest… but Michael was on company property when the explosion happened, so he would have had to have been trespassing."

"Smells fishy," Celeste said. "Turnblast just happens to be on company property when there just happens to be an explosion killing him?"

"Exactly." Brian pulled into the parking lot. "But everyone at the company is being very tightlipped. No one with the environmental organization seems to know why Michael would have been trespassing. Everyone with the organization wanted to talk more about what a horrible company, Tube Solutions, is than what could have happened to Michael. Apparently, one product Tube Solutions makes is used in oil drilling, but the product was defective and caused an oil leak in the ocean."

"Oh, no. That's not good. No wonder they were pro-testing."

Arriving at the bowling alley brought them together with Celeste's best friend Veronica Owens and her boyfriend, Tom Fitzpatrick. "Hello you two!" Veronica gushed, jumping up and down a few times. She held up her left hand to Celeste, pointing to a large diamond ring on her ring finger.

"Congratulations!" Celeste hugged Veronica while Brian shook Tom's hand.

"Will you be my bridesmaid?" Veronica asked, her eyes twinkling.

"Of course!" Celeste put her hand over her heart, feeling the friendship.

Tom chimed in, "Let's hope our wedding goes better than the last one we were all at." (You can read all about it in a book called *A Harbor of Resentment*.)

Brian rubbed his stomach. "Oh, man. That was a rough night!"

"Who wants to bowl?" Veronica asked, kicking off the night. She wore the cutest pink and white gingham dress with pink bowling shoes. "Should we team up by couples or boy girl?"

Brian stood tall. "If we team up by boy girl, you girls will get crushed."

Seeing the look on Veronica's face, Celeste told her, "Don't mind him. He's so sexist, he doesn't even know how sexist he is." Celeste squared off, and turning to Brian, she said, "I think we should play the men against the women."

Brian raised an eyebrow. "OK. Have it your way, but I warned you. You are gonna crash and burn."

"Then I'll go out in a blaze of glory." Celeste placed her hands on her hips.

They all headed into the bowling alley, and the sound of crashing balls knocking pins down echoed through the stale smelling alley. Harsh, garish lights glowed from the right where the pinball machines and video games got smacked and slapped from hyper kids hopped up on soda. Celeste picked out a pair of aqua blue bowling shoes, always a color she loved. Brian suspected he and Celeste were going to have a crazy three-ring circus kind of night. He selected the clownish green and yellow shoes, and Tom took burgundy and black striped shoes.

Celeste turned to her friend and told her, "I know you just got engaged, but remember, you are not on the same team as Tom."

Veronica whispered to Celeste, "We're going to get our butts kicked."

Celeste said to her petite, blond friend, "No, we're not. I've seen you play, and you're good and so am I. I just need you to promise me you'll bring your A game and no crying under any circumstances!"

Veronica nodded, putting her manicured fingers in the red seven-pound ball in her tiny hands. Celeste selected a purple bowling ball swirled with hot pink flames, mirroring her mood.

"Remember, your fingertips give the ball spin and control," Celeste went on coaching Veronica, "good bowling is good posture. If your front foot is straight, your arm will swing where your foot is aimed."

Veronica nodded. "Got it!"

With his green ball in hand, Brian approached Celeste. "I saw you picked up a ten-pound ball."

Celeste flipped her hair back. "So?"

"So, I think it's way too heavy for you to handle. You really should consider using a smaller ball like Veronica's."

Celeste stepped back from him. "I don't need any advice from you."

"OK, baby, let's roll." Brian would show no mercy.

Celeste went first and stood in her lane, raising the ball and taking a deep breath. The ball weighed heavily, but she wouldn't let that hinder her. More momentum it will gain down the lane, she told herself. Taking a few steps forward, she swung her arm back, praying she wouldn't lose control of her grip and kept her front foot straight. She clinched her fingers, hanging on to the ball as hard as she could until her arm swung forward, her eyes glued to the markings on the lane. When she released the ball, it hit the ground and rolled down the lane, knocking all but one pin down. She smiled triumphantly.

When rolled the second time, she threw a gutter ball. Burning, she heard Veronica shout, "That's all right! Good job!"

Brian poked his fingers in his ball, and with pomp, he brought it up to his puffed-out chest. Shoulders back, he waltzed up to his lane, spinning around as he approached the 60-foot mark. In one smooth motion, he rolled a strike, never taking his eyes off the ten pins. "What a nice cracking sound that made." He smiled at Celeste, but she surveyed the bowling alley around her, refusing to acknowledge him. He clucked like a chicken, moving his arms like wings strutting past her, jutting, and jolting his neck.

What an asshole, Celeste thought, telling herself to stay calm. She cheered Veronica on, clapping as they went. With a burning arm, Celeste picked up her ball. Breathing deep she walked carefully to her lane and didn't let herself stop to feel any fear. She prayed again she wouldn't let the heavy ball go too soon when she swung her arm pack. Foot straight, eyes on the lane markings, she released the ball down the lane. The path the ball rolled down would only score Celeste a few pins. She repeated the process and knocked down a few more pins.

Tom rolled and bowled like a pro. Celeste tried not to get discouraged as she wondered how long he'd been bowling. His first roll he got all but one pin. His second roll, he moved to the left and knocked off the one pin to the far right.

As the match carried on, Celeste picked off a 3, 7, 10 split. Brian followed her and knocked off a 6, 7, 9, 10 split using a carefully controlled hook. The women gave it their best, fighting quite a battle, but the winning score went to the men.

"You ladies played one heck of a good game," Tom said. "Let's go get some more beers and burgers."

Brian put his hand on Celeste's right arm. What a gracious gesture, she thought.

"Your arm is going to be sore tomorrow." Brian's laugh felt like a hyena circling her.

"So is yours, but for different reasons." She walked away from him towards the bar.

Hot on her back, Brian ordered, "A pitcher of beer, please!"

Celeste interjected, "I'll have a milkshake."

"You don't want a beer?" Brian asked.

She snipped, "No, and I can order for myself, thanks."

"You're being a sore loser," he said to her under his breath.

"I'm not a loser!"

"Celeste, you just lost the game."

"Well, we'll see what happens in the rematch because I was just getting warmed up!" She swiveled her barstool away from him.

He swiveled her back. "Maybe next time you'll be smart enough to use a smaller ball so you can handle it better."

"Do you know what you did tonight?"

Brian smiled. "Yes, I was bowling—at a *high* level!"

"No, I mean your behavior."

Seeing the look on her friend's face, Veronica jumped in, "Let's talk about our wedding! Where do you think we should get married? I always wanted to get married on a boat, but after what happened at Jeff's wedding, there is no way I want to do that now."

Brian offered, "You two should just elope and go to Vegas and get hitched."

Celeste turned to Brian. "Is that really your advice?"

"What?" Brian wondered. "It's easy, no fuss, and kind of romantic."

Tom said, "I don't mind the idea."

Looking at her fiancé, Veronica said, "You're just trying to save money."

Tom grinned. "We could have Elvis marry us."

Giggling, Veronica squeaked, "Immediately NO!"

After hanging out for a while, Brian said they'd need to get going because he had to work an early shift the next day. Celeste hugged her friend goodbye, congratulated her again. "I'll call you soon so we can start planning your wedding… *not* in Vegas." She glared at Brian.

"Sounds good! And I won't be doing a peacock theme," she said, giggling. "Probably pink, lots and lots of pink!"

On the drive home, Celeste remained silent and turned the volume up on the radio so as not to have to talk to Brian.

He turned the volume back down. "I didn't realize you were so competitive."

"I'm not competitive." She turned the volume back up. She thought about what all she'd need to do to help Veronica. That's what she had to keep her mind on to avoid a fight.

Brian broke her mental list and asked over the music, "Do you want to go out again next weekend? I have an early shift on Friday. We could try that new Greek place that opened up by your place."

"Sounds good." Celeste kept her focus on her phone screen scrolling around looking at pictures of white rose bouquets… white and pink… Veronica would like white and pink.

"Maybe we could go to a movie, too." Brian's phone binged when he pulled up to Celeste's place and he took it out. The police chief sent him a text telling him to get over to the mayor's house. Looked like his shift was going to start earlier than planned.

"Maybe." Not extending a much-wanted invitation in, Celeste said, "I know you have to get up early tomorrow, so I'll just see you next Friday." She pecked his cheek and quickly pulled back. She hopped out of his car and on her way up to her front door, she twirled around like Brian did when he approached his lane. It felt like an involuntary ridicule of his behavior. When in history has a chicken dance ever gotten a man laid? Celeste slammed her door closed behind her.

Driving over to the mayor's house in Sunshine Beach, Brian thought about Celeste being frigid. He wondered why he was still dating her.

Chapter Six

Uncle Clarence

That same night, Maybel breathed in smoke sitting by the firepit, trying not to cough. The night air in the Shady Sunset garden fell cold. The courtyard was lit up by nothing but the crackling fire. Maybel buttoned up her wool cardigan and felt uncomfortable on the flimsy lawn chair beneath her. Swatting away a buzzing mosquito, the chair rocked back and forth.

"Good," Sheila said in a calming tone. "Everyone take in another deep breath to the count of four, then hold the breath for the count of seven and let it out to the count of eight. Smell the summer lilies and the roses from the garden."

Maybel couldn't smell the flowers over the smoke. She breathed in, counting to four, but forgot the other numbers, letting her breath out. She opened her eyes, spying Norma sitting to her right and Vera to her left. Across from her sat Sheila, Arnie, and Ida, the small group that gathered for the fireside chant.

"Now, let's all stare into the flames of the fire. Feel how relaxing that is. Keep taking deep breaths and remember, you are the U in the universe." Sheila watched the group of seniors looking at the fire burning in the pit. "First, we're going to chant 'om' for our inner peace. Then, for our mental health, we'll recite some affirmations like 'my body is a temple'. I'll walk you through a guided meditation."

Maybel fixed her eyes on the dancing flames from the fire. This really is relaxing, she thought, while chanting, om.

Wanting to soothe everyone, Sheila picked up the flute sitting next to her and blew into it. A sharp whistling sound pierced Maybel's ear, startling her. For a few minutes, sour noises escaped the flute, and Maybel wanted to plug her ears but knew that would be rude. Glancing around at the group, Maybel watched Vera wince at the high-pitched cries escaping Sheila's instrument. Arnie stuck his index finger in his ear, wiggling it. Maybel had heard more harmonious sounds emanate from Mr. Piddles when he got hungry and meowed for his dinner.

"Did you notice how the flames danced around and flickered to the music?" Sheila asked.

Norma wondered, "Is om a foreign language? I always wanted to learn another language like French, but I never got around to it. And I thought we were going to tell ghost stories and make s'mores."

Sheila took a deep, cleansing breath to the count of six. Speaking in a calm tone, she said, "Norma, remember how we discussed that there is a time to speak and there is a time to be silent?"

Norma nodded. "Oh, yes. I remember. I thought that was so insightful. Most of the time I feel like talking and I've been told I'm *not* a good listener, but I have so much to say that it's difficult for me to keep quiet. I've always talked a lot ever since I was a young child and–"

"Norma!" Sheila whispered, "this is a time for being quiet."

"Oh, OK. I thought maybe we were going to chat. Earlier, you said we were going to sing and chat."

"No," Sheila corrected. "I said we were going to chant, not chat."

Norma asked, "What are we going to chant? Om is not really a sentence. It's just a noise if you think about it, or does it have meaning? I'd like to know the meaning. Are we also going to chant any affirmations? I really like those, especially the spiritual ones. I've really been trying to get in touch with my higher self like you recommended the other day. Yesterday I tried meditating on what my inner spirit is really like, and I concluded that I–"

"Norma, what I said was," Sheila began, raising her hand in the air toward the heavens, "when you are open to a partnership with spirit, you form a partnership with your higher self. I encourage you all to open up your spirit and get into the flow of God's abundance."

Arnie leaned forward in his rickety lawn chair. "Speaking of spirits, has anyone heard the story about Uncle Clarence?"

"No, I don't think so," Norma said. "Is this a story about your Uncle Clarence? I had an Uncle Randolph. He had a farm in Oklahoma where we're from, and he used to cut his nails with his pocketknife. Uncle Randy was a funny man. He was my cousin Sally's father. We used to go fishing in his pond in the summer."

Arnie shook his head. "No. Uncle Clarence was one of the residents here at Shady Sunset." Arnie paused for dramatic effect. In a macabre whisper, he said, "*Uncle Clarence died on the premises under very suspicious circumstances. Rumor has it his ghost still inhabits this place.*"

"Goodness! What happened?" Ida asked over the sound of chirping crickets.

Arnie rubbed his hands together. "Oh, Ida, my beautiful wildflower, wait until you hear this story!"

Sheila, realizing she had lost control of the group, busted out the Hershey bars and put s'mores together.

The warm glow of the flames in the firepit lit up Arnie's weather-beaten face, creasing into kindly wrinkles when he furrowed his brow. His gray hair shined in the silver moonlight. In his most serious voice, he said, "Years ago, Uncle Clarence moved in after his wife passed away. He stayed in the same apartment that Violet is in now. Every night… he walked the halls crying for his beloved wife. The residents could hear him mourn her night after night. Some complained to the staff that his crying kept them up at night."

"Oh, that's so sad!" Vera wrapped her coat around her tightly to stay warm.

Sheila stuck some marshmallows on metal skewers and passed them out.

"It was very sad," Arnie said. "His hollow wails echoed out through the halls of this old mansion. He was consumed with grief. Then, one dark and dreary day, his niece Victoria came to visit him on family day. When she went to his apartment, she couldn't believe what she found!"

Norma's eyes widened. "What did she find? Was he dead? He was dead, wasn't he?"

Arnie went on, "His niece, Victoria, went to his apartment and knocked. There was no answer. She knocked again. There was no answer." Arnie reached out his hand and said, "She turned the doorknob, but it was locked. She found a maintenance man and asked him to unlock the door for her. When they opened it, there they saw Uncle Clarence. He had hung himself from the ceiling fan!"

Ida gasped, covering her mouth. Norma and Vera were glued to Arnie's every word.

Arnie said, "It devastated his niece. She felt so guilty and blamed herself. She said if only she had visited him more often, it wouldn't have happened. 'Why, oh why, didn't I visit him more often?' she cried out when she saw his lifeless body. But that's not even the worse part. They realized the door to his apartment had been locked from the *outside*! Only the outside lock had been locked! There was no way Uncle Clarence could have locked it!"

"And then what happened?" Sheila asked, crunching on a gooey chocolate marshmallow filled graham cracker.

"His niece ran down to the main office to tell the administrator, and the administrator told her, 'We've never had anyone here by the name of Clarence.' His niece couldn't believe it. She demanded the administrator check the

Shady Sunset records. The administrator asked if he went by any other names, and his niece said no. The administrator checked all their records but found no record of anyone named Clarence staying in that apartment, *ever*. The administrator told his niece the apartment had been vacant for the last six months!"

"Oh, my God!" Norma exclaimed.

Maybel rolled her eyes around like a pinwheel on a windy day.

"When they raced back to Uncle Clarence's apartment, his body was gone! He vanished without a trace. To this day, some residents say they can still hear Uncle Clarence crying in the halls late at night."

Norma clutched her chest. "I bet those are the noises I hear every night!"

"I'm sure they are," Arnie said, sticking his skewered marshmallow into the fire. He quickly pulled it back out and blew on the flame, extinguishing it and looking at the nice black char mark.

Colleen walked under the garden courtyard trellis, emerging in the dark night. She greeted everyone seated around the firepit. Her short, blue-black hair blended into the night sky. Being the administrator for the retirement home, it was her duty to keep an eye on everything. Standing tall and thin in a white pilling cardigan, she politely smiled, scanning the group.

"Norma, you don't actually believe this story, do you?" Maybel wondered.

Norma gave Maybel an indignant look. "Of course, I do. It explains everything!"

Maybel sputtered, "It explains nothing! It's not true."

Vera interjected, "It would explain a lot. I think I've heard the crying at night, too. Now I know why. It's the ghost of Uncle Clarence."

Maybel insisted, "There is no such thing as ghosts, and Arnie made that story up!"

Wiping melted chocolate from the side of his mouth, Arnie protested, "The story is true, Maybel. You're just afraid to believe in ghosts."

"Ghosts aren't real!"

"Well, all I know," Arnie said, taking a tiny black book from his back pocket, "is I'm going to start documenting these strange goings on my little black book."

Maybel shook her head. "That is so gross that you have a little black book!"

"Get your mind out of the gutter, Maybel. I only use this book to keep track of my golf scores and my bowel movements."

Shelia rubbed her tummy and whispered, "Arnie has problems with constipation, so I recommended he track his bowel movements. If he goes too long without one, that could be a sign that he has a blockage."

A disgusted look dumped out on Maybel's face.

"But now, in this little black book, I'm going to document all the ghostly activity here at Shady Sunset. I've noted the strange bursts of fog I've seen out at the cemetery," Arnie said.

Maybel crossed her arms over her chest. "Again, there is no such thing as ghosts."

"I'm not so sure," Sheila said. "The spirit world can transcend all our understanding. It would be naïve to think there isn't life after death here on earth. I'd be happy to host a séance for all of you."

"Maybe Uncle Clarence had some unfinished business, and that's why he couldn't pass on to the other realm," Vera added.

Arnie proposed, "Yeah, we could stir up the spirits and have a séance to see if Uncle Clarence wants to communicate with us."

Astonished that the entire group, except for her, believed in ghosts, Maybel wiped melted chocolate off her hand. "This is ridiculous!"

Arnie laughed, sitting back in his lawn chair, sprawling out and spreading his long legs wide. (Body language experts would call his position a crotch display.) "What are you so scared of, Maybel?"

A sneer crawled up Maybel's face as she looked away from Arnie's groin area. "I'm not afraid of anything! You're just getting everyone riled up again. You should be ashamed of yourself!"

Colleen reached for a graham cracker and said, "I'm with Maybel. It's a bad idea to summon the dead. Let them

rest in peace. In my experience, when people start believing in ghosts, problems wait ahead…"

Chapter Seven

No Signs of Forced Entry

Later that same night, Detective Bahn pulled into the driveway of the mayor of Sunshine Beach's mansion. Walking up the cobblestone steps, he ran a hand through his damp hair. The misty ocean air hung heavy. The officer who arrived first on the scene met Bahn at the gigantic double front doors of the home. After the briefing, Bahn asked, "What kind of weapon did he carry?"

"Some sort of walking stick," the clean-cut officer answered.

Bahn looked around the area. "How do we know the intruder intended to use it as a weapon?"

"The mayor said," the officer replied.

Detective Bahn walked around the outside of the mayor's lavish home. Their mansion perched majestically on a cliff overlooking the ocean. "I'd like to speak to him."

"He's in his study with his wife." The officer led the way, walking through the front foyer of the house. Detective Bahn looked up at the high ceiling and noted the expensive dangling crystal chandelier that sparkled everywhere. A spiral staircase climbed up to the left, with the library to the right. On the way, they passed a wall with some thick framed art. Bahn stopped to look at a painting of a few triangles and a long-mouthed man's face. It looked like something a child painted. Funny what the rich consider art, Bahn thought. What a typical display of wealth Bahn observed, knowing the mayor's salary, while higher than his, was not enough to cover this mansion.

"Mayor Moustrip and Mrs. Moustrip." Bahn nodded his head in a greeting to the stiff couple sitting in the ornately decorated library. Mahogany shelves were lined with books Bahn suspected had never been read. A large desk sat in the corner with a view of the ocean that the taxpayers obliged. The couple were sitting in leather chairs at the opposite end of the room. Their throne-like seats faced a fireplace burning and crackling with wood a flame. A bar stood regal behind them, glimmering with gold decanters, crystal stemware and top shelf brand bottles only.

The mayor stood and shook Detective Bahn's hand. His wife dabbed at her moist eyes with a tissue and slowly stood up to greet him, straightening out the wrinkles in her silk skirt. Bahn made note of their formal attire, thinking Mrs. Moustrip looked much younger in front of the firelight than she did the first night he met her a while back. "Mayor, Officer Nelson here told me what happened, but if you don't mind, I'd like to ask you a few more questions."

The mayor nodded and put his arm around his visibly shaken wife.

"You had a party here tonight, correct?"

The mayor answered, "Yes, that's correct. We were celebrating my 50th birthday. Our dinner party ended around 10 pm."

"How many guests were here?"

The mayor's wife spoke up. "I'd say about thirty people were here. We wanted a smaller, more intimate group for this event."

Bahn looked at the mayor's wife, and searching her face, he could see she'd had some work done. She looked flawless. "Would you be able to get me a copy of the guest list?"

"Of course," Mrs. Moustrip said.

"Could the intruder have been a guest? Or a friend of a guest?" Bahn asked.

"No," the mayor replied. "I'd never seen this man before."

Bahn looked at the mayor and a voice in his head cautioned him to step carefully on this landmine of a lie. "When you found him on your property, where were you?"

The mayor hesitated for a few seconds. "I was in the garage."

Bahn inquired, "What were you doing in the garage?"

"I heard a noise. I thought maybe we had a racoon in there again."

Bahn raised his eyebrows. "A racoon?" *Jesus, what a lie!*

The mayor nodded. "Yes, we've had a few of them get in the garage recently."

His wife added, "There's a small hole in the corner, and we haven't had time to have it fixed. We think that's where they are getting into the garage from."

"What happened when you went into the garage?" Bahn looked down at Mrs. Moustrip's shoes.

Mayor Moustrip said, "I turned on the light and I saw him."

"The intruder? Or the racoon?" Bahn wondered, performing a balancing act of pretending to believe the mayor while trying to determine the truth. Bahn was walking a metaphorical tightrope, and if he fell off, he'd make the most powerful man in Sunshine Beach his enemy.

A scowl scratched the mayor's face. "The intruder. He was standing in the garage wearing a trench coat and holding a large stick."

"Can you describe the stick?"

The mayor cleared his throat. "It was a long walking stick."

"So, a cane?" Bahn wrote a note on a small notepad, old school pen and paper.

"No," the mayor answered. "It didn't have a rounded handle like a candy cane. It was a knotted crooked stick with a slightly curved handle–like a backwards seven."

"You got a good look at his stick." Bahn smiled. "What happened next?"

"I asked him what he was doing in my garage."

Bahn glanced at the mayor's wife, who kept her eyes glued on her husband. "And what did he say?"

The mayor took a deep breath and let it out. "He said he was the rain man, and he'd come to collect what was due to him."

The worst liar ever. "Rain man? Like Dustin Hoffman?"

Another scowl twitched at the mayor's face. He spoke a slow warning. "I assure you, it wasn't Dustin Hoffman. I think the man was crazy. I asked the man to leave my property, and that's when he lunged at me with the stick, so I grabbed my harpoon gun off the wall and shot it at him."

A sob came from the mayor's wife, and she dabbed at her eyes again. She took a deep breath. "That's when I came in."

"Did you hit him with it?"

The mayor paused before speaking. "I think I made contact on his left side. I think the harpoon went through his coat. It's still stuck in the wall with a scrap of fabric on it. It tore his trench coat. I'm just glad I didn't kill him."

Detective Bahn stared at the mayor a few seconds longer than what was socially acceptable. "We've all got to die sometime." He looked at Mrs. Moustrip, who would not take her eyes off her devoted husband. Bahn burned with anger at being put in this position. "May I have a look in the garage?"

"Of course." The mayor briskly led the way.

Detective Bahn looked around the neatly organized garage. A Lexus and a Mercedes were parked side by side. A large freezer stood in the corner, along with shelves of tools and some boxes stacked up neatly. He saw the tiny hole in the side of the garage where they said the racoons were getting in. "Well, I'll be damned. You do have a hole in your garage wall." Bahn chuckled. "Those raccoons get cold at night, huh?" Bahn stared at the place on the wall where the speargun hung. "You shot the gun and then hung it back up on the wall?"

The mayor nodded.

"What did the intruder do after you shot him?"

The mayor pointed to the side door leading to the outside. "He ran out that door." He wiggled his shoulders from side to side, adding, "It all happened so fast."

Bahn watched the mayor move around, nervously observing that he looked like a snake slithering out of its skin. He walked in the direction the mayor pointed and looked at the spear sticking out of the wall. He bent down to get a closer look at it. It did indeed have a torn piece of fabric stuck to it. He stood up and said, "The spear landed rather low to the ground."

The mayor and his wife stayed silent, standing side by side like two turtle doves in love. The mayor gently and lovingly put his arm around his distraught wife.

Officer Nelson's eyes scanned the garage.

Detective Bahn pointed to the ladder in the garage that stood erect between the two cars. "This ladder seems out of place. Were you changing a lightbulb?"

"Yes," the mayor's wife answered. "I changed a lightbulb yesterday and forgot to put it away."

Detective Bahn looked back again at the speargun on the wall. "What do you hunt with that harpoon gun? Seals?" He looked at the mayor.

The mayor looked at his wife and back at Bahn. "Calico bass… halibut."

"Ah, I see. We'll need access to your security camera footage. Maybe we can identify the intruder with our face recognition software. And we'll need to take the harpoon in to examine it further."

The mayor nodded. "Thank you. We appreciate your help in finding this man. My wife is rather shaken up by the break in."

"We'll do everything we can to find him," Detective Bahn assured the mayor. Bahn took out a pair of latex gloves from his pocket. "Just one more thing. Would you mind putting on these gloves and taking down the speargun for me so we can take that with us?"

Officer Nelson frowned.

The mayor did as he was asked and slipped on the gloves. He walked over to the wall where the speargun was mounted. He stood on his tiptoes and fumbled around with it, finally pulling it off the wall.

Bahn counted the seconds it took for the mayor to pull the speargun off the wall. "If you don't mind, we'll just leave out this side door after we have forensics dislodge the spear from the wall. We don't want to take up any more of your time. I'm sure you must be tired from a long night."

On the way out, Detective Bahn examined the lock on the side door. "No signs of forced entry," he said to Officer Nelson. Walking down the cobblestone steps, Bahn asked, "What side do you think the mayor's bread is buttered on?"

Officer Nelson laughed. "So, what do you think really happened?"

"They're lying… but why they are lying? I do not know."

"You think they knew the man that broke into the garage?"

Bahn looked at Officer Nelson. "I'm sure of it. Let me ask you this: if some dirt bag broke into your house and you shot him, would you be saying you were happy you didn't kill him?"

Officer Nelson replied, "If some dirt bag dared break into my house and I had to shoot him, I would hope I killed him."

"The mayor said he took his *harpoon* gun off the wall, but it's a speargun, not a harpoon. If it was really his, he'd know that, and you'd never use a harpoon to kill bass or halibut. My guess is the speargun belongs to his wife."

"You think she shot the intruder?"

Bahn nodded. "And I bet when we dust the speargun for prints, we won't find the mayor's fingerprints on it. You saw how long it took him to get it down. He'd never handled that thing before."

"If that's the case, then we're on dangerous ground." Officer Nelson looked back at the mayor's house up the cliff. He spotted the mayor's wife's face in the second-story window, watching them.

"You know what they say… the best lies have a kernel of truth in them. We need to find out who the rain man is, what it means… and why the mayor is lying for his wife."

Chapter Eight

Someone Is So Crafty

The next day, Maybel, deciding to get more involved in some activities at Shady Sunset, walked over to the room designated for craft projects. Feeling a little nervous when she walked in, she took a seat in the back of the room.

Jo, the Shady Sunset activities director, stomped into the room and announced, "OK, ladies, and Arnie, we're going to be making flower wreaths out of pinecones!"

"With all these pinecones, shouldn't we be making a Christmas wreath?" Vera asked, loving classic traditions.

"It's almost summer, and I found a great idea for turning pinecones into flowers," Jo answered. She explained she'd gathered up a rather large stock of them from the pine trees out by the cemetery. They had already cleaned them prior to their craft class. She'd invited Vick, the janitorial maintenance man, Maybel's former neighbor, and Arnie's son, to the class. "One of the first things we must do is cut the pinecones horizontally into two or three sections, depending on the size of the pinecones and how big you want your flowers to be. Vick is here, so he can saw them into pieces for you. Everyone come up and pick out several pinecones for yourself and then give them to Vick to cut."

Vick stood by, ready with his hacksaw and a pair of bypass loppers.

The women in the craft class, and Arnie, got up and meandered over to the baskets of pinecones, taking turns picking out a few for themselves.

Norma hurried to the baskets to pick hers first. "I'm so excited! I love to create something from nothing."

Maybel frowned. "We're not creating something from nothing. Only God can do that. We're creating flower wreaths from pinecones."

Norma bristled from the correction and went on, "I can't imagine how we're going to make pinecones look like flowers!" She handed hers to Vick, and he began sawing them in half. Vick's height and size made tools look quite small in his hands. Bits of pinecone flew out everywhere and pinecone particles hit the floor.

"Geez, Vick! Be careful! You don't want to cut your hand off," Maybel warned.

Standing a foot taller than her, Vick looked down at Maybel and snapped, "I don't need you to tell me how to use my tools, Maybel."

"Speaking of tools, where did Arnie go?" Maybel wondered, looking around the room. She spotted him in the corner, buzzing around Ida Adler, one of the younger widows at Shady Sunset. "Oh, that poor thing," Maybel muttered under her breath. Running her hand along her pinecones, she felt the pokey p.

Arnie fancied himself quite the silver haired foxy ladies' man at Shady Sunset. The women outnumbered the men four to one, and Arnie, still quite spry for his age, possessed a full head of hair. "I'd love to carry your pinecones for you," he sweet-talked Ida.

A soft giggle proceeded Ida's nod. Arnie took that as his green light. He thought if he played his cards right, he'd have another notch on his bedpost before the week was up.

Jo set up an assembly line. After they picked out their pinecones and had them cut into pieces, they were instructed to go to the painting station. There they would paint their pieces of pinecones and sprinkle glitter on them if they desired. Jo set out an entire array of pastel-colored paints and primary colors. Once they were dried, they were to move over to the gluing station. At the gluing station, Jo set out Styrofoam wreaths and hot glue guns. They were instructed to glue their painted pinecones to the wreaths. After that, they were instructed to go to the ribbon station and pick out a ribbon to attach to their wreath.

Jo stood at the painting station mixing yellow and red to make orange. When she offered the color to Vera, she shook her head. "That looks too garish for my taste," Vera said, crinkling her nose.

"Is that a new broach?" Jo asked.

Vera looked down at the pin on her lapel and replied, "No, I've had this in my family for years. It's real amethyst."

"Oh, it's just lovely!" Jo admired.

With the class in full swing, Sheila Anderson, dressed in her pink hospital scrubs, popped her head in. "Hello everyone! I just wanted to remind you that my brand-new nutrition class will start tomorrow. Hope to see all of you there. I know for some of you, this class will be very help-ful. I'll be teaching you how to test for food sensitivities that can cause inflammation that leads to a whole slew of health problems like arthritis pain, gas, and bloating," she said, rubbing her stomach and looking at Maybel.

Maybel looked over at Arnie. His flirting with Ida kept him from hearing a word Sheila said. "That figures," she said. If she did one more eye roll, Maybel thought her eyes would fall out of her head. She squirted some more glue out of the hot glue gun, attaching another painted pine-cone to her wreath.

Colleen also popped her head into the class to see how everyone was doing. Walking around admiring everyone's wreaths, she said, "I've always thought pinecones are like little treasures that drop from the trees and wait like new friends to be found. Pinecones show us that we are all dif-ferent, all beautiful, all perfect in our imperfection." With one in her hand, she turned it around, examining it.

"What a lovely sentiment," Norma replied. "I agree. I've always loved pinecones."

When Maybel completed crafting her wreath, she stepped back and looked at it. Thinking it looked like a craft a five-year-old would make in kindergarten, she knew she wouldn't hang it on her door. Looking around the room again, she saw Violet sitting alone with her pinecone pieces. Knowing Violet probably couldn't maneuver around all the craft stations with her oxygen tank, Maybel walked over to her to help.

"Here Violet, let me carry your pinecones over to the painting station," Maybel said with a smile.

"You're such a dear friend, Maybel."

Maybel carefully helped her go to each craft station, completing all the steps. She sat with Violet while she tied a ribbon to her wreath of brightly painted pinecones. Maybel noticed Violet painted her pinecones in shades of yellow and orange.

"Bright and cheery," Maybel complimented her. "I only used purple and pink."

Vera walked up and said to them, "Well, I know we were supposed to be making summer flowers, but since we were using pinecones, I painted mine red and green. I felt that was a more traditional use of them. I'm going to save mine and hang it on my door for Christmas."

"What a wonderful idea!" Violet smiled and put her oxygen mask back on.

Norma showed off her wreath. "I painted mine to look like daisies, so they're white with a yellow center. All it needs now is a bumblebee!"

"Now ladies, don't forget to come back tomorrow! We're going to be making Hawaiian leis for the luau we're having tomorrow night!" Jo's chipper demeanor rang out in the craft room.

Arnie let out a hearty chuckle and winked at Ida. "Oh, I'll be back tomorrow to get *'leid'* for sure!"

Maybel rolled her eyes like dice on a Vegas Craps table. She turned to Violet and said, "Why don't I help you carry your wreath back to your place?"

Once they got to Violet's, on a hunch again, Maybel turned the knob and found it unlocked.

"Oh, dear! I forgot to lock it again!" Violet let go of the handle on her tank and wrung her spotted hands.

"We all forget things sometimes, Violet," Maybel said, comforting her. "Don't be too hard on yourself." She helped Violet get settled in, made her a cup of tea, and hung her summer flower wreath on Violet's front door before she left.

Back at her own place, Maybel skipped going down to the dining room for dinner. As social as she used to be, she still didn't feel completely at home at Shady Sunset. She sure missed George and thought about going to visit his grave, but decided to save that for another day since a rainstorm was moving in. She prepared herself a toasted cheese sandwich, heated a can of tomato soup, and sat down in front of her tv. Mr. Piddles sidled up to her, and she knew it wasn't affection he craved. She saved a few bites of her sandwich for him, which he devoured quickly. He curled up next to her, scratching at the stuffed mouse Jeffrey bought for her at the amusement park on her birthday.

Maybel turned down the volume of her television to hear the dripping rain outside. She found the rat-a-tat-tatting of rain soothing. Looking out her window after a jagged flash of lightning lit up her living room, she heard rumbling thunder and fierce wind. Sheets of rain cascaded down her window. She asked Mr. Piddles, "How about a cup of hot cocoa?"

In her kitchen, a saucepan full of half milk and half cream heated gently. Adding some chunks of milk chocolate, she stirred it continuously. After sprinkling cinnamon into it, she poured herself a cup. Mr. Piddles was served his own saucer of plain cream. Carrying her cup carefully back to her couch, she set it down on her end table and grabbed the pink blanket she'd knitted years earlier that hung over the back of her couch. Spreading the afghan across her lap, she remembered how George joked about it, looking like Pepto Bismol pink, but she loved her blanket. In between sips of hot cocoa, she laughed at the memory. Jeffrey had chimed in that the pink blanket on the brown couch looked like Baskin Robbins. Missing those days of her family being altogether, she looked out her window again. The storm subsided a bit, and she stared at the light rain drops drizzling and squiggling down her window. Growing drowsy from the soothing pitter patter of rain, she soon drifted off to sleep.

A beastly wind rattled her window, waking Maybel and Mr. Piddles from their nap. Mr. Piddles jumped off the couch and climbed up to the top perch of his cat tree. He curled up and went back to sleep. Even Mr. Piddles leaves me, she thought, picking up her knitting and listening to the light rain. Not being fully settled into Shady Sunset, it seemed more like a stay at a hotel than in her home. Skilled at moss stitching, she wove blue and green yarn around and around in a beautiful pattern while pushing thoughts of George out of her mind.

Maybel's phone binged. A group text from Arnie read: **I just saw it again! The burst of fog is back!**

"Oh, that imbecile!" Annoyed, Maybel looked out her window that gave her a clear view of the Heavenly Souls Cemetery. She stood carefully. Because of the weather, arthritis in her knee made it a little stiff. In disbelief, she spotted it. The rain had eased and through the night air, she saw a small, strange, foggy cloud billowing around in the cemetery. "Good grief! He's right!"

The lights in her apartment flickered and went out. Maybel used the flashlight on her phone and poked around in a kitchen drawer, taking out a candle and some matches. Carefully carrying the candle with her, she poked her head out her front door. The light from her candle cut dancing patterns on the walls. Looking down the hall, it appeared all the lights at Shady Sunset were out. Her phone binged again. Norma, unable to stifle her excitement, texted the group: **The storm knocked the lights out and a painting just fell off my wall! The ghost of Uncle Clarence is back!**

"Oh, geez! Here we go again!" Maybel said. She closed her front door, carried the candle with her, set it down on her coffee table, and sat on her couch. She texted the group: **Uncle Clarence wasn't real!**

Arnie texted the group: **Oh, he was real alright!**

Maybel reached for her battery-operated book light and popped it on, knitting by the rays of the tiny bulb. Her clever kitty curled up next to her and slept peacefully.

Sometime later, Vera texted everyone: **I heard the dragging noise coming from the attic again!**

Maybel texted: **That's probably where the fuse box is. Someone probably went up there to get the power back on.**

Sure enough, a minute later, the lights came back on. Maybel texted everyone again: **See!**

Arnie texted the group: **I'm sure my son Vick got the lights back on and saved the day!**

"He's such an idiot," Maybel said to Mr. Piddles. A flick of his tail signaled he agreed.

Another text from Vera binged: **Before the lights came back on, I poked my head out of my place, and I saw a ghost in the hallway!**

Arnie texted: **I'm noting all of this in my little black book!**

"Oh, good heavens! This is out of control." Maybel called Vera and asked, "Tell me exactly what you saw."

Vera replied, "I looked out into the hall and saw a figure in a filmy white gown floating around. Her shadowy face leered at me!"

"What did she look like?" Maybel asked, remaining calm.

"Just some woman… with a pale green wraith-like face…"

"How long was this object in the hall?"

"It wasn't an object! It was a ghost! But it wasn't Uncle Clarence. A female ghost haunted the hallway. I think it was the ghost of Beatrice Parkins! I know you don't believe me, but I know what I saw. Norma was right. This place is haunted!"

"Where exactly did you see this female ghost?"

Vera replied, "Like I said, at the end of the hallway against the wall. She wore a flowy gown made of white gossamer fabric. It must have been her wedding dress; the dress she wore the night she died. Her face glowed! She flittered about, and then she vanished! It gave me quite a fright! Maybel, it was so eerie!"

Maybel mulled over the information and speculated, "Someone could have projected an image against the wall."

"I guess that could have been what happened, but who would do that?"

"That's a good question… but isn't there a mirror on the wall at the end of your hallway?"

"Yes."

"Do you think you could have seen your own image in the dark?"

"No! I know what I look like, Maybel! And there was one other really strange thing."

"What's that?"

"I am positive that when I looked out in the hallway, I smelled lavender."

"So?"

"So?! According to all the stories and reports, Beatrice Parkins wore lavender perfume. People say you can still smell her perfume when she walks the halls at night."

"Alright. If you see the ghost-like image again, try to get a picture of it," Maybel suggested, wanting to get to the bottom of this hoax.

"OK, I'll try." Vera signed off.

Maybel didn't believe Vera saw a ghost in the hallway, but she believed Vera saw something. Wondering what it could be, she heard a shuffling sound. Looking over, she saw her front door ajar. "I thought I closed that." Gingerly peeking out into the hall, she saw nothing unusual. A powerful gust of wind screeched at her window, startling her. She closed her door, locked it, checking it twice to make sure she secured the latch. "No such thing as ghosts," she assured herself.

Chapter Nine

Aloha

"What do you think you saw last night?" Celeste asked Maybel during their phone call the next day.

A light spring rain drizzled on Maybel's window, and a cloud covered sky cast a dark hue in her tiny apartment. "I'm not sure… guess the fog rolled in again. I think that happens when cold air comes in quickly moving over the warm air."

"That sounds so scientific."

"It does, doesn't it? But it really looked spooky… a small billowy patch of fog swirling around. Maybe we should investigate some night," Maybel said.

"The last place I want to be is in a cemetery late at night."

"You don't believe in ghosts, do you?"

Celeste paused before speaking. "No, I guess not, but it just seems kind of creepy. Like the stage is set for a horror movie."

"Oh, well, we wouldn't want that," Maybel replied.

"What do you think happened with Norma's painting?"

"She probably just didn't hang it right, and it slipped off the wall," Maybel reasoned.

"And the ghostly face I saw in the window *and* the ghost Vera saw in the hallway last night… how do you explain that?"

"Maybe you saw just someone's reflection in the window, and I told Vera someone could have projected an image onto the wall at the end of the hallway. I'm sure there is a reasonable explanation for all these mysterious midnight shadows. Either that, or the ghost was a creation of Vera's hysteria. It doesn't help that Arnie is making up all these stupid ghost stories."

"Why would he do that?"

"Because he's full of doo doo! But I will tell you, I did discover something interesting."

"Do tell!"

"I woke up early this morning before sunrise and couldn't get all this ghost business off my mind, so I went downstairs to the library room."

"I didn't know Shady Sunset had a library."

"Yeah, it's not very big. It's in a room off to the side of the lobby. It has a comfy couch. It's olive green and burnt orange plaid and reminds me of a couch George and I had when we first got married. The library has some rocking chairs, too. It's even got a stone fireplace, and they put some gorgeous silver candlesticks on the mantle. Above the mantle is an old painting of some hunting dogs on a country hillside. There are mahogany bookcases with lots of books. The library has one window that overlooks the garden area, and they put a side table in the corner where residents can play chess, backgammon or checkers."

"That sounds nice and cozy."

"It is, but I'm getting off track. I normally avoid the library because Norma likes to hang out there. She talks so much I'd never be able to concentrate on my reading. But early in the morning, there's no one in there. I went down to the library because Norma mentioned there's a binder that has information about Shady Sunset before they remodeled it and turned the mansion into a retirement home."

"Did you find the binder?"

"I sure did! And as she said, there was lots of information and photos in it. Based on the photos I saw; this old mansion had all kinds of outdated features. Before the remodel it had push-button light switches, razor slits in the medicine cabinets, a dumbwaiter, a milk door, transom windows, a servant's entrance and a root cellar."

"A root cellar? That's unusual for California."

"Yes," Maybel agreed, "unusual, but not unheard of, especially a hundred years ago. Anyway, based on the original blueprint of the property that was tucked in the binder, I really learned a lot."

"Like what?"

"Like there was never a pool on this property."

"Why does that matter?" Celeste wondered.

"Vera said she heard a rumor that a young girl drowned in the pool and is one of the ghosts that haunts this place…

but that just can't be, because there was never a pool on the property."

"So, you just debunked the rumor?"

"Indeed… and Vera told another story about a cook being cut in half when he got caught by a heavy door to the pantry."

"Oh, that's horrible!"

"Well, yes, it would be if it actually happened."

"You don't think it did?"

"Absolutely not. On the original blueprints of this property, all doors are clearly marked. There was no door to the pantry… but even if there was, that's not the only discrepancy. Vera also said that Beatrice Parkins, the original homeowner, died here too. She said she was to get married here on the property and when she was walking down the curved staircase, she tripped and fell to her death."

Celeste gasped.

"Dear, don't worry. I don't think it happened. The blueprints show a straight staircase in the original house. This place didn't get a curved staircase until the remodel. People are just making stuff up. But the most interesting thing I found was that originally, the servant's entrance was a staircase on the side of the mansion. So, I went looking for it."

"How exciting! Did you find it?"

"Most definitely. According to all the blueprints, the entrance from the staircase into the house is on the floor Vera's apartment is now on, at the end of her hallway where she said she saw the ghostly image. I walked up to her floor to the end of the hallway. There's a full-length gilt mirror at the end of the hall. I examined the frame for a minute and then pushed on the mirror carefully. When I did, the door the mirror is attached to popped open. Viola!"

"Oh, wow! Good thing you didn't break the mirror, or you'd have seven years' bad luck."

"Dear, I don't believe in luck. I believe in the Lord."

"Was the staircase still there? Or did they take it out during the remodel?"

"Well, I poked my head in but couldn't see much at first. I looked behind me in the hallway to make sure no one saw me snooping around. There was no light switch in the secret passageway, but once I stepped inside, I could see the stairs. I walked down the staircase to find out where it led to."

"Maybel! You didn't! Do you know how dangerous that is? At your age, walking down a dark staircase! You're lucky you didn't fall and break a hip or twist a knee or sprain an ankle. And if you'd fallen, no one would have known you were there! Oh, I get chills just thinking about it."

"I appreciate your concern, dear, but I had my cellphone with me. I used the flashlight on it. It's not as bright as a real flashlight. I could only see a couple of steps at a time, but I held tight to the railing that ran along the staircase. It was hard to see, but I had to check it out. The scariest part was when I got about halfway down the narrow staircase that runs parallel along the side of the mansion, the door with the mirror on it swung closed… probably because the mirror was so heavy. I no longer had any light from the hall-way. Even with my flashlight, it was dark and hard to see. At one point, I felt like I was descending into an abyss, and all I could see were the cobwebs that filled every corner of each step. I even got wrapped up in one. That was icky! But it was too dark to go back up the stairs. I couldn't see the landing down in front of me, either. I was engulfed in darkness, and it smelled musty. I took each step carefully, and I placed my right foot on the step below, then placed my left foot on that same step. I just kept slowly repeating that process. I let the light from my cellphone be a lamp unto my feet and said a silent prayer, hoping I wouldn't fall."

"A lamp unto your feet... why does that sound familiar?"

"It's a Bible verse. God's word is a lamp unto our feet. It guides us. In scripture, it's used metaphorically, but I was using it literally. Anyway, as I got closer to the bottom, I saw a crack of light. I joyfully moved towards the light."

"Was the light from a door to the outside?"

"Yes, indeed. When I finally got to the bottom ledge, I found the door to the outside to the left and another door to the root cellar to the right."

"Tell me you didn't go down into the root cellar!"

"No, I didn't have the nerve, but I was hoping to find a clue that would help me get to the bottom of all this. I feel like we're being duped into thinking there is all this ghostly activity at Shady Sunset."

"Did you find any clues?"

"I'm not sure. I found the doorknob on the door that led out to the side grass area, and it was unlocked. I stepped outside and right into some clumps of willows. I was so glad to be out in the light again! I walked along the willows, but it was dark under the heavy foliage, and I almost tripped over some roots. The projecting underbrush kept catching on my pants. I came to the gate that surrounds the cemetery. I examined that closely too and found a hidden latch that opened a gate. That's a secret entrance into the cemetery from Shady Sunset."

"Someone could go back and forth from Shady Sunset to the cemetery without being seen."

"Exactly!"

"Why would anyone want to do that, though?"

"That's a good question. I'm not sure, but if this place is ever supposed to feel like my home, I need to get to the bottom of it."

"And knowing you, you will."

"In hindsight, it probably wasn't very smart for me to walk down that staircase."

"Did you walk back up it?" "Oh, heavens no! I used the gate to go into the cemetery and I had to walk all the way through it and around to the front of Shady Sunset. I definitely worked up an appetite for breakfast."

"You know, if the door at the bottom of that staircase was unlocked, it doesn't sound very safe for Shady Sunset."

"When I was on the outside and looked back at the door, it's completely camouflaged by the shrubbery. No one would ever guess you could enter the mansion from there."

"Promise me you won't do that again."

"I won't. So, what's new with you, dear?"

"Not much. I was supposed to go to dinner with Brian to try this new Greek place that just opened up, but he canceled on me."

Picking up on the tone in Celeste's voice, Maybel said, "You don't sound happy."

"He said he has to work late, but things have been weird between us lately," Celeste said.

"Trouble in paradise?"

"It's hardly paradise. I feel like he's pressuring me to get a lot closer, and I'm just not ready," Celeste informed her. "I just can't move as fast with my heart as he can with his body."

"Love waits," Maybel said.

"I think he's getting tired of waiting, and sometimes he's so arrogant. It makes me angry," Celeste replied. "You should have seen the stupid chicken dance he did right after he bowled a strike. It was so obnoxious!"

"Maybe he's not arrogant. Maybe he's confident and his confidence brings out your insecurity," Maybel suggested.

"If he weren't so ridiculously good looking, I wouldn't have even gone past a first date with him."

"Ah, hormones. I remember those." Maybel laughed. "By the way, we're going to be having a luau here tonight.

We're making leis for it today. Guests are welcome if you'd like to come."

Celeste thought about it and said, "I was going to invite you over for lunch this weekend, but I could come to the luau instead. That sounds like fun. It's a date!"

"Great," Maybel said. "I better sign off now. I promised Sheila I'd attend her nutrition class today."

Maybel said goodbye to Mr. Piddles, who was perched at the top of his cat tree, and walked over to the craft room, which was being used for the nutrition class. She was the first to arrive, and Sheila rushed up to her. "I'm so glad you decided to attend! Everyone who attends today gets a free test kit to find out what their food sensitivities are. I know you've been having some gas lately."

"I don't have a problem with that," Maybel protested, grabbing one of the test kits.

"Oh, sure you do, Maybel!" Arnie said, walking up behind her and slapping her on the back.

Maybel's face reddened, and she took her seat.

Slowly, other seniors entered the room and took their seats. Vera sat next to Maybel. "I hope Sheila doesn't tell us we can't have chocolate. I think I'd rather die than give up chocolate," she said with a giggle.

"Alright everyone, thank you for coming to this class today. Your body is going to thank you too! Let's jump right in. I'm going to show you step by step how to do the food sensitivity tests. We won't be able to find out today what your sensitivities are because we have to send the tests off to the company who makes these tests and then wait to get the results in the mail." Sheila went over in minute detail how to use the food sensitivity test kit. After that lecture concluded, she talked about healthy food choices, what foods to avoid, and which foods cause the most gas.

When she got to the last part, Arnie, who was sitting behind Maybel, leaned forward, slapped her on the back. "Pay attention, Maybel!"

With her back stinging, Maybel felt livid listening to the laughter rip through the room. Turning around, looking Arnie in the eye, she snapped, "Arnie, you're too old to display such childish playground antics!"

"Oh, don't get into a tizzy, Maybel." Arnie chuckled.

Once the class concluded, Sheila passed out some protein bars she recommended as being the healthiest ones on the market. "Great for controlling blood sugar spikes," she said to Maybel when she grabbed hers.

***

When Celeste's workday ended, she drove home to change and feed her bird, Birino. She cleaned the bottom of his cage, changed the water, and gave him more bird seed. Her little finch cooed with delight. After a few minutes of watching him peck at his dinner, she set her finger on the edge of his cage. Little bird feet walked up her finger to her hand. Stroking his wing with her other hand, she felt how soft his feathers were. He flew out her hand and up to his ring perch that hung from the ceiling. "My little free bird."

After putting on a lime green sundress, she fastened a bright flower in her long dark hair. "This looks Hawaiian," she said to her reflection in the mirror. She grabbed her bag and headed over to Shady Sunset.

Pulling up to park, she took a good long look at the building that housed the seniors. Watching the trees cast windy shadows everywhere, she thought it really looked like a haunted mansion. Celeste peered over to the right, seeing the graveyard with tombstones sticking up from the flatland sprinkled with trees. The light storm broke, and a beautiful rainbow stretched over the cemetery. There was something peaceful about it, a loved one's final resting place.

She entered the lobby of Shady Sunset, and an attendant seated at a desk in the foyer told her the luau was behind the main building in the dancehall. She made her way there, and when she went inside, she heard lovely Hawaiian music. The sound of the ukulele tickled her ears. They decorated the dancehall with flowers, grass skirts, birds, and a beachy backdrop. She smiled, feeling transported to an island oasis. Lots of residents were seated at tables with tropical printed tablecloths decorated with coconut centerpieces. She found Maybel at a table in the back with her friends.

"Hello everyone!" Celeste greeted the table. Maybel stood and hugged her.

"Hello, dear. Have you met everyone? This is Norma, Vera, and Violet," Maybel said, doing the introductions.

Pointing to Celeste's hair, Vera said, "I love your flower."

Handing her a flower lei, Norma said, "Here, put one of these on like the rest of us."

Celeste admired the beautiful purple and white orchids on the lei, hung it around her neck, and sat down.

"Hello, hello, hello ladies!" Jo greeted them, clipboard in hand. "Get ready to do some dancing later! We've got some real Hawaiian dancers coming for entertainment, and the pig only has an hour more to roast. We just put out the Hawaiian punch, too!"

"Wow, they really went all out for this," Celeste said to Maybel. "Why don't I go get us all some punch?" she offered, excusing herself from the table.

Arnie, dressed in a vivid pink and green Hawaiian shirt, slipped a flask of bourbon out of his pants pocket, and poured it into the punchbowl. "That outta liven things up!" He was still snickering when Celeste approached the punchbowl. "Oh, hello my lovely! We meet again!" Arnie's eyes danced at the sight of Celeste.

Celeste greeted Arnie with a polite smile. "Hello Mr. Arnold."

"Arnie, you must call me Arnie. We are definitely on a first name basis, my fair lady," Arnie said, putting his hand back in his pocket to make sure the flask didn't slip out.

"Maybel said she saw the burst of fog over by the cemetery that you've been talking about," Celeste prompted.

"Finally, she saw it! I know she thought I made it up, but now she knows I told the truth," Arnie declared.

"Is there some reason Maybel would think you would lie?" Celeste smiled and tilted her head.

"Maybel and I go way back." Arnie looked over at the table where Maybel sat.

"She's a fine woman, isn't she?" Celeste asked.

"Why do the prettiest flowers always have the sharpest thorns?" Arnie smiled back.

"Well, if you'll excuse me, I need to take some punch back to the ladies."

Arnie jumped in to ladle some punch into paper cups. "Here, let me help you with that. Four hands are better than two."

"This punch is delicious!" Norma went bottoms up with her cup.

Vera added, "I'm going to have a second cup."

After Maybel finished her punch, she felt her head spin. Giggling, she said to Celeste, "I feel a little tipsy-turvy."

"I think you mean topsy-turvy."

Maybel looked at Celeste. "Isn't that what I said?"

In no time, the entertainment began. The luau music pounded with Hawaiian flair. Hula dancers came out onto the stage and performed several dances. With the drumbeat hitting fast and hard, the hula dancers shook their hips.

Jo and Sheila were working at the event, and they encouraged the residents to get up and dance with them towards the end. "It's good exercise. Exercise is good for digestion!" Sheila shouted to Maybel over the music, rubbing her tummy.

Maybel shook her silver-haired head and asked Celeste if she wanted to dance. They danced the hula side by side, having a great time. When Celeste shook her hips, Arnie didn't know what hit him. He tried to dance with her, but she sidestepped, leaving him to dance with Maybel.

Sipping a second cup of punch, Celeste watched everyone dance the hula.

Colleen approached her. "Looks like Maybel is having a good time with Arne."

Celeste nodded. "It's about time."

"She's a pretty good dancer, and I should know. I used to dance professionally." Colleen stood taller than Celeste. Her blue-black hair cut short on the sides and spiky on top elongated her slim face.

Celeste turned to inspect Colleen, noticing she possessed the long lanky body of a dancer. "And now you work here?"

"I was in a car accident that broke my ankle. It's never been the same since. My dreams ended… sometimes the lemons life deals you are just too sour to make lemonade with." Collen chuckled.

"You should be out on the dance floor with them."

"Oh, no. My dancing days are behind me, but I was so good, I was getting calls from famous New York play producers. Now, the only calls I get are from my creditors," Colleen said with a bitter laugh.

Celeste noticed a price tag sticking out of Colleen's Hawaiian shirt. She pointed to it, letting Colleen know.

Colleen's face blushed slightly as she tucked the price tag under her collar. "Thank you."

"So, you gave up dancing completely?"

Nodding, Colleen replied, "It's just too painful, but I don't mean physically. I mean emotionally. I just can't do what I used to because I lost some of my mobility, so I felt it was best to give it up all together. These days to get my exercise, I go bicycling and I do some bird watching. I'm not a real bird watcher. I mean, I don't track their migration patterns or take note of their reproductive habits. But I have been known to climb some trees to wait and really get a good look at them. I just find them so fascinating. I love watching them build their nests and flutter their beautiful wings." Shifting gears, she said, "I've been a little worried about Maybel. I think she's been struggling to fit in here and feel like this is her home. Sometimes people entertain certain delusions to help them cope."

"What delusions are you referring to?"

"She thinks she's some sort of amateur detective."

"She kind of is. She and I helped solved a few murders recently."

"Oh… really?" Colleen looked back at Maybel, watching Arnie dancing around with her. "I find that hard to believe."

"She's quite resourceful when she wants to be." Celeste threw her cup in the trash.

"I think she may need some grief counseling. Many of the residents here at Shady Sunset are widows or widowers. In my counseling, they can better process their grief and move through it in a healthy way. I fear Maybel is letting herself get too preoccupied with silly things as a coping mechanism. Some people do that to avoid facing their grief."

"Silly things?"

"Yes," Colleen said, looking back at Maybel. "I'm afraid some residents here think they're seeing ghosts."

"Oh, no. That's not Maybel. Maybel doesn't believe in ghosts."

"Well, that's good." Colleen smiled.

Heading back to their table, Celeste observed an elderly man in a wheelchair sitting at another table by himself. Feeling the tug on her heartstrings, she walked over to him and sat down, introducing herself.

With a croaky frog sounding voice, he said, "I'm Anthony Trutelli. My friends used to call me TT." He smiled, revealing a few missing teeth.

Celeste smiled and asked, "Are you enjoying the luau?"

He nodded. "Reminds me of the old days."

"You used to live in Hawaii?" Celeste inquired.

"My brother and I were stationed there. It was all fun and games until the bombs dropped."

"You were at Pearl Harbor?" Celeste's eyes widened.

"Yes, we spent our spare time chasing hula dancers… up until that day…"

Celeste felt the honor of being in the presence of a real American hero. "Were you in the Navy?"

Anthony shook his head. "No, my brother and I were stationed in the Army. When the bombing started, we got the orders to start shooting down the airplanes. I'll never forget that day. There was so much smoke in the air… it was hard to see what we were doing." His eyes filled with tears.

Celeste fought back her own tears. "Can I get you some punch, TT? It's really good. Arnie spiked it."

Anthony smiled and accepted the gesture. While sipping his punch, Celeste asked him if he had any hobbies.

"I like music. I listen to big band music, and I can still play the trumpet."

Celeste smiled at him. "My grandfather liked big band music too, and so do I. I have a few Glenn Miller records."

When the dancing settled down, Vick carried the pig in on a large platter for Jo to slice up and serve, along with other Hawaiian foods. Celeste rolled Anthony's wheelchair over to the table with Maybel and her friends. There was no way Anthony would sit alone, not when she was around.

After dinner concluded and everyone had a piece of pineapple upside down cake, Maybel and Celeste took Anthony back to his tiny apartment, helped get him settled in, and said goodnight. Celeste rested her lei around his neck, and a grateful smile beamed on his face.

Maybel walked Celeste out to her car, and as they were saying their goodbyes, Maybel saw the burst of fog again.

She pointed. "Look!"

Celeste turned and saw a cloud of fog rolling over the ground by the cemetery. "Well, what do you know…"

"I think we should go check it out!" Maybel urged.

Celeste shook her head. "No way. I'm not doing that."

"Oh, you party pooper!" Maybel huffed.

Celeste laughed. "Like you said, it's probably just fog. The days have been hot, and the nights have been cold. Hey, speaking of hot, how did you like dancing with Arnie?"

"Ugh, he moved like an octopus with eight hands everywhere. I haven't been felt up like that in years!"

"You're a grown woman," Celeste said. "You're free to do whatever you want."

Maybel looked down and said, "I miss George. Being here makes me miss him so much."

"I wish I could ease your pain."

"Oh dear, you do. More than you know. Well, if you're not going to go with me, then I guess I'll have to walk over to the cemetery by myself… all by myself."

Celeste exhaled sharply. "OK. I'll go with you." They walked from the parking lot to the cemetery in the general area, where they saw the fog. Under the moonlight, Celeste looked around at the headstones. "I'm not sure what we're looking for." A powerful gust of wind barreled around, forcing her hair to whip her face. Tree leaves danced and fluttered in the breeze. Looking up at the sky, she spotted clouds rolling in. Goose bumps popped up on her arms, and the wind pierced her dress, cutting through to chill her bones. "I can't believe I forgot to check the weather. I didn't even bring a coat."

"It's so dark out here, it's hard to see." Maybel looked around at the headstones. "Oh, look at these Chocolate Cosmos. How beautiful!"

"Chocolate what?"

Maybel pointed to a bouquet of some deep red velvety flowers in a grave vase in front of one headstone. "It's a rare flower called Chocolate Cosmos. They get their name from their smell. You can't find them just anywhere. I wonder if the person who brought them grows them in their own garden." Maybel bent down to admire the flowers and breathe in their fragrance.

A faint hoot in the distance called out, startling Celeste. "Did you hear that?"

"Dear, it's just an owl," Maybel said, looking around. A powerful gust of wind rustled her short silver hair and almost blew her off her feet. A jagged bolt of lightning cut the sky, followed by a heavy roll of thunder.

Feeling misty rain drops kissing her bare skin, Celeste cautioned, "This is a bad idea. Let's head back before this rain turns the ground into a mire of mud. Like I said, there's nothing out here to see."

Once back at Celeste's car, Maybel bid Celeste farewell. "Drive carefully, and text me when you get home, so I know you arrive safely."

Maybel went back into Shady Sunset and took the stairs back up to her apartment. Mr. Piddles greeted her with a soft meow and wound himself around her ankles. "Hello, you little rascal. Were you good while I was gone?"

Mr. Piddles meowed his answer. Maybel took a box of Cheez-It crackers out of her cupboard and fed him a few. He looked up at her for more, his green marbled eyes hopeful. "OK, two more." He ate them quickly and Maybel took the lei from around her neck and put it around Mr. Piddles' neck. Laughing, she said, "You look so cute. Hold still. Let me get a picture." After taking one with her cellphone, she texted it to Jeffrey. She included the caption: **Pass me a Mai Tai!**

Chapter Ten

There's Always Room for Jell-O

The next day, Maybel attended the luncheon event Jo coordinated. 'Gumbo & Games', she called it. The kitchen cooks whipped up some gumbo and different board games were set out at all the tables in the dining room. Jo assigned seating so residents of Shady Sunset could mix and mingle. Maybel ended up at a table with Anthony, Ida, Arnie, Sylvia, and Morton.

After a leisurely lunch, Ida said, "That gumbo tasted delicious!"

Maybel, knowing she could make a better gumbo, stayed silent. Watching Arnie ogle Ida just about brought her lunch back up. She shook her head and looked away.

Ida went on, "I hope that andouille sausage doesn't give me heartburn."

Arnie opened the vintage boxed board game of *Operation* with the unclothed man pictured in the center with a red buzzer for a nose. "Speaking of sausages, where is this guy's sausage?"

"This is a children's game, Arnie! That is inappropriate." Maybel scolded.

Buzz after buzz rang out as each player tried to operate with the little tweezers. Anthony tried unsuccessfully to take out the broken heart, and Ida failed at pulling on his funny bone. Maybel almost got the Charlie horse free without touching the side, but at the last second, she hit the edge, and the buzzer rang. Only Arnie could keep his hand steady enough to pull the wishbone loose without touching the side.

Gloating puffed out Arnie's chest. "See, I told you all I can do sleight of hand! Who wants to play another round?"

Maybel, unable to stomach his showmanship, said, "I'm going to go to the dessert table and get some sugar free Jell-O. Does anyone else want one?"

Anthony raised his hand, and Maybel nodded at him, walking away. When over at the dessert table, she heard Jo talking to another resident about the talent show. "Oh, Maybel! I've been meaning to talk to you. You still haven't told me what you'll be doing for the talent show, and it's in a few days."

Maybel let Jo know what she decided on, and Jo scribbled more notes on her clipboard. "I won't need any props or a microphone. I'll bring everything I need," Maybel told her.

"Wonderful!" Jo bubbled.

"Is that a new ring?" Maybel queried, looking at Jo's hand.

"This? Oh, no. It was my mother's. She passed it down to me," Jo answered.

"It's lovely," Maybel admired. "I've never seen you wear it before."

"I always tried to save it for special occasions," Jo went on, "but lately I thought what the heck am I saving it for?"

"Well, those are beautiful diamonds. Now if you'll excuse me. I need to get this Jell-O back to my table." With two small dishes of cherry Jell-O in her hands, Sheila, the healthcare facilitator, approached her.

"Maybel, you're just the lady I wanted to see," Sheila began. "Oh, I see you chose Jell-O for dessert… probably a good choice since most likely you're lactose intolerant. That cheesecake would make you gassy again."

Maybel frowned. "Is that what you came over here to talk to me about?"

Sensing the tone, Sheila said, "No, no. Uh, I came over here to let you know I'm starting up a new guided meditation class. I think it would be perfect for you! It will help with your anger issues."

With a raised eyebrow, Maybel asked, "Why do you think I have anger issues?"

"Well, I know you are a widow. Sometimes we misplace our grief. Meditation can help you get in touch with that."

Maybel replied, "I think you mean displaced grief, not misplaced."

"Yeah, yeah, that is what I meant. I can also come over to your place and do a one-on-one hypnosis session which can also release grief and get you in touch with your past lives," Sheila said.

"I assure you that I have no past lives," Maybel responded, thinking how garish Sheila's blue eyeshadow looked.

"Can I at least count you in for the guided meditation class?" Sheila looked at Maybel, eagerly awaiting her reply.

"Sure," Maybel said with no intention of going to the class.

Sheila squealed with delight. "Great! I'll see you later."

Back at their table, Arnie had been trying to convince Ida to be the woman in the box he was going to saw in half during his magic act for the talent show. He said, "No, I swear! It's perfectly safe."

Maybel handed Anthony his Jell-O and sat down. With Ida still giggling at all of Arnie's jokes, Maybel held her eye rolling at bay.

"Maybel, I was telling Ida that you saw the strange burst of fog over by the cemetery too," Arnie said.

Nodding, she said, "I've seen it twice now."

Ida's eyes widened. "What do you think is causing it? It sounds so mysterious."

"Probably just June gloom, or May gray," Maybel answered.

Ida went on, "But there have been so many other goings on that can't be explained… like Violet's missing necklace, the strange sounds Norma keeps hearing in the hall, the footsteps Vera hears in the attic–and the ghost she saw!"

Maybel grew tired of everyone's imagination running away with them and said, "The noises Norma hears are probably just residents or staff walking down the halls, and the noise in the attic could be mice or opossums."

"I guess that's possible," Ida said. "The other night I saw Violet walking down the hall. It was late, and I felt a little afraid to look out into the halls. I swear, sometimes I can feel the ghostly midnight shadows leering at me! But I stayed up watching tv, and I heard her rolling her tank along."

"See, there you go. It's all explainable. No ghost, just Violet," Maybel concluded and excused herself from the table. Exiting the dining room, she saw Violet wave her over.

"Maybel, I'm not feeling well. I was wondering if you could help me back to my place," Violet said, looking pale.

"Oh, of course!" Maybel helped Violet up out of her chair.

The two ladies carefully and slowly walked back to Violet's tiny apartment. With a tired, shaky hand, Violet got out her key and unlocked her door. Maybel helped her get settled in and asked if she wanted some tea.

Violet pulled off her oxygen mask and sipped her warm beverage. "You're always so helpful." She smiled at Maybel.

"It's my pleasure," Maybel replied, admiring the tea service she set out. She'd gotten quite good at it, but still didn't like the taste of chamomile.

"I've been thinking. It would be a good idea if I gave you the extra key to my place… just in case something happens." Violet set her teacup down and reached into her pocket.

Maybel accepted the extra key and asked, "Have you been sleeping well?" "Yes, why do you ask?"

"I was just wondering because Ida said she saw you walking the halls late at night."

Violet's puzzled looking face concerned Maybel. She asked, "Were you walking in the hall late at night the last couple of nights?"

Violet shook her head. "I go to bed around 9 pm, and I don't wake until 6 am."

"Ida must have been mistaken."

"I had been having trouble sleeping a few months ago, but after a one-on-one hypnosis session with Sheila, I sleep like a baby now."

Frowning, Maybel said, "I don't trust that Sheila gal. Do you think it's possible she could have taken your necklace when she performed her hypnosis session?"

Violet wrung her hands. "Oh, I don't know. I don't think so, Maybel. She's such a nice lady. I really enjoy her visits. I don't get many visitors, you know."

Maybel smiled and changed the subject. "Did you decide to do something for the talent show?"

Violet responded, "No, I'm going to pass, but I will be there to watch the rest of you. I'm really looking forward to it. I can't wait to see Arnie's magic show!"

"I invited my son Jeffrey, Celeste, and her boyfriend Brian. It should be a fun night."

"I'll go to visit John and my son at the cemetery earlier in the day. That always takes me a long time because I walk so slow with this tank. Then I'll go to the talent show in the evening after my nap. That's my plan, anyway." Violet put her oxygen mask back on.

Maybel smiled at her friend. "Sounds like a good plan."

Back at her place, Maybel poured Mr. Piddles a saucer of milk and sat down in front of her tv. After he finished lapping up his snack, Mr. Piddles joined Maybel on the couch, his wispy whiskers covered in creamy droplets. She checked her cellphone and saw a text from Jeffrey that read: **Can't wait to see you back in action at the talent show! See you soon!**

That reminded Maybel she needed to practice. She got up and went to her kitchenette and pulled open a drawer, taking out the item she needed to practice with. That filled up the rest of her afternoon until dinner time. Deciding to forgo going down to the dining room, she prepared a tuna fish sandwich that she shared with Mr. Piddles. He sat next to her and purred until he fell asleep. Once he fell asleep, Maybel got out her knitting from her sewing basket, reaching for the sunny yellow yarn to add a little harmony to her green and blue symphony. Knit one, pearl two, knit one, pearl two, knit one, pearl two…

Chapter Eleven

The Hand Is Quicker Than the Eye

"I'm telling you; I heard the ghost again!" Norma stated.

Maybel sat down at the table for breakfast with the other ladies. "What exactly did you hear, Norma?" Maybel decided even though she knew Norma didn't hear a ghost, she wanted to investigate the strange goings on.

"I was having trouble sleeping and so read one of my Martha Stewart magazines. I just love her. She has so many fantastic ideas for crafts and food. She even has this fun way of organizing your scissors. You need a different pair for every job, like kitchen scissors, craft scissors, hair cutting scissors, and sewing scissors, because let's say you use hair cutting scissors to cut paper. Those scissors will get dull and then not cut hair very well. Anyway, I was sitting in my recliner reading an article on how to hand paint designs on cloth napkins, and I heard a tap, tap, tap sound in the hall that I thought sounded like footsteps. I got up, put my robe and slippers on, but by the time I looked out in the hallway, the ghost disappeared."

"Are you sure you heard footsteps? Could it have been something else?" Maybel asked.

"Well, I heard a foot tapping sound," Norma explained.

"I see…" Maybel went deep into thought, trying to figure out what it could be.

"I still haven't found my necklace," Violet said, looking at Maybel through sad eyes.

"Ladies," Vera began, "I hate to tell you all this, but… I had kept some cash in the top drawer of my nightstand in case of emergency. I went to check it this morning, and it's gone!"

Norma gasped. "So, it's a thieving ghost!"

"It's not a ghost," Maybel reasoned. "But I think there is a thief. Vera, who all has been in your place lately?"

Vera listed everyone. "The cleaning people and Vick the maintenance man. Jo stopped by to look at some bags of beads I have that I suggested we could use for a craft project. Sheila came over to cleanse my aura. Colleen and I had a counseling session, and Norma stopped by for tea."

Maybel slipped back into deep thought. As much as Vick annoyed her, she really didn't think he was a thief. It was also unlikely that Norma took the cash. Sheila, it had to be Sheila. She decided after breakfast to talk to Colleen to see if they could look into this. "Do you ever leave your door unlocked?"

Vera thought about this. "Why, yes. I usually leave it unlocked when I come down here for breakfast. We're never down here for very long, and if I put my keys in my pocket, they make my slacks look bulky. I lock it at night, though, just to be safe."

"OK. Until we figure out what's going on around here," Maybel warned, "we all need to keep our doors locked. No matter what!"

Everyone nodded.

"Hello, hello, hello ladies!" Jo chirped, dancing up to them. "Don't forget, the talent show is tomorrow night!"

"We wouldn't miss it for the world." Violet placed her oxygen mask back on.

"What a lovely top! Is that new?" Norma inquired.

Jo looked down at her shirt. "No, I just dug around in the back of my closet and found this. I forgot I had it and haven't worn it in ages."

Norma smiled. "Blue is really your color, Jo. People often tell me that blue is my color. It brings out my eyes. I had my colors done one time and I'm a winter so I can wear blue, black, gray, burgundy—"

Arnie approached the table wearing a tall black magician's hat and a full tuxedo complete with cummerbund and cape. He took his hat off and pulled a rabbit out of it. Arnie winked at them and said, "Just a preview of what you ladies will get tomorrow night!" He set the rabbit down on the table in front of Maybel, who pulled her coffee cup away from it. A little fireball burst from Arnie's free hand.

Vera picked up the rabbit and snuggled her while Maybel coughed from the fireball smoke she inhaled. The other ladies giggled, oohing and awing with delight. Waving her hand around to clear away the smoke, Maybel said, "You're going to catch something on fire if you're not careful, Arnie."

"Maybel, I do not need you to tell me how to do my craft! I've been practicing magic since I was a boy."

Jo interjected, "Then I think we're in for a real treat tomorrow!"

"Anyone can purchase spirit lights, invisible decks and vanishing hankies from the magic shop, Arnie. That hardly makes you a real magician."

"If I wasn't a real magician, could I do this?" He pulled a quarter from behind Norma's ear.

"We already saw you do that trick, Arnie." Maybel huffed.

"I'm saving all my good stuff for the talent show. Just you wait and see, Maybel." He took his rabbit back from Vera. "Now, if you ladies will excuse us, Bun Bun and I are going to hop into the kitchen to get her a carrot to snack on, and then we're going back to my place to take a nap."

"He's so funny," Norma said, chuckling

Rolling her eyes, Maybel replied, "Yeah, he's a laugh a minute."

After breakfast, Maybel went to Colleen's office to speak to her about the strange goings on. After relaying everything to her, Colleen said, "We will look into this. I wasn't convinced we had a thief on the staff when it was just Violet's necklace. I figured she just forgot where she put it. Many elderly people have trouble with their memories. But now that Vera is missing something, I'm a little worried. I'll start by asking some questions. Thank you for bringing this to my attention."

"Maybel, I do not need you to tell me how to do my craft! I've been practicing magic since I was a boy."

"No problem. I've been known to solve a few mysteries in my time," Maybel replied.

Worried she'd become delusional again, Colleen asked, "Emotionally, how are you feeling about being at Shady Sunset? Sometimes residents have a hard time transitioning."

Maybel took a deep breath. "I'm OK. I miss my old place. You know I had lived there since 1958 and all my memories were there."

Colleen smiled and put her hand on Maybel's. "Your memories are still in your heart, no matter where you live. Sometimes keeping a journal and writing down your beloved memories can help."

Maybel looked down at her hands and nodded, fighting back tears.

Colleen continued, "Let me know if you'd like to schedule a time to chat. I'm not only the head of administration here, but I'm also a certified counselor."

Impressed, Maybel asked, "You do two jobs for the price of one?"

Colleen laughed. "It's not even a good price, either. But I've been able to help other widows here at Shady Sunset. I feel confident I can help you too. I also do a group grief counseling session I think you should attend."

Maybel, never having considered counseling in her life, was intrigued by the offer. "That might be a good idea. I'll think about it."

Back at her place, before practicing some more for the talent show, Maybel poured another saucer of milk for Mr.

Piddles to enjoy. He tucked himself in the space between her couch and the wall, but when he heard her open the refrigerator, he came running. After lapping up the milk, he began his hunt for spiders. He'd gotten quite good at catching them.

Maybel felt a little rusty, but the more she practiced, the more it came back to her. She heard her phone bing and a text from Celeste read: **Looking forward to the talent show tomorrow night. It will be just me because Brian said he got called to work another shift. Someone broke into the mayor's house and tried to attack him.**

Upon seeing the text, Maybel called Celeste. "Please let Brian know he will be missed. I'm disappointed he won't be there, but I understand."

"This is the second date he's canceled on me," Celeste told her.

"You sound like you're taking it personally."

"I guess I am." Celeste let out a deep breath.

"He has a very demanding job. I don't think you should take it personally."

Celeste went on, "It's just that things have been awkward between us, and I think he's pulling away… and I can't even blame him because I think I'm pushing him away."

"Dear, I'd like to give you some advice from all my years of wisdom. Don't overthink this. He likes you, and you like him. You're afraid of getting hurt, so you're pushing him away. But there is no relationship you won't get hurt in. That's what we do as human beings. We hurt each other… sometimes intentionally and sometimes unintentionally. But if you don't risk anything, there is no reward."

"You sound like Dr. Fisher, my therapist."

"Your therapist is wise," Maybel said, laughing. "I might start doing some therapy myself. I spoke with Colleen, the head of administration here, and she said she's also a licensed counselor."

"That's great. I highly recommend it. It helps give you a different perspective."

"I'm ready for a new perspective. Now, tell me, what's this about the mayor's house getting broken into? I didn't hear about that on the news."

"Brian said they wanted it kept out of the news for privacy's sake."

"Privacy goes out the window when you hold a public office like that. You know, I've never liked mouse trap. I always thought he could do more for the city of Sunshine Beach."

"It's pronounced mousse trip—like chocolate mousse. I think it's French."

"I know how to pronounce it. I just don't like that guy. He's got shifty little beady eyes. Who could ever trust him?"

"Brian said it's a really strange case."

"Strange how?" Maybel pet Mr. Piddles along the sleek fur down his back.

"He said he has a strange feeling about it, like nothing the mayor said sounded true."

"He doesn't think it was just a routine break in?"

"No. He said something is fishy, and when he watched the footage on the security camera, he said the man looked familiar to him or moved around familiarly. But their face recognition software came up with nothing because he wore a hat and had his head down. There were also no finger-prints or forced entry."

"Do you think the man who broke in could have been the mayor's secret gay lover? I've always thought the mayor of Sunshine Beach has a little sugar in his tank."

Celeste giggled. "I don't know."

"Tell me, what happened when he broke in?"

"Brian said the intruder went in through a side door to the garage, and that's where they mayor found him and shot him with a speargun."

"A speargun? Good grief!"

"Yeah… and Brian said the mayor seemed relieved he didn't hurt the intruder."

"Oh, then it was definitely his illicit lover!"

"Who knows? He still hasn't figured out what hap-pened with that explosion at the manufacturing plant. I guess that's why he's so busy lately," Celeste paused before going on, "He's really not supposed to tell me anything, so mum's the word, OK?"

"OK. I've got my hands full anyway, trying to catch the thief that's running around Shady Sunset."

"Are you ready for tomorrow night?" Celeste asked.

"As ready as I'll ever be. I haven't done this since Jef-frey was a boy," Maybel explained, keeping her act a secret.

"If you're as good at this talent as you were at aerobics dancing at the Halloween party last year, then we're all in for a real treat."

Maybel laughed. "I'm still quite spry for my age."

"I know."

"And I'm not dead yet!" Maybel proclaimed.

"You have many years still ahead of you, Maybel. I'll see you soon."

Chapter Twelve

Walk the Dog

The morning of the talent show, Maybel decided not to go down to the dining room for breakfast or lunch. She cooked a late breakfast for herself in her kitchenette. She no longer kept a fully stocked kitchen, but she stocked enough ingredients to prepare some scrambled eggs and toast. Not wanting to make small talk with everyone, she ate in solitude, except, of course, for Mr. Piddles begging for some scraps from her plate.

Later that morning, Violet called Maybel to check on her. "When you weren't at our table for breakfast this morning, I got a little worried."

"How sweet of you to check in on me, Violet. I'm OK. I just want to spend as much time as I can rehearsing before the show tonight."

"Today I'm going to visit my husband and son at the cemetery, and then I'll go back to my place and take a nap before the festivities tonight. I have so little in my life that gives me joy now, but I've been looking forward to the talent show for weeks."

"Well, in that case, I better get back to rehearsing because I don't want to disappoint you!"

Violet's frail voice croaked, "I'm sure you won't. I'll see you tonight, my friend."

Pulling her wheeled oxygen tank, Violet sauntered over to the cemetery next door, making her way carefully through the dew-laden grass. Most of it evaporated from the early afternoon sun by the time she arrived at her husband and son's graves. Except for a favorite purple coat, Violet mostly wore black, the color of mourning. A gauzy black dress hung loose on her tiny body. She rolled her oxygen tank over their graves and set down some daisies she'd picked from Shady Sunset's garden. Winded from her slow walk, she sat on the cold cement bench under the great pine tree. Shade covered the area, cooling her and calming her labored breathing. With a shaky hand, a flower embroidered hankie tucked in her pocket came out to wipe the sweat beads from her brow. No matter how tiring the walk to the cemetery, Violet would not be deterred from visiting her loved ones.

Too exhausted to speak, she prayed silently for quite a while, making her daily requests. One particular concern bothering her made her seek God's guidance. Tears flooded Violet's faded eyes. A subtle but spirited breeze bristled her thin gray hair, interrupting her holy thoughts. The branches on the giant pine tree swayed and cracked in the wind. Looking down at her feet in despair, she felt a sharp pain in her head. Toppling over into the dirt, she couldn't move, for the pressure on her back restricted her.

Violet heard a voice telling her to stop fighting it. Her oxygen mask ceased to help her. She couldn't breathe. Oh God, will my daughter ever forgive me for what I did to her? Violet lost consciousness. The spirit interceded, pulling Violet towards the light… the soft, warm comforting light… she heard the clank of the golden gates opening… Jesus, is that you? John… Tim… Her earthly body grew colder and colder. Grace called Violet home. Joy unending…

***

Maybel distracted Mr. Piddles with another saucer of milk while rehearsing her act for the talent show again. It proved to be difficult rehearsing in front of him since he kept trying to go after her prop for the talent show. While grabbing the box of Cheez-It crackers from her cupboard to feed him another snack, she accidentally spilled some on the floor. Mr. Piddles quickly hoovered them up.

Maybel moved to her bedroom, closing the door to keep him out. She looked through her closet in search of an outfit for the show. She gave away a lot of her clothes before moving to Shady Sunset because her new place was smaller than her old place, but she found a royal blue sequined dress. Smiling, she remembered wearing it when she and George went on vacation to Atlantic City. Holding the dress in her hands, she closed her eyes and felt warm tears flow down her cheeks. She and George had such a delightful time at a carnival by the boardwalk. They strolled hand in hand, looking out at the golden sand. How she wished she could see George again. He took her out for a nice steak dinner before they did a bit of gambling. Later, he bought her a box of saltwater taffy. She wouldn't dare eat taffy now for fear of breaking a tooth. The sharp ache of George's absence stabbed her heart. Opening her watery eyes, she wondered if the dress was too fancy for the show, but she remembered Arnie in his tuxedo. Chuckling, she said, "No, it's not too fancy."

Later in the afternoon, Mr. Piddles scratched at her bedroom door, and she let him in. After perching himself on her bathroom counter, he watched her style her hair pretty. Digging through her bathroom cabinet drawer, she found a silver beaded hair comb. She pulled one side of her hair back and fastened the comb, leaving a curly tendril hanging down the side of her face. Mr. Piddles swatted at her can of hairspray, knocking it over before she could get to it. "You little rascal!"

Maybel took out the pearl necklace from her jewelry box she only wore on special occasions. It went perfectly with her royal blue sequin dress, complete with pantyhose and high heels. She dabbed some mauve lipstick on and blotted it on a tissue, and she lined her eyes with charcoal-colored eyeliner. Looking in the mirror, she drew in a long breath. "Oh, George… I wish you were here." Mentally, she told herself not to cry. She didn't want to redo her eye make-up.

All the residents performing in the talent show were to meet in the dancehall at 4 pm. The show started at 5 pm, and a soup and salad dinner would be served immediately after the show. At 3:45 pm, Maybel said goodbye to Mr. Piddles, who had moved out to her windowsill. He kept a close eye on a butterfly outside the window while he sunned himself. Taking her prop with her, she walked over to the dancehall.

Another burst from a tiny fireball popped out of Arnie's sleeve. Maybel asked him, "Isn't that a little premature? Shouldn't you be saving that for the show?"

Arnie snapped, "I'm never premature, Maybel."

Norma tapped away in the corner in her tap shoes, practicing her dance. The bun atop her head bobbed around with her movements, and her red dress sparkled. Vera tickled the ivories to get herself warmed up before the show and looked elegantly dressed in all black.

"Alright, everyone, gather round!" Jo shouted over all the commotion.

The talent show contestants stopped what they were doing and stood around her. She instructed them, "I've come up with the order that you will all perform in." She passed out some tags with their numbers. "We're getting close to the time when we'll be letting the audience in. I hope you all invited your families. Now, let's head to the backstage area."

The talent show performers made their way behind the thick red velvet curtain on the stage to the hidden backstage area and continued rehearsing. Other residents filtered in and took their seats in front of the stage. Colleen helped take tickets from the outside guests, who were also arriving. The dancehall filled with chatter as everyone took their seats, awaiting the show. When Celeste arrived, she made a special effort to look around for Anthony and sit next to him, but she couldn't find him. Jeffrey showed up soon after her, and she waved him over.

"Hi Celeste! How are you?" he asked, giving her a friendly hug.

"I'm doing good. I can't wait to see what your mom is going to do for the show," she said with a smile.

"Me too! I haven't seen her do this since I was a kid. She taught me how to do it!"

Jo took the microphone on stage and got everyone's attention. "Quiet please! Quiet! Our show is about to begin. We also have a panel of judges," Jo said, pointing to a table off to the side where three residents of Shady Sunset sat with notepads and pens to decide on a winner.

"The winner will receive one month's free rent here at Shady Sunset, and this grand gift basket that was so generously donated by Cookie Hut from down the street!" Everyone applauded and when that died down, Jo went on, "Now the first contestant in our talent show is Vera Myers, who will play the piano for us! Please enjoy as she performs Beethoven's Moonlight Sonata!"

Everyone remained quiet as Vera played skillfully. She tickled the ivories with quite a finesse from years of playing. When she concluded, applause filled the air. Jo continued to announce the contestants in the talent show, and one by one they performed various things like lip-syncing and joke telling. One lady demonstrated how to make a flambé and almost caught the table on fire. Fortunately, Vick stood by with a fire extinguisher. Norma tap danced her heart out. Celeste got teary-eyed when Anthony Trute-lli rolled out in his wheelchair, picked up a trumpet from his lap, and played '*Taps*'.

Then it was time for Maybel's act. She took a deep breath and walked out onto the stage. The lights were much brighter than she anticipated, and they blinded her for a few seconds. Luckily, she really didn't need to see to per-form her act.

With the string on the yoyo slip knotted around her middle finger, she held the yoyo in her shaky hand. She took another deep breath and flung the yoyo out, then back again doing the gravity pull move. After a few times of repeating this, she executed a power throw down. Next, she made a forward pass, flipping her hand around and catch-ing it. Joyfully, she executed outside loops and inside loops, never missing a beat with her neon green yoyo. From that, she proceeded into the sleeper move. With a loose arm, she brought her elbow up to her nose and threw it out in front of her. She tugged it back up to her hand and repeated it a few times. For her finale, she executed the walk the dog movement. The yoyo glided across the floor and then she pulled it back up to her and repeated it one more time. Done with her performance, she took a bow.

Applause roared through the audience, and Maybel saw Jeffrey and Celeste stand up to clap and cheer. This gave a smile to her face. Walking off the stage, she passed Arnie and said, "Try to top that!"

Arnie rolled his magician's box with Ida's head poking out of it onto the stage after Jo announced him. Using Vick's hacksaw, he sawed the box in half and pulled it apart. The audience oohed and awed. He put the box back together and opened it. Ida jumped out in one piece, and the audience went wild.

"Everyone knows how that trick is done," Maybel mumbled under her breath, watching from the side of the stage behind the curtain.

Arnie performed various magic tricks with a grandiose demeanor that Maybel found nauseating. Card tricks, fireballs, spirit lights, vanishing hankies, a rabbit out of a hat, all the classics. He waved around a red scarf and called Ida out onto the stage with him, announcing to the audience she would climb into a box, and he'd make her disappear. Handing her the red scarf, he told the audience, "Keep an eye on this scarf. You'll see it later." Ida climbed in and Arnie closed the box. He locked the box and waved his magic wand over it, and a fireball shot out from his sleeve. He spun the box all the way around and then opened it. Ida was nowhere to be seen. Applause filled the auditorium, and the audience insisted on an encore.

For the crowning piece of his act, Arnie released a dove from his jacket pocket. The dove fluttered its wings, flying over the auditorium, and the crowd went wild with applause. He indicated the conclusion of his act by pulling off his top hat and taking a bow. The audience loved Arnie's bravado and roared with more applause. Maybel thought it sounded louder than what she received.

After the judges tallied their scores, Jo, with Arnie's red scarf in her breast pocket, announced who won the talent show, "And the winner of the 2019 Shady Sunset Talent Contest is….," she paused for the drumroll, and then shouted, "Arnie Arnold!!!"

"Hhhmmmppff! Now I'm never going to hear the end of it," Maybel grumbled.

Arnie laughed with delight, lightly pushed Maybel aside, and proudly strode back out onto the stage to receive his prizes. He took another bow. "Thank you! Thank you!" He waved to the audience, taking a third bow.

Chapter Thirteen

Soup to Nuts

After Vick and another maintenance man moved all the audience chairs around, dining tables were set up for the soup and salad supper. Maybel squeezed her way through the crowd, finding Jeffrey and Celeste.

"You were wonderful!" Celeste gushed. "I had no idea you could do that!"

"Mom, you were fantastic! Better than I remember!" Jeffrey hugged her.

"It's been years since I worked with a yoyo, but it all came back to me." She smiled.

Standing with her loved ones, Maybel heard cellophane crinkling in her ear. She turned and Arnie bumped his large gift basket from the Cookie Hut into her. Cellophane scratched her cheek, and she pushed the basket away from her face.

Arnie said sorry, not looking sorry at all. Triumphantly, Arnie told her, "Better luck with your little yoyo act next year, Maybel!" He laughed and pushed through the crowd, his grand gift basket leading the way. A throng milled about Arnie, congratulating him, and he soaked it up like a sponge. A pat on the back from his son Vick brought a beam to

Arnie's aging face. Father and son stood head and shoulders above the crowd.

Celeste suggested, "Let's get in line to get some soup. I'm hungry."

"OK, but I'd like to find Violet first and make sure she sits with us because she said her daughter couldn't make it. I don't want her to be by herself," Maybel agreed, scanning the room for Violet.

Celeste walked around with Maybel looking for Violet, but they couldn't find her. "Maybe she went back to her room," Celeste said.

"Yeah, maybe. I guess we should get some dinner and sit down." Maybel conceded the search.

With empty bowls of clam chowder in front of them, Jeffrey said he had to work the night shift and needed to get going.

"I'll walk you back to your apartment," Celeste offered after they said goodbye to Jeffrey.

Walking through the halls of Shady Sunset, Maybel said, "Dear, if you don't mind, I'd like to walk to Violet's and see if she's OK."

Arriving at Violet's, Maybel knocked, but no one answered. She frowned and knocked again, louder. No answer. "She gave me a spare key. I think I should use it," Maybel said, taking it out of her dress pocket and unlocking her door. A quick scan of Violet's place found it empty. "Where could she be? If she wasn't at the dancehall for the show and she's not here..."

"Why don't you try calling her cellphone?"

"It went to voicemail," Maybel said, hanging up. "Today was the day she went to the cemetery to visit her husband and son. I wonder if she's still there."

"You'll do anything to get me out to that cemetery at night, won't you?"

"Dear, I'm worried. Something is wrong. I can feel it in my bones."

"OK, let's go look for her."

At a hurried pace, they walked out of Shady Sunset and made the short walk next door over to Heavenly Souls Cemetery. "She said she always sits on the cement bench that's under the big pine tree at the cemetery."

When they got closer to the cemetery, in the darkness, they saw the empty bench under the pine tree. Upon moving closer, a horrifying sight presented itself. Violet lay sprawled out on the ground, face down in front of the bench. The sun had long since set on her. The oxygen tank had been knocked over on the ground next to her. Maybel gasped, rushing to Violet with Celeste right on her heels.

Maybel steadied herself by placing one hand on the bench and carefully kneeled on the ground next to Violet, giving her a little shake. "Violet! Can you hear me?" Violet didn't answer. Maybel placed her fingers on the side of Violet's neck to check her pulse. Seeing the look on Maybel's face, Celeste knew something bad had happened, and she called 911.

"She's dead," Maybel uttered. Celeste helped Maybel stand up. "She's cold and has no pulse. Do you think she had a heart attack? A stroke?"

Celeste examined the vicinity around Violet using the flashlight on her cellphone. Bending down, she looked at everything carefully, her eyes roaming in every direction. She saw footprints where the ground was soft.

Tears stung Maybel's eyes, and she could feel herself shaking. "This was her crying place. Right here under the giant pine tree. This is where she came to grieve for her husband and son. Oh, how awful! She died out here all alone."

Celeste walked around the grass surrounding the dirt area Violet was lying on. "The tank is on the wrong side."

"What?" Maybel looked blankly at Celeste, wiping tears from her eyes. "Maybel, her oxygen tank is on the wrong side. She's right-handed, right? The time I met her, I noticed she kept her oxygen tank on her right side."

Maybel nodded. "Yes, that's right."

"The oxygen tank is on her left, but there are track marks from the wheels on her tank on her right side, but the tank is laying here on her left side. There's a red spot on her scalp… and look at these footprints. There are two sets of footprints… and there is dirt on her back… the surrounding dirt is displaced like she struggled a bit. Look, these stones were overturned."

"She could have fallen on her back and then tried turning over," Maybel said.

Celeste bent down again, shining the cellphone light over Violet. "No, Maybel, I think there is a footprint on her back… it's faint, but I can see it." Celeste stood up and looked around again. "We're missing something…"

Maybel sniffled and asked, "What could that be, dear?"

Celeste shook her head. "I don't know… but I can feel it. My instincts are telling me there is something else to this… she didn't die of natural causes." Celeste made a second phone call.

"Celeste," Detective Brian Bahn continued, "I told you I had to work tonight. I'm sorry I missed our date, but I'm in the middle of something."

"That's not why I'm calling you. I'm here at Shady Sunset with Maybel, and I think one of the residents has been murdered."

"Did you call 911?" "Of course," Celeste said, "but you're probably going to get the call to come investigate."

"I'll be there as soon as I can. Don't touch anything!" Brian ordered.

Chapter Fourteen

Cold Shoulder

The yellow tape sectioned off the area where Violet's body lay. Celeste and Maybel gave their statements to the officers who arrived on the scene first. Celeste made a point of letting the officer know why she suspected foul play. Residents gathered near the cemetery trying to find out what happened.

Shortly after the coroner arrived, Detective Bahn arrived. He walked past Maybel and Celeste with long, wide strides and without greeting them. He spoke with the officers on the scene, and they briefed him.

With hands on hips, Brian watched the coroner examine Violet. He stood with his body still, scanning the area and turning his head almost all the way around from side to side like a wise old owl. The initial panoramic view gave him a crucial first impression of the crime scene. No science, just instinct. He shined his flashlight on Violet and studied what he saw. She lay face down in the dirt, and he saw some redness on her scalp through her thin silver hair and the faint footprint on her back. He looked around again, wondering why someone would kill an elderly grieving widow. What enemies could she possibly have? Observing the crowd that had gathered, he looked from face to face. He could feel the killer watching him.

Celeste approached him as close as she could without crossing the caution tape. "Brian," she began, "I'm not sure if this matters, but Violet was right-handed and always kept her oxygen tank on her right side. When we found her, the tank was on her left side."

He turned and looked at her. His voice sounded deep and flat. "Thank you for the information." He turned back around.

She spoke again to his back, "Also, I don't know if you noticed, but there is a second set of footprints in the dirt around where her body is, and I think there is a footprint on the back of her shirt."

"Celeste, if I need your help, I'll ask for it. I got your statement from the officer in charge."

Flabbergasted by his brusque manner, Celeste stepped back. Feeling dejected, she walked to where Maybel stood surrounded by her friends, who were taking turns embracing her.

"Dear, did you let him know about the footprints?" Maybel asked.

"I did." Celeste crossed her arms over her chest and told herself to remain calm.

Rushing up came the staff, Colleen, Jo, Sheila, and Vick. "Good heavens, do you ladies know what happened? Who is over there?!"

"It's Violet. We found her," Maybel answered Colleen.

Colleen covered her mouth in shock.

Sheila spoke up. "She must have had a heart attack. She mentioned at her last check-up, her doctor told her she had a heart murmur."

"Oh, Maybel. Are you OK? I know you and Violet were close," Colleen said, putting her hand on Maybel's shoulder.

"I'm OK. I think I'm in shock." Maybel shuddered, feeling buried in sadness.

Celeste watched Vick approach Detective Bahn. Upon seeing Vick, Brian met him halfway, and they did a fist bump greeting. Brian's face filled with animation when he spoke with Vick.

"What the…," Celeste uttered.

"What did you say, dear?" Maybel queried.

Maybel is right, it really is a man's world, she thought. "He practically stared daggers at me and gave me the cold shoulder. Then Vick goes over there, and he's all smiles and manly man handshakes."

"Maybe he's giving you a taste of your own medicine," Maybel said. "Don't look at me like that. Look, I know you have a sweet and warm heart, but sometimes… outwardly you act cold to him."

Celeste cleared her throat. "Well, he said he didn't need to speak to me, so I'm going to leave. You'll be alright. Vera and Norma are here. I'm sure they can walk you back to your place."

Maybel called after Celeste, "Will you call me later?"

Celeste's stride moved fast while her mind told her a woman was dead, and this was no time for her to be angry. But…. ugh! Unlocking her car door, she heard her name.

"Celeste," Arnie called. "Do you know what happened? I saw you leave the area where the police are."

"I'm sorry to have to tell you this, Arnie, but Violet died. Maybel and I found her fallen over by the bench under the pine tree at the cemetery."

Arnie's face saddened at the news. "Oh, no! Do they think she had a heart attack?"

"They won't know yet."

"Is Maybel OK?" He removed his top hat and scratched his head.

"I think so. Vera and Norma are with her." Celeste jiggled her keys.

"I should go check on Maybel," Arnie offered.

With a tired smile, Celeste said, "I think that's a good idea, Arnie. Goodnight."

Burning on the drive home, Celeste stewed over how Brian treated her. She'd practically solved Brian's last two cases for him, and now he blows her off when she tries to help. He didn't even want to hear her important information. If that's how he wanted to act, she wanted no part of that!

Chapter Fifteen

If the Shoe Fits

"Based on what you're saying, it doesn't sound like the contusion on her head caused her death," Detective Bahn stated to the coroner, who completed the autopsy of Violet.

"No, it's not deep enough," he replied.

"Can you tell what type of object she was hit with?" Bahn asked.

"Not really. It looks more like an abrasion than a contusion."

"And toxicology came back clean?"

"Yes. She just had a blood thinner in her system for her heart condition."

"Did she have a heart attack?"

The coroner replied, "No."

"Anything else I should know?" Bahn inquired.

"I believe she suffocated," the coroner informed Bahn. "Forensics showed the oxygen tank was empty, but she was face down with her mask on. There were markings around her mouth made by the mask being held tightly over her mouth."

Bahn tapped his pen on his desk. "So, someone knocked her out and then suffocated her with the oxygen mask connected to an empty oxygen tank."

"It seems so, yes," the coroner confirmed. "There were slight signs of a struggle."

"Could she have accidentally suffocated when she fell over and landed face down on her mask?" Bahn asked.

"That's a possibility, but there was a footprint on the back of her shirt. I think someone held her down, but like I said, she didn't struggle much."

"What was the time of death?"

"Approximately 2 pm."

"Some residents said they saw her in the dining room for lunch around 1 pm. She probably went out to the cemetery after that, and then it happened," Bahn said, thinking aloud.

After signing off with the coroner, Bahn went over the forensic reports to see the note about the oxygen tank being empty. "No prints on the tank... not even hers," he said. He noted that the report said the serial number on the oxygen tank lined up with where her other tanks were issued from. He read further into the report, and it confirmed there was a second set of footprints in the dirt that didn't match Violet's. They were estimated to be size eight and a half, and Violet's shoe size was 7.

Bahn read Maybel and Celeste's statements again, noticing Maybel mentioned Violet claimed her diamond necklace had been stolen. Again, he asked himself why someone would kill an elderly grieving widow?

He drove back out to Shady Sunset to ask some more questions of the staff. Upon entering the lobby, he ran into Colleen in the foyer and remembered she was head of administration. "May I ask you a few questions about Violet?"

Colleen ushered him back to her office and offered him some coffee.

"Yes, black, please."

Colleen handed him a bitter cup of coffee. "It's so sad what happened to Violet, but I guess now she's in a better place and with her husband and her son. Her daughter asked if she could hold the funeral service here for her at our chapel, and I told her of course she can. That's the least we can do for her."

Bahn nodded and sniffed the air. "Someone must be baking something. It smells like chocolate cake. When was the last time you spoke to Violet?"

"Let's see." Colleen looked at some notes on her computer. "I spoke to her last Tuesday in a one-on-one session. I'm a licensed certified counselor, and I meet with some residents from time to time for mental health checks, grief counseling and such."

"And how was her mental health?" he asked. Noticing Colleen's hesitation he said, "The sessions you had with her are no longer covered under any doctor patient type of privilege since she's deceased."

"She was severely depressed. I was concerned about her. Over the course of time that she'd been at Shady Sunset, I never saw any progress with her depression. I recommended all kinds of things like the art therapy class, group grief counseling, but nothing seemed to help her."

"Did you prescribe any anti-depressants to her?"

"No, I don't do that," Colleen said.

"One resident here said that Violet claimed someone stole her diamond necklace," Bahn went on, "but no one filed a report with the police. Do you know why?"

"Well, the residents here are elderly, Detective Bahn, and sometimes they get forgetful and misplace things. Some of them even get a bit of dementia and think they're seeing ghosts."

"Is that what you think happened? She misplaced her necklace?" Bahn sipped his bitter coffee.

"Most likely, but thanks to Maybel bringing it to my attention, we also questioned the cleaning staff. I called Myra into my office. She's the manager of our apartment cleaners. Now, I didn't want her to think I was accusing her of anything because she's been with us a long time. So, I said to her, 'There's been some theft reported lately, and I really need for you to be my eyes and ears and let me know if you see anything suspicious.' See, that way, I've alerted her we're aware of what's going on without making her feel threatened. I also watched her reaction closely to see if she got uncomfortable."

"Did she?"

Colleen shook her head.

"And did anything come from that conversation?"

"Nothing really. I mean, no one admitted to taking anything. We do background checks on all staff before they're hired. I assure you we don't hire anyone with a criminal background, so I really doubt it was an 'inside job', as they say. And quite frankly, I think Maybel might have an overactive imagination. I know her friend said they've helped solved a few murders, but now I think Maybel is seeing crime everywhere." Colleen chuckled.

"Did any other staff that have one-on-one contact with Violet?"

"Let me think… she participated in a lot of the activities Jo oversees, but that wasn't one on one. Oh, and there's Vick, one of our maintenance men. He helped Violet with a clogged sink, so he was in her apartment, and I think Violet had a hypnosis session with Sheila."

"Did you ever observe Violet not getting along with anyone?"

"No. Violet got along with everyone. She was such a gracious lady. No, no, wait. There was that one time I heard her and Norma arguing. I'm not sure what that was about, but Violet seemed pretty upset."

Detective Bahn stood and thanked Colleen for her time. He asked if he could speak with Norma, and Colleen escorted him to her apartment.

Norma welcomed him, and he sat on her floral print sofa. The powerful aroma of pot-pourri stung his nostrils. "You and Violet were good friends, weren't you?"

"Why yes, we were. How did you know?" she asked.

"You've been crying, and I doubt you'd cry over someone you didn't care about."

"She was such a nice woman, and I'd seen her every day for the last two years that I've been here. I'd gotten quite attached to her," Norma said. "I'm a widow too, and we widows need to stick together, you know?"

"The day of her death, did you see her?"

"Yes, I had lunch with her in the dining room," Norma said.

"Did you notice anything unusual about her?"

"No, not at all. She was looking forward to the talent show," Norma said, wiping her eyes.

"Colleen mentioned you and Violet had an argument recently. Tell me about that."

"Just politics, I think. She can't stand, I mean, she couldn't stand our current president," Norma answered. "I told her you don't have to like him. He just has to do a good job, and then she said he's a balding maniac, and I said a lack of hair doesn't mean anything, and she said he acts so unpresidential, and I said it was time we had someone run this country who isn't a career politician, and then she said—"

"OK, I got the idea. I just have one more question. What size shoe do you wear?"

"Eight and a half. Why do you ask?" Norma looked at him through startled eyes. "You don't think I had something to do with Violet's death, do you?"

"Just routine questions. What did you do after lunch yesterday?"

"I came back here to practice more for the talent show. I was tap dancing in my kitchen."

"Can anyone vouch for that? Did you run into anyone?" Detective Bahn asked.

"Well, no… but I assure you I was here. There are scuff marks on my floor," Norma said, pointing to her kitchenette.

"Thank you for your time." Detective Bahn stood and asked, "Do you know where I can find Sheila?"

Minutes later, Brian entered Sheila's on-site apartment. He looked around, noting all the bright colors she decorated with, and a beanbag sat in the corner next to a lava lamp. He asked Sheila with a smile, "Ms. Anderson, can you tell me a little about your interaction with Violet? It is Ms., isn't it?" The burning incense smelled like cinnamon to him.

Giggling like a schoolgirl, Sheila instantly melted at Detective Bahn's charms and good looks. "Yes, it's Ms. Are you married?"

"Twice divorced," he responded, noticing her wiry red hair looked like a Brillo pad.

"You know what they say. Third time is the charm!" She ran her hand through her long frizzy strawberry blond hair and licked her lips.

"Did you know Violet well?" Bahn inquired, aware of the effect he was having on her.

"Oh, about as well as any of the other residents. She was always kind of depressed, but she had a few friends she'd eat in the dining room with. She attended some activities we have here, and once I did a hypnosis session with her. I tried to help her with her grief. The poor lady had lost both her husband and her son."

Bahn raised an eyebrow. "And did it help?"

"No, I'm afraid not," Sheila responded. "She still seemed as depressed as ever. I could hypnotize you if you'd like. Anything you're struggling with? Stress? Sexual repression?"

Bahn smiled and thought of Celeste. "No offense, but I don't really go in for that sort of stuff."

"Well, if you change your mind, you know where to find me." Sheila winked.

"Can you tell me where you were around 2 pm yesterday?"

"Let's see… I treated Sylvia with a hypnosis session."

"And what size shoe do you wear?"

Sheila stuck her foot out and wiggled it around. "Eight and a half. Do you have a foot fetish?"

"This little piggy went wee, wee, wee all the way home," he said, winking.

"Every cop has his kink."

"Thank you for your time."

Later, an inquiry to Sylvia Martin confirmed Sheila was with her from 2:30 pm to 3:30 pm the day Violet was murdered. That left about a half hour in her schedule that couldn't be accounted for.

Chapter Sixteen

The Graves of a Household

"**D**ear, I know you have your pride, but I think you should reach out to him," Maybel urged Celeste a few days after Violet's passing.

"If Brian wants to talk to me, he can contact me," Celeste said. "I think those were his last words to me."

"Those won't be his last words to you. I assure you of that."

"How are you coping with Violet's death?" Celeste asked.

"Cried every day since it happened. Colleen suggested we do a special group counseling session to help everyone process this. I think I'm going to go to that."

"I think that's a good idea. I know you really liked Violet," Celeste said.

"Everyone has been very supportive around here. Even Arnie reached out to me."

Celeste smiled.

Maybel went on, "It's disturbing to me to think someone could have killed her. I mean, I left Regal Palms to get away from all the murder, and then this happens!"

"I guess murder just follows you wherever you go," Celeste reasoned.

"Dear, I've been thinking…"

"Uh oh," Celeste said, laughing.

"I think we should investigate," Maybel proclaimed.

Celeste reminded her that was what Detective Bahn was for.

"Well, I know, but he can always use a little help from us, and I'm sure he's busy with the mayor's case."

Celeste moved her phone from her right ear to her left. "I assure you, he doesn't want our help."

"What is going on with you two?" Maybel asked.

"Nothing, absolutely nothing." Celeste stared at her computer screen.

"Violet gave me a key to her place. I think we should go look for clues," Maybel suggested.

"The police already searched her place," Celeste responded.

"They may have missed something. Besides, I have a hunch I want to check it out. Are you in or are you out?"

Emphatically, Celeste said, "I'm out."

"No, no, you're not! We always work on cases together."

"Maybel, this isn't our case," Celeste reminded her.

"She was one of my best friends," Maybel said. "You're quiet. What are you thinking?"

"I was just thinking I need to pack my bags because you're taking me on a guilt trip."

"If you thought someone murdered Veronica, what would you do?"

After a pause, Celeste said, "OK, I'll come by tonight after work, but I'm pretty sure this is breaking and entering."

"No, no, this is what Violet would want me to do, and it's not breaking and entering if you have your own key. I'm sure of it."

Celeste sighed. "I'll see you tonight around seven."

"Wear black, all black."

Maybel sat in silence on her couch and Mr. Piddles cuddled up next to her. She felt his comfort and pet him with one hand, wiping tears away with the other. In the short time she'd been at Shady Sunset, she'd really grown to like Violet. She'd felt a genuine bond with her. She stared out her window, looking at the graveyard in the distance. "Who could have done this to you, Violet?"

***

After work, Celeste drove to Sunshine Beach and parked in the guest parking of Shady Sunset. Nightfall crept up, and spring storm clouds hung heavy in the sky. She walked through the lobby and up to Maybel's apartment.

Maybel scolded, "You're not in black."

Celeste stepped in and said hello to Mr. Piddles. She found him curled up on Maybel's couch, purring like he didn't have a care in the world. She scratched him under his chin and behind his ear. "This black patch of fur across his eye is so cute! He kind of looks like *Starchild* from *Kiss*."

"Who from what?"

"Never mind. So, am I supposed to be the lookout while you go into Violet's place? Because I'll tell you right now, I'm not going in. Brian would kill me if he found out."

"Yes, you're the lookout. Just whistle like a bird if you see anyone." Maybel put on George's black ski cap, and they walked down the empty hallway over to Violet's place. Maybel quickly unlocked the door and slipped in.

Celeste waited out front, hoping Maybel would hurry. Feeling as if someone was watching her, Celeste looked around the hallway but didn't see anyone.

A few minutes later, Maybel came back out. "Just as I thought!"

"What?" Celeste asked.

"Let's go back to my place so we can speak privately."

Maybel brewed some decaf coffee and carried a tray with a plate of walnut brownies to her coffee table. "Would you like one?" she offered to Celeste.

Celeste took a bite of one and closed her eyes, feeling the rush of endorphins from the chocolate. "These are so good!"

Maybel sipped her coffee. "I add a little espresso to really bring out the chocolate flavor. I've been craving chocolate ever since I smelled that delightful chocolate cosmos bouquet. Dear, before Violet died, she told me she had some Bearer bonds in her safe. I just found out they're gone!"

Celeste's eyes widened. "How do you know?" After finishing her brownie, she stroked Mr. Piddles. "She told me the combination of her safe was her birthday. I know how old she was, and her birthday was a week before mine. I calculated it and opened the safe."

"Could she have cashed them in?" Celeste wondered.

"No, I'm positive she didn't do that. She said they were sentimental to her, and that she didn't need the money. There's no way she cashed them in between the time she told me that and the time of her death."

"Well, this is interesting. Can you check with her daughter? Maybe she took them, or Violet gave them to her."

"Something else has been bothering me. Ida mentioned she saw Violet walking down the hall late one night, but when I checked with Violet, she said it wasn't her. She always goes to bed early."

Celeste sipped her coffee, petting Mr. Piddles with her other hand. "That is strange."

Maybel picked up her cellphone and made a call. "Hello, Ida, how are you?"

Celeste sat and listened to Maybel's side of the conversation over the sound of Mr. Piddles purring.

"Oh, I'm sorry. I didn't mean to interrupt you and Arnie. I just wanted to ask you a quick question. You mentioned you saw Violet walking out in the hall late one night. I was just wondering why you thought it was Violet… Oh, I see… OK… Thank you. Have a good night."

"What did she say?" Celeste asked.

"The person she saw in the hall wore a purple coat and rolling an oxygen tank. Ida said she didn't see their face but remembered that Violet wore a purple coat. She said she remembered that because she always thought it was so cute that Violet wore a violet-colored coat."

The women sat in silence for a few moments before Maybel spoke. "This is puzzling. I think we should go out to the cemetery and look around again."

"What is your obsession with making me go to the cemetery in the dark?" Celeste giggled.

"Dear, this is serious. I can't rest until I know who did this to Violet. I will leave no stone unturned!"

"No stone unturned? I'm not touching anything out at that cemetery, especially not a headstone!"

"I was speaking symbolically, not literally."

"With you, I never know. Sometimes you get carried away."

"Dear, I never get carried away."

Mr. Piddles flipped over on his side, stuck his four legs straight out, and dug his claws into Celeste's leg. "Ouch!"

"Oh, I forgot to warn you. He does that sometimes. He claws at my feet, too."

"His claws sure are sharp," Celeste said, rubbing her leg. "Bad kitty!"

Maybel laughed. "Scolding him does no good. I think it only encourages him. He's feisty."

"Well, if we're going out to the cemetery, we better bring our umbrellas." Celeste got up and took their coffee mugs to the sink, and Maybel slipped on her coat.

Creeping down the creaky staircase and through the dimly lit lobby, Celeste whispered, "Why do I feel like we are doing something wrong?"

"Don't be silly," Maybel replied, opening the huge front door to the retirement home, hinges groaning.

Under the cover of darkness, they trekked through the lush lawn on the property grounds of Shady Sunset to the trail leading to the Heavenly Souls Cemetery. The wrought-iron gates of the graveyard swung back and forth in the brisk wind as if moved by an unseen hand. There was a chain and padlock on the gate.

"Oh, it's closed at night. Guess we can't go in," Celeste said with a giggle.

"Don't be silly, dear. I know where there's a secret opening in the gate, remember? Follow me." Maybel walked along the gate surrounding the cemetery and walked back behind all the trees and shrubbery in front of Shady Sunset. She pointed to the side and whispered, "See that way? That's where the hidden door to the hidden staircase is. Then over here is the section of the gate with the latch that opens it and leads into the cemetery."

"Oh goodie," Celeste said, watching Maybel pull the latch, popping the gate open.

They entered the cemetery, passing the old tombstones marking the places of the dead, their etchings faded from years of sunlight and now barely legible. To avoid stepping on the sunken headstones, they walked carefully along a rutty section of the path lined with knee high California Wildrose bushes.

"It smells like rain."

"I know. The arthritis in my knee is killing me." Maybel turned up the collar of her coat against the chilly wind that kicked up.

A glorious weeping willow swayed in the far corner of the cemetery. The moon peaked out from behind the clouds, revealing the sad face of a stone angel statue. Traveling into the cemetery, they passed a statue of the Virgin Mary, whose lovely face looked down at the infant in her arms. Foggy clouds encircled the statues, and the wind blew them up to the heavens, whispering a warning.

Celeste shivered.

"Oh, dear, are you cold?" Maybel wondered.

"Have you ever seen those movies where the dead come out of their graves?"

"That's just make believe. Only God can raise the dead, and I doubt He's going to do that tonight."

"How do you know?"

"You just have the jitters. The Bible says when God comes back, He's going to come like a thief in the night. You never know ahead of time when a thief is going to break in, do you?"

Celeste shook her head, but the eerie graveyard under an inky indigo sky ignited all her fears. Surrounded by damp ground and mossy green patches of grass, the chilly breeze blew, and branches full of pine needles dipped, poking the murky air.

Passing a cordoned family burial plot, Maybel asked, "Do you think we should let Brian know all of this new information we got tonight?"

"You can tell him if you want," Celeste said flatly.

"Dear, it seems like you are holding a childish grudge against him. I wish you'd let me know what is going on."

"Childish? You're one to talk. You can't even be around Arnie for more than two minutes without getting into a fight with him."

Maybel sputtered, "That's different. We have a history."

"I know the history, the meeting about his flatulence."

"The meeting wasn't about his flatulence. He was flatulent during the meeting. Well… actually, it was right before the meeting. But it's more than that. He also made a pass at me many years ago, and I rejected his advances. I told him I was a married woman and that nothing could happen between us. But you know Arnie has such a big ego that he never forgave me for spurning his advances. I really think that's why he undermined my presidency of the board of the Regal Palms Homeowners Association."

"You're both single now. Maybe it's time to light that fire… just don't light it too close to his rear end."

"Don't be absurd. Besides, he's with Ida," Maybel protested.

"But what if he wasn't? How would you feel?"

"Don't worry about that. We've got clues to search for," Maybel said, looking at the ground under the pine tree, shining her flashlight around.

"Alright," Celeste said, looking at the ground. She walked a few steps more and looked up. Behind a spider's web, she spotted something. From under the great big pine tree, she called out, "Here's something interesting…"

Maybel looked up. "What am I looking at?"

"Don't you see it? There is a broken branch up in this pine tree." Celeste pointed.

Maybel moved around, almost tripping over a pine-cone on the ground, grabbing Celeste's arm in a viselike grip to steady herself. "Oh, now I see it. What do you think that means?"

"I'm not sure, but look at this," Celeste said, pointing to a carving on the trunk of the pine tree lit up by her cell-phone flashlight.

"V + J inside of a heart. What do you think that stands for?" Maybel wondered.

"What was Violet's husband's name?"

"John."

Celeste ran her hand over the carving and speculated, "It looks fresh. Perhaps Violet carved it while she sat here at this bench."

A burst of lightning and a rumble of thunder startled the ladies. "Maybel, we should get out of here. I don't like being here at night."

"Just a few more minutes, dear. Let's go look at that well over there."

Approaching the circular stones, Maybel noticed a hatch in the middle of it. "I always thought this was a wishing well, but there's no water in it, and it's not very deep." Tugging on the handle of the hatch, she pulled it open. "I wonder where this leads to. Maybe it's another secret passageway leading back to Shady Sunset. Should we check it out?"

"No! Absolutely not! It's too dangerous and it probably just leads down to the sewer. You already found one secret passageway. That's plenty."

"But I feel like we're missing something," Maybel said, walking further into the cemetery. Slowly, she passed headstone after headstone, reading the names. She found Violet's husband's headstone, the place for Violet's headstone next to John's. A few headstones further, she saw their son's headstone. She walked along, reading names.

"Look at this one!" she shouted.

Celeste rushed over.

"Josephine Stelliano."

"Do you know her?" Celeste asked.

"Our activities director is Jo Stelliano, but I assumed Jo was short for Joanne. Do you think it could be a family member of hers? Maybe her mother?"

"Maybe it's her own plot. Could she have bought a plot and had her headstone made in advance?" Celeste asked, speculating.

Deep in thought, Maybel mused, "No… it has a date of death on it… and the date of birth would make her about 90 years old. Jo is young… about 35. This is really a coincidence."

"You know what they say, there is no such thing as a coincidence… especially when a murder is involved." Celeste popped her umbrella open to protect them from the drizzling rain.

Maybel placed her hands on her hips. "Well, that settles it! I'm launching a full investigation!"

"It's off to sleuthville we go… again…" Celeste smiled.

Chapter Seventeen

The Jig Is Up

Celeste drove home carefully along the coast through the rain, thinking about Brian. She didn't understand why he acted so cold to her… maybe he was just in business mode, which she could relate to… but he was rude to her, and that had to be personal because he was friendly to Vick.

When she got home, she changed into flannel pajamas, put her hair up in a messy bun, applied a clay facial mask with avocado oil and gave Birino fresh water and birdseed. His fluffy wings fluttered with delight. Eagerly, he pecked at his meal. She turned on the tv, but it didn't hold her attention. Still fuming about how Brian treated her, she poured herself a glass of wine. Sipping it, she thought of a quote she'd heard; "Rejection is God's protection." Perhaps, she thought, this was God's way of showing her Brian wasn't good for her. After all, he did seem to be a bit of a womanizer.

With a second glass of wine in hand, she curled her legs under her on her plush couch. Running her hand along the velvety fabric, she remembered when she first met him. "Oh, he was so arrogant… and callous!" Birino chirped.

After munching on some potato chips, she finished her third glass of wine. "And that stupid chicken dance!" she said, remembering their date at the bowling alley. Her mind went into a full-blown negative downward spiral. "He couldn't even finish our date at the park. He ran off and left me alone at the train station."

The next thing Celeste knew, she texted Brian: **Is there a reason you gave me the cold shoulder at Shady Sunset?**

She waited for what felt like the longest hour of her life. He texted back: **You wanted to push me away, so I went away. I gave you what your behavior dictated.**

She texted him: **I didn't push you away. You had a case you needed to get to after the bowling night.**

His text back to her read: **You didn't know about that at the time you pushed me away. I told you about the case later when I canceled our next date. I think there is a disconnect between how you act and how you think you act.**

Finishing her fourth glass of wine, she texted: **You're not my therapist.**

He replied: **Good thing I'm not because if I was, I'd tell you you're being a brat.**

Celeste gasped at the words she read. While drafting a fiery text back to him, she decided to shut down instead. She turned her phone off, put it on the charger, washed the clay mask off and climbed into bed, sleeping fitfully, unable to get him out of her mind. She tried talking herself out of falling in love with him.

In the morning, she woke with a bit of a headache. Taking some aspirin, she washed it down with a big glass of water. She hopped in the shower to help wake up and get ready for work. With suds in her hair, she remembered she'd shut her phone off. She toweled dry and turned her phone on. Nothing. No new messages. Burning, she finished getting ready for work by putting on a forest green pencil skirt, a silky white blouse and a pair of black leather boots. She swept her hair up into a French twist, slapped on some scarlet red lipstick, brushed her lashes with mascara and slipped into her black wedge heels.

An hour into her workday, she received a text from Maybel. **Now Ida is missing some of her jewelry! I think Arnie is a thief! He's the only one that's been in her place besides the cleaners.**

Celeste texted back: **You should notify Detective Bahn**

Maybel replied: **I already did, and he's going to want to talk to you.**

Celeste asked: **Why?**

Maybel texted: **Someone saw us go into Violet's place and told him.**

"Well, at least she warned me what's coming," Celeste said. She finished working on the claim she'd been processing and reached for her purse to step out for her lunch break. A knock hit her office door. Assuming a co-worker needed advice, she called out, "Come in."

Detective Brian Bahn entered. Her throat closed up and her mouth went dry when she saw him. "How did you know where I work?" she managed to ask, knowing she was in trouble.

He smiled. "I am a detective… remember, Celeste?"

"So, what brings you here?" She sat stiffly in her white leather chair, running her sweaty palm on the side of her leg.

"I think you know," he said, not taking his eyes off her.

"If you came here to insult me again, I'm not interested in hearing it."

"That's not why I'm here, and you know it," he said.

Celeste remained silent and stared back at him. He stood between her and the door, and with him standing and her sitting, she felt an imbalance of power. She stood up.

He looked her up and down, admiring her work outfit before he spoke. "One resident at Shady Sunset informed me they saw you and Maybel break into Violet's apartment."

Celeste searched her purse for her keys. "I have never entered Violet's apartment."

"What about Maybel?"

"What about her?"

His voice grew louder. "Don't play dumb and don't change the subject like you always do."

"Is it considered breaking and entering if someone gives you their key?"

"And don't answer a question with a question! You always do that!"

"Why does that bother you?"

An angry laugh escaped him. "No, that's another question. Stop it!"

"You can't control me. You're not the boss of me."

He moved closer to her. "I'm not trying to control you. I'm trying to protect you."

"Well, thank you, but I don't need you to," she said, jiggling her keys.

"I can arrest you for interfering with a police investigation."

Celeste gasped. "First, you insult me. Now you're threatening to arrest me!? What is wrong with you?"

He stepped towards her. "What is wrong with you?"

"I don't know what you're talking about." She looked down at the ground and stepped back.

"I thought things were going really good between us, and then you gave me the cold shoulder the night we were at the bowling alley," he said, softening a bit.

"I didn't give you the cold shoulder."

"Stop playing dumb! You're just a sore loser."

"You're a horrible winner!"

He laughed. "But I won."

"Well, you didn't get the prize, did you?"

"No… you didn't invite me in," he said with a sigh.

"That's what this is about. You expected sex and didn't get it, and now you're giving me the cold shoulder. You're obsessed with one thing and fixated on getting your own way." She fiddled with the keys in her hand.

"No, this isn't about sex. Well, it's a little about sex. Why is it such a big deal to you?" he wondered.

"How come it is *not* a big deal to you?"

"Stop it. That's another question. Answer my question." He moved a step closer to her, putting his hands on his hips.

Hating his demand, she raised her voice, "You left me alone at the train station!"

"I had to work, Celeste."

"Yes, I know. Your job is the most important thing to you."

"Give me a reason to put it second."

Breaking eye contact, she quietly said, "I can't separate my heart from my body."

"No one is asking you to."

"My heart isn't there yet," she murmured. "Genuine commitment is mind, body and soul."

Unsure of his footing with her, he stayed calm and asked, "Is your body there?"

"Where?"

He sighed again. "A man can't wait forever, Celeste."

"I suppose not."

"Do you trust me?" he asked, stepping closer.

A half-hearted laugh escaped her lips. "I don't trust anyone."

"You know that's a sign that you grew up in a dysfunctional family," he said, stepping even closer.

"Do you and my therapist have a chat room you get together and talk about me?"

"No, but I really wish she'd give me instructions on how to figure you out."

"Well, here's a hint. Sexist and condescending remarks are a turnoff… rude behavior, a turnoff, chicken dances, turnoff… "

"I'd like to think I'm a rooster, not a chicken."

"A rooster is a chicken!"

Brian laughed. "Now I know your turnoffs. What about turn-ons?"

"Compliments… " She smiled, tilting her head.

He perked up. "Oh, so your love language is words of affirmation."

"You read that book?"

"What book?" he asked.

Laughing, she said, "Ah, now you're doing it."

Pulling her close to him, he gently, slowly kissed her like he'd never kissed her before. His lips trailed down her neck.

She held her breath, and her knees went weak. Leaning back against the edge of her desk, she hung onto it to keep from falling.

Stroking her cheek, he whispered in her ear, "Your skin is so soft… "

Trying to slow down her breathing proved futile.

Between kisses, he asked, "Don't you just want to let go of control and receive love?"

He knows the effect he has on me…

Her face flushed bright red.

He wondered why couldn't they just be on a tropical island away from the world? Choosing harmony over discord, he asked, "Why can't we just sail away to an island somewhere?"

She breathed in the intoxicating smell of his aftershave and kissed him back, feeling his body against hers. If she hadn't been at work, she might have given in to the temptation to go further. "You know I don't like being on a boat. I'm afraid of sharks."

"We can fly—let's fly to Jamaica and drink rum punch." He grinned at her.

She shook her head. "I can't drink rum. I got sick on rum one time at a bachelorette party."

"You're impossible, you know that?"

Giggling, she asked, "How about Paris? And champagne?"

"I'm in! I'm in all day long."

Her phone binged.

He pulled the phone from her hand, and she sputtered, "Hey! You can't look at my phone."

He handed it back to her. "You know I could hack into your phone if I wanted to. I could see everything."

"There's not much to see. I live a very boring life… well, I did, until you entered my life."

"Circling back to that dysfunction. Let's talk about that," he prodded.

"There's not much to tell. The short answer is my mother died when I was very young, which caused some trauma, and my dad wasn't around much. He worked a lot, but even when he was around, he was emotionally distant… and he had a very *short* fuse and a terrible drinking problem."

"Was he abusive?" Bahn asked.

Celeste nodded. "And the thing is, once you are damaged, there is no undoing it. People talk about healing and that's all warm and fuzzy sounding, but the damage is done, and it rewires how your brain works. It stays with you… it forms you. You can't change that. All you can do is learn how to function with the damage."

"I see," he said, taking her hand in his.

"From a very young age, I was just never able to build trust with anyone because of what all I went through. That's where my extreme independence comes from."

He looked at her and really saw her for the first time. "This is why you've never been in love. You've never let it into your life."

"You can look at me with that sad, sympathetic look in your eyes, and it's all very tragic what I went through. But you won't care when I'm sabotaging this relationship and holding your bleeding heart in my hands. I've been a warrior fighting this off for many years now. It's all I know." Her vision blurred from her tears.

"I'm not going to let you do that. Your negative thoughts are like weeds choking the life out of the garden of our relationship."

Celeste titled her head to the side. "May I ask you something?"

"I'm wide open, babe. What do you want to know?"

"Where did you hear that phrase 'the garden of our relationship'? Men don't talk like that."

Brian smiled. "You're not the only one that reads. You need a new vision for this relationship. You're going to break this pattern, and you're going to stop fighting it. Can you just try to keep an open mind and not push it away?"

"What is the '*it*' in that sentence?" she asked, laughing.

"This is what you do. We're having a real moment, and you make jokes. Do you harbor resentment towards men?"

Feeling his thumb run along the top of the palm of her hand sent a shiver down her spine. "I think I used to. I mean, I remember a few years back thinking about my past failed relationships… and I realized none of those chumps knew the way to my heart."

"You reinforce negativity by affirming lack and limitations. I think deep down you feel undeserving of love because of your troubled relationship with your father."

"You may be right. Love has always seemed like something for everyone else, but not for me." Closing her eyes, she felt his forehead press to her forehead, and she breathed in the moment.

His deep voice reverberated in her ears when he said, "And I think you are being selfish in our relationship."

"What!? I'm not selfish!"

"You're being selfish by not letting this relationship grow, Celeste."

"You're not going to figure me out this afternoon. I assure you of that. I'm too complex."

"I think it's very simple. Men want to love you, but you push them away, not trusting it and not wanting to get hurt… not really knowing how to form a deep attachment… not wanting to get attached to someone you might lose." He looked into her dark, shining eyes.

"What is love, anyway? I've had men say they love me, but they only hurt me."

"And you only date guys that you unconsciously know will be a letdown so that it supports your theory that no one is capable of loving you."

"I want you to stop analyzing me now." She bit her quivering bottom lip.

"Why? Is it making you uncomfortable?"

"And where do you fit into all of this? Twice divorced…"

"Oh no! You do not get to weaponize my past against me and insult me to push me away again," he said, laughing bitterly. "At least I've loved someone. I took a risk and made a commitment."

"You broke your commitment, too," she pointed out.

"It's not that simple," he protested.

With graciousness, Celeste decided not to point out his hypocrisy. "Well, Dr. Phil, I'm on my way to lunch. Do you want to join me?" she offered, putting her phone back in her purse and fixing her lipstick. She handed him a Kleenex. "You've got a little on your mouth."

"I'd love to, but I must get somewhere. I have to follow up on a lead with the mayor's case. How about we go out on Friday night?" he asked.

"I'd love to, but I already promised Maybel I'd go to Shady Sunset. The residents are putting on a play and she wants me to see it. You're welcome to go. Jeffrey and Vick should be there, too."

"It's not the night I imagined with you."

"What kind of night did you imagine with me?" She titled her head to the side and smiled.

"It involves you wearing that red dress again… remember the one you wore the night I first came over to your place?" He breathed on the side of her neck when he kissed it. "But yes, I can go to the play if that's what you want."

She looked up at him. "Yes, that's what I want. I think Maybel has been struggling with transitioning to this new place and making friends. Losing Violet is taking a toll on her."

"Alright, it's a date. We'll go to the play." Brian kissed her goodbye.

After he departed, Celeste caught her breath and the clean smell of his cologne stayed in the air of her office. She felt her flushed cheeks as she stepped outside. Once in her car, before leaving for lunch, she read the text Maybel sent her: **Did Brian question you? Is the jig up for me?**

She texted Maybel back: **No, the jig is not up. I distracted him with a fight. You're welcome.**

Chapter Eighteen

The Family Jewels

"**O**h, dear, I really owe you one! Thank you for not telling Brian I went into Violet's apartment," Maybel said to Celeste the next morning. "I spoke to Violet's daughter. First, she let me know when Violet's service will be, and second, she confirmed she doesn't have the Bearer bonds. So, my plan is to let Brian know the Bearer bonds are missing, but I would conveniently avoid telling him anymore than that."

"Sounds like you are proceeding with your own investigation." Celeste sipped slowly from her steaming coffee and read a work email.

"Indeed. And now some of Ida's jewelry is missing. I told her to file a police report, but I think I'm going to set up a sting operation."

"Just don't let Brian find out. He threatened to arrest me for interfering with a police investigation. He's serious about not letting me get involved in this one, and I'm sure he doesn't want you involved either."

"My goodness! Was he flirting with you when he said he'd arrest you?"

"I hope that's not how he flirts." Celeste deleted a junk email.

"I'll have to do this investigation on my own, then."
Maybel scratched Mr. Piddles under his chin. "I know for a
fact that Ida and Arnie have been hooking up, as the young
kids say. After questioning her, I found out that Arnie was
the last one in her place before she realized her gold bracelet went missing."

"You don't really think Arnie stole her jewelry, do you?
Isn't he well off financially?"

"As far as I'm concerned, nobody is above suspicion. I
have it from excellent sources that Arnie also paid visits to
Violet and Vera, and both of them were missing jewelry or
cash. He's the common denominator. Maybe he has a fetish for stealing. My plan is to leave my pearls out, invite
him over to my place, and see what happens."

"How do you know he paid visits to Vera and Violet?"
Celeste wondered.

"Don't worry about that. Let's just say I started up a
new phone tree. All the tea I'd been drinking caused me to
make too many trips to the bathroom. I don't know why
you are laughing. This isn't funny."

"No, no, it's not. Just be careful, please," Celeste warned.

"I don't want to exploit Arnie's lust for me, but if I
have to, I will."

"This play that's coming up, what is it?"

"We're doing Shakespeare's *King Lear*. And you'll never
guess who King Lear is!"

"Your arch nemesis?"

"Yep! Ida, Vera, and I are playing his three daughters. He really let this role go to his head. He put a gold star with his name on it on his front door. And you won't even believe what happened the other day in dress rehearsal. Arnie ripped a hole in his tights."

"Oh boy. You don't need to tell me anymore than that."

"I didn't see all the detail, but I could feel it looking right at me! The part that protruded out of his man tights looked bubble gum! It poked through and–"

"Really, I got the idea! You don't need to go on."

"He told me to stop staring, but *it* was looking right at me!"

Giggling, Celeste asked, "Do you realize that you've now seen both Vick *and* Arnie's private parts?"

"Oh, good heavens, I hadn't thought of that, but you're right," Maybel continued, "and speaking of Vick, I have it on excellent sources that he's been shacking up with Jo!"

"Your phone tree?"

"You know she lives on site, and so do Colleen and Sheila. Well, someone spotted Vick leaving Jo's place early one morning. The walk of shame, I think they call it. Like father, like son. Neither one of them can keep it in their pants!"

Celeste pointed out, "If it's true that Vick and Jo are romantically involved, then maybe the V + J on the pine tree is for Vick, plus Jo."

"I hadn't thought of that. You could be right. I'll need to investigate it further. But I need to get going because I booked a counseling session with Colleen, and before that I need to clean out Mr. Piddles litter box. Then I'm going to set my trap for Arnie."

"Promise me you will be careful," Celeste urged.

"I promise."

After dinner, Maybel put on a pink silk blouse and unbuttoned one extra button. She fluffed her hair up and applied some lipstick. She sent a text to Arnie: **I think I just saw that burst of fog again! Will you please come over? I'm scared!**

Arnie texted back: **I'll be right over!**

Intrigued by Maybel's tantalizing offer to come over, Arnie spritzed himself with cologne and gave his thick hair a quick comb. He put on his favorite blue V-neck sweater and a pair of pleated slacks.

A couple of minutes later, his knock hit her door. In his bold outfit, Arnie brazenly barreled through the doorway.

Playing the damsel in distress, Maybel spoke as sweetly as she could. "I'm so glad you're here! It frightened me when I saw it!"

Arnie rushed to her window and looked out. "I don't see anything. It's gone now. I didn't see it from my window either."

In her best come hither voice, Maybel asked, "Could you stay with me for a little while? It really shook me up." She batted her eyelashes faster than Mr. Piddles batted around a ball of yarn.

"Oh, sure." Arnie smiled, sitting down on Maybel's couch. Maybel noticed he wore a freshly pressed pair of mustard yellow gaberdine slacks. He patted the cushion next to him and extended one rangy arm along the back of the couch, waking up Mr. Piddles, who was napping behind it. "You smell wonderful. What's that perfume you're wearing?"

"It's arthritis cream for my stiff knee. Why don't I get us a drink first," Maybel said, intentionally leaving him alone in her living room, pearls loose.

Taking her time, she filled two glasses with lemonade from her plastic pitcher. Forcing herself to smile, she walked back into her living room and handed Arnie a glass. After taking a seductive sip, he smacked his lips from the tart beverage. Reluctantly, Maybel sat down next to him.

With one powerful leap, Mr. Piddles pounced from behind the couch, landing on Arnie's private area, causing him to spill his lemonade. Mr. Piddles scrambled up Arnie's chest to his head. Claws and cat legs caught on to Arnie's blue cashmere sweater, snagging it along the way. Mr. Piddles jumped onto Arnie's head, and Arnie reached for Mr. Piddles to pull him off, making fur fly.

Pandemonium ensued and Maybel didn't know who made worse noises, Arnie or Mr. Piddles. Upon a closer look, she realized it wasn't fur that flew. Arnie's toupee flung to the ground. Looking at his bald head, she suppressed a giggle. Mr. Piddles sprang from Arnie's neck down to the carpet, landing on the hairpiece.

Arnie jumped up. "That damn cat!" With his anger fully aroused, Arnie reached for his toupee and pulled, but Mr. Piddles dug his claws in further, hanging on for dear life. Arnie jerked and jerked at his toupee.

Refusing to release, Mr. Piddles dangled from the fuzzy molded skull cap of wiry gray hair. Arnie grabbed Mr. Piddles front leg and tugged its claws off his toupee, but the ferocious feline fought hard and dug in his other front leg claws. Mr. Piddles hissed hotly at Arnie, clawing him with his free back legs. Arnie yanked Mr. Piddles other front claws from his toupee, and Mr. Piddles plummeted to the ground, jutting off behind the couch with a piece of fluffy toupee in his jaws.

Arnie stormed out, rubbing the scratches on his bald head.

Maybel watched in dismay, setting her glass down. She checked the end table to find her pearls were gone. "I knew it!" she shouted, hurrying out of her place. She caught up to Arnie in the hall, grabbing at his wet pants, reaching into his pockets.

"Geez, Maybel! Control yourself! I know you wanted to get together, but your cat killed the mood," Arnie said, pushing her hands off him.

"I don't want to get together, you idiot! I'm trying to get my pearls back!"

"Your what?" "Oh, don't act so innocent. I know you're the one stealing everyone's jewels!" The accusation burst off Maybel's tongue like one of Arnie's fireballs.

"I don't have your jewels or anyone else's," Arnie said, pulling his pockets inside out so she could see they were empty. "You can pat me down if you want."

Maybel huffed, "You should be so lucky! By the way, you look like you peed your pants. I think Sheila would recommend it's time for you to wear adult diapers!"

Looking down at his wet crotch, Arnie shouted, "You know your stupid cat did this to me!"

"I know no such thing, Arnie Arnold! And I still think you have my pearls! You probably did your sleight-of-hand trick and stuck them up somewhere I can't see!"

Arnie's face and bald scalp reddened at the accusation. "That's lunacy! I did no such thing!" He put his toupee back on and stormed off.

Several minutes after getting back to her apartment, Maybel received a call from her new phone tree. The person on the other end congratulated her for getting lucky with Arnie.

Chapter Nineteen

Don't Throw Your Pearls to the Pigs

The next morning, over Celeste's laughter, Maybel said, "It's not funny! Now everyone here at Shady Sunset thinks I hooked up with Arnie, *and* my pearls are still missing!"

"Gossip is a dangerous thing, Maybel," Celeste warned. "What kind of bed does Arnie have?"

Maybel huffed, "OK, OK, you made your point!"

"Sounds like the tea got too hot for you."

"Dear, I assure you I would not have let Arnie's sexual advancements advance that far."

Celeste asked, "So, Sherlock, what's your next move in this investigation? You know I'm sitting this one out since Brian threatened to arrest me if I interfere, but perhaps I can coach you from the sidelines."

"Well, I have to report my pearls missing, and I need to tell Brian about the Bearer bonds."

"Tread carefully when you speak to him."

"I will."

After signing off with Celeste, Maybel had a strategically worded conversation with Detective Brian Bahn in which she let him know about the missing Bearer bonds but did not let him know she'd been in Violet's place and opened her safe. He told Maybel that since she searched Arnie and he didn't have the pearls on him, there wasn't much he could do, but he agreed to speak with Violet's daughter about the Bearer bonds.

"I know Violet had a safe in her bedroom, and she told me the combination was her birthday. She said that's where she kept the bonds. You should search and make sure they're still there," Maybel said.

Bahn smiled. He knew she knew they weren't there. "I'll send a police officer over there now to check. Thanks for the tip."

"Wonderful! By the way, how are things going with you and Celeste?"

He let out a breath. "She is the feistiest woman I've ever known."

Maybel laughed. "She's also a kind soul."

"She's a sass master."

Maybel smiled. "She's worth the time you invest in her, despite her sass. I assure you that."

"She tried to convince me she's damaged goods, but she's the most put together woman I've ever known."

"She's one of a kind for sure, but she's more fragile than she lets on."

"Yeah," Bahn agreed. "That tough outer shell is just a cover."

As soon as she ended her phone call with Detective Bahn, Maybel went downstairs to the dining room to eat breakfast. When Vera and Norma spotted her, they were all smiles. She sat down and placed her napkin on her lap.

"Maybel, you're glowing!" Norma said.

"Oh, please. Nothing happened. I tried to get Arnie to steal my pearls," Maybel protested.

"Is that what they're calling it now?" Norma asked, laughing with Vera.

With a snicker Vera added, "I hear Arnie has a magic touch with the ladies."

Chuckling, Norma said, "All the ladies call him the silver-haired fox."

"There is nothing between Arnie and I!"

Arnie approached the table. "Oh, come on Maybel. You couldn't keep your hands off me!"

Maybel stood up and fumed in his ear, "Listen Houdini, I swear to God I'll make that toupee disappear right off your head in front of everyone if you don't let them know what really happened!"

Arnie spoke sternly, "Ladies, I assure you. Nothing happened between Maybel and I. She spotted that strange fog again, and I went over to her place to watch for it."

"Speaking of spotting, did you get your pee pants dry cleaned?" Maybel chuckled.

With hands on hips, Arnie insisted, "I didn't pee my pants!"

Vera adjusted the cuff on her plaid jacket. "So, you just went over to Maybel's to see the strange fog? Is that all that happened?"

Arnie scoffed, "And she thought I took her pearls, but her dumb cat, Mr. Shittles, probably swallowed them."

"His name is Mr. Piddles!" Maybel hit her limit and turned on her heel, exiting the dining room. When she arrived back at her apartment, she put some toast in her toaster and gave Mr. Piddles a saucer of milk. She cooed, "You're a good kitty! I'm glad you pulled that dumb toupee off his stupid head!"

A short time later, they were to have another dress rehearsal because the first one went so badly. Maybel changed into full Shakespearian garb and waited around for everyone to get ready. Ida, also decked out in Shakespearian garb, approached Maybel. "Have you been practicing your lines?"

"Every night."

"Well, except for last night." Ida giggled. "I heard you were busy with Arnie. Isn't he a tiger? And he's still got a full head of hair! I can't say that about any of the other men here."

"It wasn't like that!"

"Maybel, you don't have to deny it. Nothing is exclusive around here," Ida said, winking.

"Oh, good heavens!" Maybel let out a disgusted sigh, but before she could go on, something in the corner of the backstage dressing room caught her eye. She walked over to a clothing rack lined with various costumes and reached for a purple coat. She pulled it off the rack and motioned

Ida over to her. "Ida, does this look like the purple coat you thought you saw Violet wearing?"

Examining it, Ida said, "Why, yes. It looks just like it."

"It's definitely not Violet's coat, but it is similar. Violet's coat had silver buttons, and this one has gold. Plus, Violet's coat color was almost a periwinkle, and this one is a bit darker like a wine-colored purple… but it's the same length and style," she said, putting it back on the rack.

Jo's chipper voice squawked, "Hello, hello, hello ladies! Are you ready to get back on stage and give it another go?"

"As ready as I'll ever be," Maybel answered. "Jo, do you know where all these clothes on this rack came from?"

Jo looked over at the rack and said, "I'm not sure. People have donated items over the years. All that stuff has been there for a long time."

Maybel concluded that anyone would have had access to the purple coat and could have borrowed it to appear like Violet walking down the halls. She checked the pockets, but they were empty. She turned back to Jo again, asking, "I've been meaning to ask you… is Jo short for Joanne?"

Jo looked up from her clipboard. "No, it's Josephine. It's a family name."

"Oh, I see. Is your mother still alive?"

Jo frowned. "Yes, why do you ask?"

"The other day we saw a headstone out at the cemetery with the name Josephine Stelliano, and I was wondering if it was someone related to you. Do you have any family buried in the cemetery next door?"

Jo breathed in a sharp breath. "No. All my family lives out of state. Now, if you'll excuse me, I need to help Vick with the props. I heard the balcony he erected isn't very stable." She scurried away.

Maybel turned to Ida. "Are you sure the person in the halls you saw late at night wearing the purple coat pulled an oxygen tank with them?"

"Oh, I'm positive! Why do you ask?" Ida wondered.

"Just curious," Maybel said.

Arnie entered the backstage dressing room clothed in Shakespearian garb and wearing a new pair of tights. "Maybel, when we run through our lines, try not to over-act this time."

"Try not to rip your man tights this time!"

Bending his legs in a plie, Arnie said, "Not that it's any of your business, but these are new leggings—not tights. They're much sturdier."

"I hope so. This is a family show, Arnie!" Maybel tugged at the itchy wig on her head.

"Just don't fumble your lines, OK? I don't want you to make me look bad."

"You do a fine job of that all on your own!" Maybel's face reddened.

The second dress rehearsal of *King Lear* flowed much better than the first one, and Jo deemed them to be ready for opening night, which would be the next night. "Break a leg, everyone!"

The cast filtered out of the dance hall and back to their apartments.

Chapter Twenty

A Man on the Inside

After the second dress rehearsal, Maybel went back to her place and settled in on her couch with lunch and Mr. Piddles purring next to her. A family name, she thought. What are the odds? Something was off, and Maybel could feel it in her bones. She hated what she had to do next, but it needed to be done. She texted Vick and asked him to come over to look at her leaky faucet.

"It's not leaking, Maybel. You're wasting my time," Vick scolded, his prematurely balding head standing tall over her.

"Well, that's strange. It leaked earlier, but since I have you here, maybe we could have a chat. I think Detective Bahn needs some help to solve Violet's murder."

A puzzled look appeared on Vick's face. "Didn't Violet die of natural causes? I thought Sheila said she probably had a heart attack."

Maybel shook her head. "That's what the murderer wants us to think, but Violet had been hit on the back of the head, and there was a footprint on her back."

"This is news to me." Vick's eyes narrowed.

"Celeste and I were the first ones on the scene of the crime, and we saw the contusion," Maybel assured him.

"What does this have to do with me?"

"We suspect that it was an inside job. We need your help."

Vick, always wishing he could have been a cop, loved the idea of helping in another case. "I'm in. What do you need?"

"You have access to all the cleaning crew's lockers, right?"

Vick stated proudly, "As head of maintenance, I have keys to everything."

"The first thing we need for you to do is search all their lockers. Perhaps one of them is the jewelry thief and they haven't pawned the jewelry yet."

"OK, that's easy enough. Anything else?"

"The second item is a very delicate matter, and you may have a biased opinion… since rumor has it you've been… shacking up with Jo."

Vick corrected her, "Jo is a lady. We don't 'shack up'. We make love."

Maybel crinkled her nose. "Despite all the love you're making, she may not be the person who you think she is. When Celeste and I were out at the cemetery, we saw a headstone with the name Josephine Stelliano engraved on it, near where Violet's husband's headstone is."

Vick didn't budge. "So?"

"Well… we think it's too much of a coincidence. We think maybe Jo stole someone else's identity… and maybe she got the idea for her fake name from one of the head- stones out at the cemetery and has been stealing from the residents here. She has keys to lots of things too, and she pays visits to the residents here."

Angered by the accusation, Vick said, "You're crazy. My Jo would never murder anyone!"

"No offense, Vick, but you don't have the best judgement when it comes to women."

"Do you want my help, or are you just going to insult me?"

"Look, I need a man on the inside. The next time you're at Jo's place, maybe you can pick up a little intel and search for clues. You know, look for anything that might indicate she's using a stolen identity. If I'm wrong, you can gloat later."

After a long pause, Vick agreed to search Jo's place. "The only reason I'm agreeing to search her place is to prove to you that my angel is as pure as the driven snow." He crossed his arms over his puffed-out chest.

"By the way, did you and Jo carve your initials out on that pine tree at the edge of the cemetery?"

Vick dropped his arms and giggled like a schoolboy. "Yeah, I went out there with her to help her collect pinecones for her crafts class, and I took out my pocketknife and carved our initials inside a heart. I thought it would earn me some brownie points with her, and boy oh boy did it! That night she grabbed me by the–"

"No, that's OK. You don't need to tell me anymore. Did either of you climb the pine tree?"

"No. Now I must get going. I'll search the staff lockers later tonight, and then I'll go over to Jo's, proving you wrong." Vick exited Maybel's place, slamming her door loudly.

Once he left, Maybel turned to cat and said, "I'm going to solve this case if it's the last thing I do, Mr. Piddles. My friend Violet deserves justice." He meowed for another saucer of milk, and Maybel lovingly poured it.

After changing into a black sweater and skirt, she made her way over to the tiny non-denominational chapel on the Shady Sunset property for Violet's funeral service. Seeing a woman who looked a lot like Violet, she figured that must be her daughter. Maybel turned to look at the picture collage hanging on an easel in the foyer. Maybel smiled, admiring all the photos that told the story of Violet's life. Wiping tears from her eyes, she approached the open casket. Violet looked good; all things considered. Maybel whispered to her, "I'm going to find out who did this to you, Violet. I swear."

She took a seat next to Norma and Vera before the funeral began and read the funeral program. On the front, was written, '*Those we love don't go away. They walk beside us every day. Unseen, unheard, but always near. Still loved, missed and held so dear.*'

Vera leaned over and whispered to Maybel, "Are you going to the cooking class tomorrow?"

Maybel shook her head. "I already know how to cook."

Norma whispered, "Oh, we were really hoping you'd go. It sounds like a lot of fun. Jo is going to teach all of us how to cook a soufflé."

Remembering she was trying hard to fit in, Maybel conceded, "OK, I'll go."

The three ladies sat quietly listening to the sermon the pastor gave and memories some of Violet's family members shared. After singing hymns, the service concluded. Everyone walked out to the cemetery for the graveside committal to the ground ceremony. Maybel noted that the same headstone, located by Violet's headstone, had a fresh bouquet of Chocolate Cosmos inside the in-ground vase. After Violet was laid to rest, everyone gathered in the dining room for a luncheon hosted by the family.

Maybel approached Violet's daughter Leah, where she was standing alone. "My deepest condolences to you, Leah. I'm so sorry for your loss. Your mother was such a dear person, and you're the spitting image of her. I know you had your differences, but she loved you," Maybel said, patting her arm.

"Differences? That's putting it mildly. My mother was a bitter, selfish old woman who treated my younger brother like an infant and drove him to drink. After he drank himself to death, she cared more about her deceased son than her living daughter. She was controlling and never wanted Tim to grow up, so she financially supported him, but the *one* time I asked for help, she refused. And you call that differences?" Leah laughed bitterly.

Taken aback by Leah's words, Maybel stammered, "I know she did a lot for Tim, but that didn't mean she didn't love and care for you."

Leah narrowed her red-rimmed eyes. "Did more for Tim? She was going to leave him her entire estate because she didn't think he could take care of himself. Tim used her as his cash cow and never financially supported himself. She did everything for him and *nothing* for me. Did you know that she didn't leave me any inheritance? She left it all to charity… didn't even give me a dime. I had to come out of pocket for her funeral and burial expenses! She was a hateful woman. It took every ounce of grace I have to give her a funeral service, but I figured her friends and other family wanted to say goodbye to her."

"Dear, I'm so sorry she didn't leave you anything… but please know that doesn't mean she didn't love you."

"That's exactly what it means. My mother was very manipulative, and you weren't even smart enough to realize that. But don't be sorry she didn't leave me anything. My mother was not my source of wealth. My wealth comes from God. Every good thing I have is from the Lord, not her."

Trying not to feel insulted, Maybel replied, "Well, I think your mother did more for Tim because he had less… he didn't have the independence and wherewithal you have. You can't put a price tag on how valuable your faith and independence are… and your real inheritance is the kingdom of heaven… that's priceless."

Leah spat her words, "It doesn't matter how much money my mother had. She just used it as a tool to hurt me, but she couldn't take it with her, could she?"

"You seem angry and that's understandable, but I'm sure your mother did a lot of good things for you, too."

"You didn't know the first thing about who my mother really was. You're ignorant, and I don't blame you for being ignorant, but please don't try to speak to me from a place of knowledge when you're ignorant."

Maybel blinked a few times, struggling to process what she heard. Keeping her tone soft, she said, "You're right. I'm sure there was a lot that transpired between you and your mother that I know nothing about… and I know your mother wasn't perfect. I just want you to know that in time, I think it will be good for you to forgive your mother. The Bible commands us to forgive. In the book of Matthew, it is written, '*For if you forgive others their trespasses, your Heavenly Father will also forgive you, but if you do not forgive others their trespasses, neither will your Father forgive your trespasses*'. You don't want to live or die in a place of unforgiving anger. That's a dangerous place to be. Forgive her for your own wellbeing."

Leah stuck her chin out and folded her arms across her chest. "I hope you told my mother that because no one could hold on to a grudge better than her."

Nodding, Maybel whispered, "I told her."

Leah looked down at the ground, fighting back tears. "I don't know what hurts worse, her death or her betrayal."

Maybel wrapped her arms around Leah, embracing her. "I am so sorry, dear. I know how difficult it is to make allowances for a loved one's flaws. In time, this will hurt less…"

Leah sobbed on Maybel's shoulder.

Later, with Violet's funeral behind her, Maybel quietly went back to her apartment, feeling completely drained. Staying in for supper, she shared another toasted cheese sandwich with Mr. Piddles.

Chapter Twenty-One

To Rise or Not to Rise

The next day, after the breakfast service concluded, the kitchen was turned over to Jo and those residents who were attending her cooking class. "Hello, hello, hello everyone! I'm so glad you could all make it today for the cooking class. But before we begin, Colleen wanted me to remind you that her group counseling session will be later this afternoon. She hopes you can all attend that as well.

"Now, let's get started. I'm going to demonstrate how to make a soufflé. Then we'll break out and you'll each make a soufflé of your own. I have two different recipes here, sweet and savory. Chocolate if you want a sweet one and a cheese soufflé if you want a savory one." Jo tied an apron around her trim waist and did her cooking demo. "Soufflés intimidate lots of people, but they're really quite easy to make." Her students watched while she separated eggs, beat egg whites to stiff peaks, folded in her rue, added cheese, greased ramekins, and poured the batter into them.

"We don't have enough of these mini ramekins for all of you, so some of you will have to make one large soufflé," she said, sliding her pre-heated cookie sheet filled with ramekins into the oven. "And remember! Do not peek, no matter what! Do not open the oven door before the baking time is up. Who wants to make the chocolate souffles?"

Norma and Vera and a few others raised their hands. When Jo asked who wanted to make the savory souffle, Maybel, Arnie, and a couple of other residents raised their hands. Jo passed out the recipe cards accordingly and assigned everyone to their cooking stations. "Maybel and Arnie, you take station #1 over there," she said, pointing to a double stove and oven set in the corner of the giant kitchen.

Maybel got started quickly, as she was already familiar with how to make a soufflé. Arnie fumbled around, and Maybel thought about helping him, but decided against it. She greased her giant soufflé dish and sprinkled breadcrumbs around on it. After pouring her batter into the dish, she put it on a heated cookie sheet and popped it into the oven. She stood back and watched Arnie place his soufflé into the bottom oven.

Norma melted chocolate at her cooking station, and Vera greased their ramekins. They gently folded beaten egg whites into the rest of the batter and popped them into their ovens, while others grated cheese at their stations and separated egg yolks from the egg whites.

Later, when the cooking time was up, Maybel took hers out and it rose gloriously with a nice golden brown top hat. She set it on the stove to cool. Arnie took his out, and his also rose nicely. He set his next to hers on the stove to cool.

"OK everyone, gather round!" Jo said. "I want you all to try a taste of the soufflés I made."

"Mmm," Norma said, smacking her lips. What a nice chocolate flavor. I hope mine tastes as good." She dug her spoon back into the ramekin for another bite.

Maybel tasted one too. "Not bad."

After everyone tried Jo's chocolate soufflés, they went back to their stations to present theirs to the rest of the class. Maybel walked back to the stove at their station, but before she could pick up her soufflé, Arnie grabbed it. "Your soufflé fell, Maybel. That's too bad," he said, laughing.

"My soufflé most certainly didn't fall. Yours did! You're holding *my* soufflé." Maybel's cheeks burned red.

Arnie retorted, "My soufflé didn't fall. You watched me beat mine into the stiffest of peaks!"

"Oh, you rat! Put my soufflé down this instant!"

Colleen entered the kitchen, reminding everyone of her group counseling session after the cooking class. She walked around, looking at everyone's soufflés. "Why, they all look delicious!"

"Arnie, I watched you make yours. You didn't let your rue cool, you over mixed your egg whites, *AND* you peeked in the oven before the cooking time ended because you couldn't resist the temptation. Your soufflé was on the right side of the stove. You're holding my soufflé!" Maybel huffed.

"Maybel, what's going on?" Colleen asked, approaching the arguing pair, feeling the need to referee.

"Maybel here thinks my soufflé is hers. She can't accept that *her* soufflé fell," Arnie said, holding the savory soufflé with a risen top hot.

"Maybel, is this true?" Colleen asked, and students gathered around to find out what was going on.

"No, of course not. I've been cooking soufflés for fifty years! They never fall. Arnie is holding *my* soufflé, not his." Maybel stared daggers at Arnie, pointing her finger at him. "You stole my soufflé!"

Arnie set the soufflé down. "You know what they say, Maybel. When you point your finger at someone, you have four fingers pointing back at yourself."

Norma interjected, "I think you only have three fingers pointing back at yourself. Your thumb doesn't point back at yourself. But is the thumb considered a finger? I can't remember."

Arnie gave Norma a thumbs up and smiled.

Colleen, always one to give wise advice, suggested the two of them throw out the fallen soufflé and cut the risen one in half. Maybel couldn't bear to see her soufflé cut in half. "Just let him have it." She untied her apron, set it down on the counter, and walked out of the kitchen.

Colleen called after her. "Don't forget the group counseling session in half an hour!"

Chapter Twenty-Two

God Is Always with You

Cold metal folding chairs sat in circle formation in the Shady Sunset Retirement Home dancehall, and Colleen looked around at everyone. "Thank you all for attending this grief counseling session. I know most of you are widows and widowers," she looked at Arnie and went on, "but I also wanted to talk about Violet since most of you knew her."

Maybel folded her hands and rested them on her lap. She fought back her tears, but she wasn't thinking of Violet. She knew Violet was in heaven with John and Tim. Maybel thought of George. She missed him so much; it ached like no other ache.

"She's in a better place," Norma said, bottom lip quivering.

Arnie and some others nodded.

"Yes," Collen said, handing a box of Kleenex to Norma. "Violet is in a better place now. It's OK to cry. Think of crying as cleansing your eyes so you can see better and aren't blinded by pain. And, at times like this, it's good to remember we are more than just our bodies. We have souls. Plus, remember that what we keep in our memories of our loved ones remains ours, forever unchanged. I wanted to have this special session to check in and find out how everyone is doing."

Vera spoke, "The funeral service helped. I feel like a got a little bit of closure, and I think her family gave her a proper service."

Norma wiped her eyes. "What a sweet lady her daughter is. I'm glad I got to meet her, but I feel bad for her. Now, she's lost both her parents and a brother. As a widow, I understand how grief becomes your constant companion."

Maybel remained silent about what she knew about Violet and Leah's relationship.

Colleen added, "Grief is the cost of loving someone who died. Without love, we cannot grieve. It's like the good book says, '*Blessed are those who mourn, for they shall be comforted*'."

Vera asked, "How can mourning possibly be a blessing?"

"The context of that verse refers to feeling remorse over your sin, not the loss of a loved one," Maybel replied.

"I remember after my husband passed away," Vera continued, "I felt so angry. I felt like God had abandoned me. People kept quoting scripture to me, and I didn't want to hear one more Bible verse. They kept telling me that one, '*He will wipe every tear from their eyes*', and I wondered, where is the comfort in that? If God really wanted to be good to me, He wouldn't have taken my husband away from me."

Norma handed the box of tissues to Vera.

"That's a very normal reaction, Vera," Colleen went on, "and as most of you know, anger is part of the five stages of grief. There's nothing wrong with being angry at God. Some people think being angry at God means you don't believe in Him, but if you didn't believe in God, you wouldn't even be angry at Him. The caution would be don't stay in that place of anger. You must move through it."

"I felt a lot of anger towards my husband, too." Vera said. "If he would have just taken better care of himself, then he wouldn't have gained so much weight and his cholesterol wouldn't have gone up and he wouldn't have had that heart attack. He was always so lazy!"

Maybel shook her head. "You shouldn't speak ill of the dead."

"Yeah, it's like that Bible verse 'speak of the devil and the devil appears'," Arnie interjected.

"That's not a Bible verse. It's just an old saying," Maybel said.

"Well, excuse me if I'm not the theologian you are, Maybel. I don't know as much about the devil as you do."

"Don't call on the devil, Arnie! That's a bad idea!" Maybel folded her arms across her chest. "You should call upon the Holy Spirit. The Holy Spirit is like a gentle wind that comes along to assist us… knowing just the right time to help us… only letting us bend and not break."

Arnie snickered. "Well, if anyone would know about breaking wind, it would be you."

"You are so immature, Arnie Arnold!" Maybel felt her face burn.

Norma spoke, "The Bible verse that really comforted me is the one that says, '*No eye has seen, no ear has heard, and no mind has imagined what the Lord has prepared for those who love Him.*'"

Vera shook her head. "My grief was so painful that no Bible verse was of comfort to me. I still don't want to hear them." Vera folded her arms across her chest.

"That's so bleak. How do you grieve if you don't have any hope in an afterlife?" Maybel wondered.

Vera shouted, "We are all allowed to grieve in our own way, Maybel! Your religion isn't superior!"

Maybel lifted her chin up. "Jesus had those scars on his wrists for a reason."

Vera blinked. "What scars?"

"From the nails," Maybel replied.

"Not all of us believe that Jesus being nailed to a cross means anything." Vera bristled, stuffing her tissue into her pocket.

Maybel replied, "Vera, you have nothing to lose by believing, and you have everything to gain."

Colleen interrupted, "We're all entitled to our own beliefs. Let's move on."

"For me, losing my husband taught me to not take anything for granted. I have so much hope in God's promises," Norma said.

Colleen nodded. "That's good, Norma. Death teaches us how to live, and life is a gift."

Vera snapped, "Hope in what promises?"

"Well, I suppose hope that suffering will end. There will be no suffering in heaven," Norma replied.

"If God really loved us, He wouldn't let us suffer like this." Vera wiped her eyes.

With a gentle tone, Colleen suggested, "Vera, maybe it's time you forgave God. You know, when you hold on to grudges, the only person you hurt is yourself."

Arnie spoke, "When I found out my wife had cancer, I told God if he healed her, I'd start going to church again."

Colleen gave a sympathetic smile. "That is normal, too… and it's part of the bargaining stage of grief. I'd also like to remind everyone that it's OK to cry. Crying is healing and tears cleanse the soul."

"Well, my bargaining didn't work. I lost her anyway," Arnie said, looking down. "She was in so much pain. I remember one day she asked me how much longer she would have to suffer before she could pass on to heaven, and I told her 'In no time it will be time.'… and it was so fast after that conversation she died. I felt lost after she died. I didn't know what to do. There were so many things I took for granted. I even had to learn how to cook for myself."

Vera handed the box of tissues to Arnie.

Colleen looked at Maybel. "Maybel, what about you?"

Maybel said, "I already knew how to cook."

"Except for soufflés," Arnie mumbled under his breath.

Glaring, Maybel reproached him. "You stole mine! You know, that was my soufflé, Arnie."

Colleen interrupted, "I mean, what about your grief? What did you go through when your husband passed away?"

Maybel thought for a moment. "I don't understand the bargaining stage of the five stages of grief. I mean, what is there to bargain for? The person is gone."

"Well, it sort of fits in with the denial. People struggle to accept that someone is gone or will soon be gone, and it comes into play when someone finds out a loved one is terminally ill," Colleen replied.

"I had to figure out how to handle my finances. George always handled that… and I just missed him so much. Jeffrey tried to comfort me, but nothing took the pain away." Maybel looked down at the floor.

"Do you ever do anything in remembrance of him?" Colleen looked at Maybel.

Maybel nodded. "When I lived at Regal Palms, every Saturday morning, I would make George's favorite breakfast. It was tradition for us, and I kept that going even after he passed away."

"What was his favorite breakfast?" Norma asked.

"Cream of Wheat and toast. I thought it was too starchy and preferred having protein for breakfast, but that's what George wanted, so that's what I made for him. I always sprinkled a little cinnamon on it, too. He loved that."

Colleen smiled. "Maybel, that's a lovely memory, and we never really truly lose our loved ones. They live on in our hearts. They are always with us, and God is always with us."

Maybel nodded. "That's what one of God's names means. Emmanuel… the name means *God with us.*"

Norma said, "I'm glad Violet is in a better place now. She had so many health issues, and I think her grief weighed heavily on her. Now she is at peace in her heavenly home."

"Peace is an illusion," Vera interjected.

"Is peace an illusion? Or are we walking miracles?" Colleen asked, smiling.

Vera cleared her throat. "There is no such thing as miracles, only science."

"I'm very learned, Vera," Colleen continued, "and while I will admit I don't know everything and I certainly don't know what lies beyond the grave, I do believe in God's peace."

"Is Violet really at peace?" Maybel asked. "Or does she want us to find out who murdered her?"

"Maybel," Colleen scoffed, shaking her head. "Why on earth do you think someone murdered Violet?"

Maybel folded her arms across her chest. "We saw a footprint on her back."

Colleen stared at Maybel. "You fancy yourself as an amateur detective, don't you? I don't think you'll be happy until you prove everyone in the cemetery is a victim of foul play."

Deeply troubled by Violet's death, Maybel stared at Colleen and replied, "No, just Violet."

"Maybel, I think you are in denial. That is a perfectly normal part of the grieving process."

"We'll see. Time will tell…"

"You seem angry, Maybel." Colleen rolled back the cuff of her old white cardigan sweater. "That's a normal part of the grieving process."

"I am angry. I'm angry that someone murdered my friend!"

"I think this is a good time to put a pin in things and shift gears." Colleen coached the group to do some additional grieving exercises, like drawing a picture for their loved one or writing a poem.

Maybel drew cinnamon sticks, wrote George's name next to them, and circled it with a heart. When the others shared what they did, she tuned them out. Relieved when the session concluded, she excused herself and went back to her apartment.

Sitting on her couch, teardrops fell on Mr. Piddles' sleek fur. She pulled a tissue from the box on her end table and wiped her eyes. Reaching back to the end table again, she picked up her journal and pen. Normally she just noted things she didn't want to forget, but this time, she wrote a poem for George, too personal to share with the group.

Chapter Twenty-Three

Role Play

That evening, Vick, taking his assignment from Maybel seriously, went into full stealth mode. He slipped into the employee lounge that housed the employee breakroom, bathrooms, and lockers. Checking carefully to make sure nobody was around; he pulled his master key for the lockers from his giant ring of keys jangling from his belt. One by one, he searched lockers, moving aside clothing, shoes, hair products, and duffle bags. While he found some interesting things, he found no jewelry and nothing incriminating. Feeling his stomach growl, he grabbed a protein bar from an employee gym bag and stuck it in his pocket.

Earlier, he'd made a date with Jo. With his libido leading the way, he sauntered over to her onsite apartment. A bottle of wine in one hand and the protein bar in the other, he scarfed it down, knowing he needed it to keep his strength up.

Opening the door in a scantily clad Shakespearian wench's costume, she greeted, "Romeo! You've risked your life to come see me!" In her hand, she held a Shakespearian costume for Vick. Jo wanted to project her fantasies onto Vick like a blank wall on movie night.

Vick seized the costume and handed her the wine. "Excuse me while I go change into this," he said, winking. He went into the bathroom, slipped out of his maintenance uniform, splashed a little water on himself to freshen up, and dawned on the tights and thick dusty old coat. Glancing in the mirror, he had to admit he looked rather dashing. He put on the pointy high-heeled boots and fitted the wig over his balding head. On top of the wig, he fitted the fancy feathered Peter Pan type hat over it.

"My lovely lady, Juliet," he said in his most seductive voice, walking out of the bathroom.

Clad in a corset and in her most theatrical voice, Jo exclaimed, "Romeo, Romeo, where for art thou Romeo?" Clutching her bosom with one hand, she placed the back of the palm of her other hand across her forehead.

Vick reached for Jo's hand, kissing the back of it.

Jo giggled with delight. "Come dwell with me, my lord!"

Vick's nylon sheathed legs created friction warming his loins when he walked towards Jo. He extended an arm out to her. "Shall we sit out on the balcony under the moonlight and drink our wine?"

"Oh! Romeo! We might get caught if our families see us together!"

Tights chafing, Vick proclaimed, "My Juliet, I would die for you!" He rolled the sliding glass door open, stepping out onto the balcony. The purple, puffy plume on his hat tickled the top of the door frame. He took sight of the lavish feast by candlelight that awaited the two lovers.

"Kiss me!"

Embracing passionately, Vick pressed his lips to hers. In his heightened state of arousal, Vick's nostrils flared, and he breathed in the sweet scent of Jo's lilac perfume.

After serving him a goblet of wine, she fed him a chicken leg. Holding the drumstick up to his lips, she fed him like a baby. He ferociously tore off the meat from the bone. She slid a chunk of cheese into his mouth and dangled a cluster of grapes over his head. Vick leaned his head back, and she lowered them. He wrapped his lips around a few grapes and tugged them free from their stem.

Vick pulled her down onto his lap, and Jo's nose tickled him with Eskimo kisses. Her hand caressed the coarse wig resting on his balding head.

Feeling his tights giving him a rash, he asked, "Shall we move into the bedroom?"

"Carry me there!" Jo insisted.

With her still on his lap, Vick struggled to stand up. On his way to getting upright, he accidentally dropped her. He bent down to help her get up, but she pulled on his tights and ripped them. She grabbed his hand and pulled him down on top of her. Under the pale moonlight on the balcony, they copulated quickly.

Breathless, Jo whispered, "That was wonderful!" She ran her hands across his hairy ape chest.

"You were magnificent," he complimented. With sexy time over, they moved to Jo's bedroom, slipped under the covers, and both drifted off to sleep.

In the middle of the night, Vick awoke and got out of bed. With Jo sound asleep, he searched her apartment. Looking through drawers, cabinets and under her bed produced nothing. On a whim, he looked through her purse. He took out her wallet and found three different driver's licenses, all with her picture but displaying three different names, addresses and dates of birth. Stunned, he set them out on the table, reading the names.

After dialing Detective Brian Bahn's number, he said, "Hey, I've got some bad news. I found three different fake ids in Jo's purse."

"Who is Jo, and why are you in her purse?" Brian asked.

"Jo's my new girlfriend. She works here at Shady Sunset as the activities director. Maybel suspects Jo may have had something to do with Violet's death. She saw a grave out by where Violet's body was found, and one headstone had the name Jo Stelliano… same name as my Jo,"

A heavy sigh blew out of Brian's mouth. "Maybel is not supposed to be interfering with a police investigation… but send me a photo of the IDs and see if you can get something with Jo's fingerprints. Then we can run them and determine who she really is.

"Alright. This really bums me out. I really like her. She's so fun, and she's into role playing."

Laughing, Brian said, "I wouldn't know about fun right now."

"Nothing happening with you and Celeste?"

"Zip. Zilch. Nada."

"Aw, that's too bad. Dude, you guys have been dating for a while."

"Believe me, I know. I took a step back from her for a time-out and then she drunk texted me."

Chuckling, Vick replied, "Buddy, that's a good sign."

"Is it?"

"Oh, yeah! She wants you. She's just repressed or something." Vick looked out at the moon through the window.

"I think we had kind of a breakthrough the other day when I went to her work. We talked about some past trauma that I think is still holding her back."

"We've all got our shit, you know? But don't give up on her because you've already put in the time, and she's a quality woman." Vick laughed. "Either that or dump her and go out with someone new who will put out."

"We've got another date in the books. We're going to the play at Shady Sunset."

"Cool! You'll get to see my dad. He's the star. He's playing King Lear."

"Awesome. I got to get going. Text me a photo of Jo's ids and see if you can get her fingerprints."

"Will do."

Vick walked out onto the balcony; glad they hadn't cleaned up after their love fest. He placed her wine goblet in a Ziploc bag, got dressed, and left Jo's place. Vick drove to the Sunshine Police department and dropped it off with instructions. He drove back to Shady Sunset, entered Jo's place, undressed his hairy body again, and slipped back into bed with her and fell into a deep sleep.

In the morning, he showered and got ready for his shift. As charmed as he felt by her feminine wiles, his call to law and order came first, or at least that's what he told himself when he pushed his guilt aside. He stepped out of Jo's bathroom and found her in the kitchen, cooking breakfast.

"How do you like your eggs?" Jo asked.

"I'm not hungry."

"Well, at least let me feed you some strawberries and whipped cream," she said, smiling sweetly.

Vick could not resist. He opened his mouth like an infant while she popped whipped cream dipped strawberries into it. He chewed and giggled. Then he remembered the mission and asked, "So, where did you work before you worked here?"

"I worked at another retirement home in Iowa."

"Iowa? Is that where you are from?" he quired.

"No, I'm from Illinois, but I've moved around a lot."

I'll bet you have, he thought. "Have you ever been married?"

"Nope, but maybe someday," she said, winking at him.

"Have you ever changed your name?"

She frowned at him and put the strawberries down. "Why would you ask me that?"

"I was just curious. Have you?" Vick swallowed nervously.

Twisting like a pretzel when Vick tried to pin down an answer, she said, "You know what they say about curiosity."

Vick grabbed her hands, bringing them up to his mouth, and kissed them. "I better get going. I don't want to be late for my shift."

"I'll see you later, my love machine!" Jo blew him a kiss.

Vick reached up into the air, grabbed the imaginary kiss, and put his hand to his mouth. "Goodbye, my love." Stepping out of Jo's place, he wondered if he had just made love with a murderer… again.

Chapter Twenty-Four

Under the Covers

"Vick didn't find anything in the staff lockers, and he tried to say he found nothing incriminating at Jo's. But when I cornered him about it, he admitted she had three different driver's licenses in her wallet with three different names on them all with her photo," Maybel said to Celeste the next morning during their phone call.

Celeste observed, "This is the second time you've asked Vick to go undercover."

"With Vick, it's more like *under the covers*," Maybel said with a chuckle.

Celeste added, "I'm sure Brian can run all that information and figure out who Jo really is."

"Yes, he can. I've already spoken with him, and he said for now, to keep all of this on the down low, and after the play tonight, he's going to question Jo."

So much for our romantic date, Celeste thought, feeling slighted. "I guess I'll take my car over to Shady Sunset and just meet Brian there, since he'll have to work after the play is over."

"Should be a lot of fireworks after the play!"

"But Vick didn't find any jewelry at Jo's place, right?"

"Right, but she could have pawned it already or taken the diamonds out of the necklace and made a ring with it. She had a new diamond ring on a few weeks ago. She said it had been her mom's, but if she's lying about her identity, who knows what else she's lying about? Vick said they were the ones that carved the V + J into the pine tree, but they didn't climb the tree, so they weren't the ones that broke the branch."

"Maybe lightning hit the tree and broke the branch."

"Could be," Maybel said. "I've got another counseling session with Colleen soon. The first one went well."

"Oh, I'm glad to hear that. It sounds like, despite what happened to Violet, you're feeling more comfortable there."

"I am except for all the rumors going around about Arnie and I."

With a giggle, Celeste proposed, "You should just start a new rumor and that way; everyone will forget the rumors about you and Arnie."

"That's not a bad idea, dear. Normally I'm the one gossiping, but now I know what it feels like to be the subject of it."

"I think there's a lesson in there for you, Maybel."

"Did I tell you that I spoke with Violet's only daughter, Leah?"

"No, you didn't. I assume you met Leah at Violet's funeral."

Maybel let out a long breath. "Yes. It was extremely emotional. Leah is very angry at Violet."

"Why?"

"Violet didn't leave her anything in her will. She left it all to charity."

"Oh! That is horrible! Leah has every right to be angry!"

"Dear, I'm sure Violet had her reasons."

"Maybel, I know Violet was your friend, so you feel you have to defend her, but not leaving anything to her only daughter is despicable!"

"There was a charity very near and dear to Violet's heart."

"Regardless, that's still no excuse to not leave her daughter anything. That is selfish of her. It seems obvious to me that Violet did that out of anger or pettiness."

"She may have…"

"Over the years, I've had insurance clients that call in and say they're mad at one of their kids and they take them off as a beneficiary on their life insurance policies. I've always thought you have to be a real scum bag to take one of your kids off."

"I guess I'm lucky I only have one son, and I don't have to deal with that."

"Violet had one daughter. There is no excuse!"

"I think Violet and Leah had a lot of water under the bridge. I probably shouldn't tell you this, but in Violet's original will, she was going to leave everything to her son, Tim. Then, after Tim passed, she changed it and left it all to charity."

Celeste let out a disgusted sigh. "Ugh! That's even worse! Violet sounds like a very spiteful person!"

"Wow, you really feel strongly about this."

"I do, Maybel, and I'm surprised you don't feel stronger about it. I think you're blinded by your feelings of friendship towards Violet. I can't believe you're defending her behavior."

"While I agree that what Violet did to her daughter is bad, Violet was nothing but nice to me. Sometimes the same person can be different things to different people."

"Or you just didn't know Violet very well."

"Well, maybe I didn't, but the little bit that I did know her, she was kind to me when I needed a friend. You're so upset over this you'd think Violet did it to you."

"My father was a drunk and a gambler. He pissed his money away and didn't leave me anything. He didn't even set up a trust for the home he owned, but it was mortgaged to the hilt. I had to go through probate to get what little value it had, and that amount barely covered his burial expenses. He was irresponsible and didn't take care of anything. It was bad enough that I lost my mother at a young age, but then my dad just checked out. I basically had to raise myself *and* take care of him!"

"Oh, dear, I didn't know that about his estate. That must be why you're so hyper-responsible. I'm so sorry."

"You don't need to be sorry. It's not your fault. Just make sure to take care of Jeffrey and do the right thing."

Maybel smiled, thinking maybe she should add Celeste to her will since she was like a daughter to her. "I have definitely designated Jeffrey as the beneficiary of my little estate."

"Good!"

"You seem like you are still angry at your father."

"I try not to be. I've accepted that he never was the father I needed him to be."

"Well, despite your misfortune, you've turned out to be an exceptional human being."

"Thank you. I just remember feeling so much fear and anxiety after my dad passed… and I didn't know why. It's not like I relied on him for anything."

Maybel thought for a second before she spoke. "Perhaps it was the fear of death."

"That could have been it. After he died, I just kept thinking about my own death, you know, like wondering when and how I was going to die. Would I die a slow and painful death? And what if heaven isn't real? The worst thoughts plagued me, and I worried maybe I wouldn't even make it to heaven, even if it is real."

"Remember, God is good, and heaven is real."

"How can we truly know what's going to happen to us after we die?"

"Faith! Faith in the promises God has made to us."

"But what if we don't have enough faith?"

"Dear, faith is a gift from God. It is not of ourselves. If you think you don't have faith, ask God to give you faith."

Celeste smiled, feeling peaceful. "You're right. Thank you for reminding me of that. I need to stop worrying. I worry about everything. I worry about something happening to Brian because his job is so dangerous."

"And that's why you push him away… you don't want to get close to someone you might lose."

"I don't push him away!"

"Dear, you do."

Celeste breathed deep.

Maybel changed the subject. "I just hope Leah gets to a point where she can forgive her mother for what she did."

"What's that old saying? To err is human, to forgive divine."

"Indeed. No one is perfect. Sometimes we're called to love the unlovable."

Celeste thought of her father and the grudge she'd been holding against him. "It's difficult, isn't it?"

"Yes… I'll see you tonight, dear."

"Since I won't see you before the play, break a leg!" Celeste signed off.

A short while later, Maybel sat on her couch with Colleen and discussed her marriage. "We were happy for the most part. Sure, we had our problems from time to time, but I never doubted his faithfulness to me. He was a good father to Jeffrey, too. I miss him more than words can express."

"How fortunate you were to have that," Colleen said. "You know, even when our loved ones pass away, we never truly lose them. They never really leave us because their memories live with us in our hearts."

"That's a nice thought," Maybel said, contemplating that idea.

"I'm going to ask you an uncomfortable question," Colleen paused before speaking again, "Are you afraid to die?"

Frowning, Maybel thought about this. Finally, she said, "I updated our will after George passed, and I updated the beneficiaries on our investment accounts."

Colleen shook her head. "I asked if you are afraid to die, not are you prepared to die."

Maybel blinked. "Well, I guess so. Aren't we all afraid of the unknown?"

Colleen smiled. "I suppose so. How do you think you're fitting in here?"

"OK. It helped that I already had a few friends here, and then I've made some new ones… like Violet. I'm still trying to process her murder. Attending her funeral helped bring me closure. I'm going to take flowers to her headstone. I need to take flowers to George, too. I keep saying I'm going to do that, but I've been procrastinating."

"Yes, lots of people try to push their grief aside, avoiding it, but it's best to meet it head on." Colleen wrote a note on her pad of paper. "You mentioned Violet's murder. Maybel, I'm a little concerned you're not accepting reality. Violet was elderly and had a lot of health problems. She couldn't even fully breathe on her own. It's most likely she passed away from natural causes."

"She had a footprint on her back and a contusion on the back of her head. We think someone knocked her out and then suffocated her."

Colleen frowned. "We?"

"Celeste and I," Maybel answered.

"Oh, that's right. You two fancy yourselves as amateur detectives," Colleen replied. "Maybe you imagined the footprint on her back as a coping mechanism."

"No, Celeste saw it too! It's bad enough to think we have a thief running around here at Shady Sunset, but a murderer too! We need to catch this murderer soon!"

Colleen wrote another note. "Isn't that what the police are for?"

"We can all use a little help sometimes."

"I've questioned all the staff about the missing jewelry, and so far, no one has admitted to it," Collen replied.

"The thief won't admit to their thievery. We're going to have to catch them in the act," Maybel said.

"I suppose so. Why don't we stop here for today? You're making a lot of progress. Are you looking forward to the play tonight?"

"Yes! Our second dress rehearsal went well. I have a little bit of stage fright, but I should be fine."

"Well, break a leg," Colleen said, concluding their counseling session.

Chapter Twenty-Five

Two Can Play at That Game

After work, Celeste went home and took a quick shower to freshen up before going to the play, using a new scented shower gel. Standing with a towel wrapped around her, she stared at her closet. Feeling excited to see Brian again, she reached for a little black dress with a keyhole in the back, slipped into it, and put on her kitten heels. She combed her hair, putting it up in a messy bun. She brushed her teeth and freshened up her make-up, adding some more red lipstick and darkened her eyeliner. Slathering lotion on her arms, she breathed in the divine scent and looked at the name on the bottle, *Cashmere and Snowflakes*. Nice, she thought. She fed Birino his birdseed and headed over to Shady Sunset.

Driving along the coast, Celeste thought of Brian and his criticisms of her. She hated to admit it, but she knew he was right. Pulling up to the retirement home, she spotted Brian standing in front of Shady Sunset, leaning against one of the large columns with hands in pockets.

When Brian saw her car pull up, he straightened out his tie and put his hands back into his pockets, rubbing his sweaty palms against his pants. Watching her glide towards him, he remembered the first time he met her. He smiled and watched the wispy wind blow the tendrils along her pretty face. He looked down at a puddle on the ground; the water rippling in the breeze.

Approaching him, Celeste gave Brian a look that lit up his libido and caused a ripple in him. Brian knew she was the one. Completely forgetting he had to question a suspect later, he reached for her hand, brushed the hair from her cheek, and kissed her. "You smell good," he said with a grin.

Looking up at him, her eyes sparkled, and her flushed cheeks gave away her excitement. "Thank you. Are you ready to see some Shakespeare?"

"As ready as I'll ever be." He led the way, hurrying to open the door for her. They walked hand in hand through the lobby and out to the back to the dancehall. Celeste and Brian sat side by side on the uncomfortable folding chairs Vick set up for the play's audience. The lights dimmed, and Brian rested his arm on the back of her chair, whispering, "It's nice to be with you again. You look wonderful tonight." His eyes perused her little black dress.

Celeste felt the cold from the metal chair against the open space in the back of her dress. Happy he put his arm around her to keep her warm, she rested her hand on his thigh, making him ecstatic to be touched below the waist for once. She kissed his cheek. "It sounds like you're ripping off Eric Clapton, but I like it."

"Well, they may have been his lyrics, but it's my sentiment."

She leaned her head on his shoulder and breathed in the moment, knowing it couldn't last because of his call to duty later that night. An outsider watching them from behind the stage's curtain thought they looked like two little love birds nestled together out there in the audience.

The red velvet curtain on the stage rose and the audience's chatter gave way to applause. Anthony Trutelli blew a trumpet to announce King Lear. A few other residents of Shady Sunset carried out a royal throne and set it on the stage. Arnie, wearing a glorious crown on his toupee, marched onto the stage. With outstretched arms, he proclaimed his lines, talking about dividing his land among his three daughters.

"Arnie really has a flair for the dramatic," Celeste whispered in Brian's ear.

Maybel, Ida, and Vera played King Lear's three daughters. Celeste thought Maybel did a wonderful job with her lines. Being one of the daughters to give false flattery to him seemed fitting, knowing Maybel's long-standing rivalry with Arnie.

During intermission, the audience was invited to get some punch and cookies at the back of the dancehall. Brian munched a peanut butter cookie, and Celeste lowered her voice, whispering to him, "Maybel said you'll be questioning Jo after the play tonight."

"That's right, but you're not supposed to know anything about that," he whispered back with a grin.

Feeling safe because she knew he had to work later, she said coyly, "It's just too bad because I was hoping we could go back to my place after the play."

His eyes lit up. "It probably won't take very long. I could swing by afterwards," he offered.

"Oh, I'm sure I'll be asleep by then. We'll have to do it some other time," she said, smiling sweetly.

"You're being a brat again," he scolded. "You just like to be chased."

"Got your running shoes on?"

"You're just toying with me. You do this, you know. You pull me close, then push me away, then pull me close, then push me away."

She giggled. "You're my yoyo."

"And you've got me wrapped around your little finger," he said, kissing her forehead.

"I appreciate you being patient with me. By the way, how is the mayor's case going?"

"You're not supposed to know anything about that either," he said, "but it's not going well."

"No leads?"

"I chased down one false lead the other day."

"False?"

"Yeah, I should have known better. His break-in was never in the news, and we got an anonymous call trying to tip us off as to who the intruder was. The whole thing smells fishy, and I knew when we checked the speargun for fingerprints that we wouldn't find the mayor's fingerprints on it—which we didn't even though he claimed he shot the intruder with it. It ripped the guy's coat, so I know someone shot the gun at him. He said it's his wife's speargun, which would explain why her prints are on it."

Celeste looked into Brian's eyes and asked, "Do you think it was really the mayor's wife that shot the intruder? Could the mayor be trying to protect her?"

Brian nodded. "That's what I think, but why?"

Celeste whispered, "Maybel had this theory that she thinks the mayor is secretly gay… or bisexual… or something."

Brian's eyes widened. "Celeste, you shouldn't have told Maybel. I shouldn't have even told you!"

"Don't worry. I swore her to secrecy. Really, she knows to keep quiet about it."

Brian paused before he spoke. "Let's walk through Maybel's theory. They host a party for the mayor's 50th birthday. The party is over. Then, the mayor's secret lover enters the garage through a side door that wasn't locked. Perhaps it was intentionally left unlocked for a secret sexy rendezvous. The mayor meets him in the garage, gets caught by his wife, his wife gets angry and grabs the speargun off the wall and shoots the intruder."

"Yeah," Celeste said. "It could be as simple as that. Maybe she called 911 before he could stop her, and they had to let it play out. Was there anything else strange about the garage?"

"A ladder set up in between the two cars, and the spear that was shot went into the wall at a downward angle. I wondered if someone stood on the ladder when they shot it."

"What did they say about the ladder?"

"They left it up because they had changed a light bulb."

"Why would someone stand on a ladder to shoot a speargun?" Celeste wondered.

"You wouldn't. Maybe the intruder had been standing on the ladder and fell to the ground when the wife shot at him, which would explain the angle."

"Why would the intruder be on the ladder? Could he have been trying to get to something packed away up in the rafters?"

"That's not what thieves do… but let's pretend Maybel's theory is correct. It's a rendezvous between two lovers in the garage… and a ladder is involved… " Brian laughed.

"What? What is so funny?"

"The mayor has a bad knee. I remember when I met him a while back when he visited the department. He limped and had a brace on it from a tennis injury. And on the security camera footage, the intruder hobbled away, limping with his walking stick. I assumed he got injured in the garage, but he could have already had the limp."

"But what are you getting at? Two gay lovers with bad knees?"

"Geez Celeste! How naïve are you? OK, I'll spell this out for you, but remember, you asked. Maybe the mayor wanted a BJ on his 50th birthday from his secret lover and they planned to meet in the garage. But since his secret lover has a bad knee, he wouldn't want to get on his knees… so the mayor stood on the ladder high enough… to… make his crotch eye level for the activity… or vice versa."

Celeste gasped, "Oh my goodness!"

"Then the mayor's wife walks in and finds them. Maybe the mayor pushed him away quickly when he heard the door and the guy fell down, and she grabbed the speargun off the wall and shoots the guy…"

"Wow…"

Brian grinned. "We just talked through it and figured it out. I knew the mayor didn't shoot the gun because he took too long to get it off the wall and fumbled around with it. He said the guy attacked him with a walking stick, but if that was true, he couldn't have taken the time to pull the gun off the wall without really getting beat up, which he wasn't. They could have been preoccupied with their activity and didn't hear his wife come in, and she got it down off the wall. I also thought the guy brought the walking stick as a weapon, but his limp meant he needed it to walk with."

"Who does the mayor know that has a limp and walks with a cane?"

Brian's face lit up with realization. "The owner of Tube Solutions! When we investigated there after the explosion, I spoke to him. He walked with a limp. I knew when I saw the security camera footage from the mayor's house that the so-called intruder's walk looked familiar, but I couldn't place it."

"Wouldn't it be easy enough to search his manufacturing plant again and see if you can find the same type of cane he used the night of the break in? Or the ripped trench coat?"

"It would." Brian smiled.

"Do you think there is some connection between the explosion at Tube Solutions and the fake break-in at the mayor's house?" Celeste asked.

"You know what they say. There is no such thing as a coincidence, especially when a murder is involved."

"What is the owner of Tube Solutions name?"

"Hayward Hamilton."

"Boy, even his name sounds rich. Oh! I think the play is starting back up. They just dimmed the lights," Celeste said, grabbing his hand and walking with him back to their seats again.

For another forty-five minutes, they watched Arnie act out King Lear going mad. All over the stage, he dramatically performed his machinations. When the play concluded, he got a standing ovation. Then, the entire cast came out to take a bow. The dancehall flooded with applause. After the show ended, Celeste and Brian went backstage to see Maybel.

"Bravo! These are for you," Celeste said, handing Maybel a small bouquet she had tucked in her big black bag.

"Violets?" Maybel wondered.

Celeste shrugged. "I figured she's here with us in spirit."

"What a lovely thought, dear." Turning to Brian, she whispered, "Jo is right over there. She stole someone's identity right off the grave! Rolled their bones to make a dollar off the dead! She may even be the murderer!"

Brian smiled at Maybel's melodramatic description. "I see her. I'll wait until things die down a bit before I approach her."

"Well, I don't want to get in the way of police business or get myself arrested, so that is my cue to leave," Celeste said, hugging Maybel goodbye. She turned to Brian and hugged him.

He whispered in her ear, "Should I text you later?"

"If you want to, but I'll probably be asleep."

He whispered in her ear again, "If we weren't in public, I'd put you over my knee and spank you for teasing me like this."

Celeste giggled, waving goodbye. Watching her pivot and head towards the exit, the keyhole shape on the back of her dress mesmerized Brian's eyes. She glided through the crowd, disappearing into the audience, shuffling out of the dance hall.

Brian waited for a good opportunity to question Jo. He waited and waited until everyone filtered out of the dance-hall. "Miss Stelliano," he began, approaching her.

"Yes?" Jo looked up from organizing a clothing rack of cast member costumes.

"I'm Detective Brian Bahn from the Sunshine Beach police department. I need to ask you a few questions."

Jo's eyes widened. "Sure. What about?"

"Something was brought to my attention, and we have reason to suspect that you may be operating under a false or stolen identity."

"Whatever would give you that idea?" she asked.

"I have a warrant to search your premises. I can do that, or you can make it easy on me and tell me the truth. If you tell me the truth, I'll go easy on you."

From the long conversation with Jo, Detective Bahn found out that her real name was Jane Brockman, which lined up with what he got back when they ran her fingerprints. She had a criminal background that made it hard for her to get hired. A violent altercation with an ex followed her around. She found it easier to use a false identity so that background checks came back clean, often using deceased people's information. She swore she didn't steal any jewels. A search later of her place came up empty.

"Did you kill Violet?" Bahn took the direct approach.

Jane assured him she did not.

"Her Bearer bonds went missing, and since they're untraceable, it would be difficult for us to know if you stole them."

"I assure you I didn't steal anything," she promised.

"We'll be doing a check of your bank account records to see if you've made any large deposits recently."

Jane nodded. "I'm sure you won't find anything like that. If I had lots of money, believe me, I wouldn't be working here. May I ask you one question?"

"Shoot."

"Who tipped you off?"

Brian paused, not wanting to answer.

"It was Vick, wasn't it?"

Brian nodded.

With her heart stinging from the betrayal of her sweet Romeo, Jane, also known as Jo, hung her head in sadness.

After Bahn concluded his interrogation, he thought about texting Celeste. But since she played hard to get, he would play as well. No one likes getting a taste of their own medicine, he thought, driving back to his lonesome bachelor pad in downtown Sunshine Beach. He knew she'd crack soon.

Chapter Twenty-Six

Extra Extra Read All About It

"Good afternoon, ladies!" Arnie, wearing gaudy pink and blue plaid golf pants, dropped a newsletter down on the dining table where Maybel, Vera and Norma were eating lunch at. "Did you see today's Shady Sunset Gazette? I got glowing reviews for my performance last night as King Lear!" He kissed his fingertips, and his hand burst open like a blooming flower.

"Arnie, you look very dapper this morning!" Norma said.

A trundling eyed Maybel replied to Arnie, "Ugh, please! Morty Handlebaum wrote that review. He's been your golf buddy for years. Try getting a *real* review!"

Arnie scoffed. "You're just jealous because he called your performance, and I quote, 'flat and overdone all at the same time'. He wrote, 'Arnie Arnold gave a dilly of a portrayal as King Lear'!"

"What does that old coot know, anyway? He's a no-neck loser and as cultured as a tomato," Maybel huffed.

"If he'd had a rotten tomato, I think he would have thrown it at you!" Arnie's laugh circled Maybel like a hungry hyena.

"At least I didn't give a flaccid performance like you did! Anyone can balter about the stage acting a buffoon like you did!"

Hearing the argument escalate between Arnie and Maybel, Colleen navigated to their table. "Good morning, everyone! What a wonderful play you all put on last night. Norma, you did such a wonderful job with the stage decorations. Jo made a good choice asking you to help with that."

Norma smiled proudly. "I had a lot of fun! I can't wait for the next play."

Arnie interjected, "Jo should ask Maybel to help with stage decorations or sewing costumes or something else that would be a better fit for her than acting."

"Arnie, I swear to God I'll–"

"Maybel! There you are!" Vick charged their table like a bull. "I need to talk to you!"

Colleen turned to Vick and said, "Vick, I've been meaning to talk to you. The pipes under my kitchen sink are leaking. Can you swing by later to look at them?"

Vick nodded. "Sure."

"Wonderful, now I need to get going. I'm meeting with some new residents in a few minutes. You all have a nice day," Colleen said with a wave.

"Maybel!" Vick said again.

"What?" Maybel pulled the napkin off her lap and set it on the table.

Vick's face reddened. "You ruined another one of my relationships!"

A flustered Maybel asked, "What are you talking about?"

"Yeah, what are you talking about, son?" Arnie wondered.

Vick sputtered, "Jo broke up with me! She knows I'm the one that ratted her out about her false identity."

"Well… I… it's not my fault she ran on the wrong side of the law. And Jo wasn't even her real name," Maybel said, defending herself.

"And Leah! I got in good with her, and then she got arrested," he went on with his accusations, "if you hadn't of meddled in that, I'd probably still be with her!"

"This is absurd," Maybel insisted.

"Son, why don't you settle down? I'm sure Maybel didn't mean any harm," Arnie said, trying to soothe his Vick.

Vick stuck his finger in Maybel's face. "Don't let it happen again!" He stormed off, fuming that his passionate relationship with Jo had been squelched.

"What was that about?" Vera asked.

Maybel divulged to the table who Jo Stelliano really was.

"Oh, that must be why Colleen asked me to teach today's craft class in place of Jo. I just assumed Jo fell ill and couldn't teach it," Norma said.

"What craft are we going to be making today?" Vera asked, dabbing her mouth with her napkin.

"Well, there are two large baskets of pinecones left. Jo had planned on having us make pineapples out of them. You paint the pinecone yellow and attach green stems out of construction paper to the top of them. But I think if we were going to do a craft like that, we should have done that for decorations for the luau. So, I came up with another idea. We can still paint them yellow, but we can turn them into bumblebees. That will go nicely with the flowered wreaths we made," Norma explained.

"That's a good point," Arnie said.

Maybel's lips curled into a snarl. "Since when did you become an expert on crafts?"

Arnie stood tall. "I have more talent in my little pinky that you have in your whole body, Maybel. Don't forget who won the talent show!"

"Ppppfffft!" A bitter laugh soured Maybel's mouth.

Vera interjected, "I didn't make a flower wreath. I made a Christmas wreath. The last thing I need to put on it is a bumblebee."

Responding to Vera's starchy attitude, Norma suggested, "You can paint yours white and make it into a snowman! There are so many crafts that can be made with pinecones. You can make owls and birds and reindeer."

"Oh, that's a good idea! I'll make a snowman!" Vera nodded.

"Since I'm teaching today, will you all promise to be there?" Norma asked, looking around the table.

Everyone agreed.

Arnie picked up his Shady Sunset Gazette and said, "I'll bring the honey!"

"Try to keep your stinger in your pants," Maybel mumbled under her breath.

"What did you say, Maybel?"

"Nothing. I'll see everyone at craft class." Maybel excused herself and left the dining room.

Chapter Twenty-Seven

Hot Yoga Class

"You should have called me sooner," Vick said, crouching down on the ground and looking under Colleen's sink. Wrench in hand, he tightened the new PVC pipe he installed. "This leak was bad, and water got all over everything under your sink." He pulled some items out, showing her. "Your cleaning products got all wet. I think we should take everything out and let it all dry off." He continued pulling items from under her sink, placing them on the ground, a dust buster, craftsmen tools, candles, some extra pipe, a box of trash bags, paper towels, vases, and sponges.

Vick stood up, dusting himself off. "Well, you're all set now. Just leave the cabinet doors open and let everything dry out so you don't get any mold." He smiled.

"Thank you! I've been so busy I kept forgetting to deal with it. I'm sure you've heard about Jo. I had to terminate her, so now on top of everything else I need to do; I have to find a new activities director."

Nodding, Vick sadly remembered his fair maiden. "I must get going. I need to move all the tables out of the way in the dancehall for the yoga class Sheila is teaching this morning. Then, this afternoon, Norma asked me to be on standby for the craft class. I may need to cut some more pinecones for a craft they're making."

"Oh, wonderful! Fortunately, between the classes Sheila teaches and Norma filling in for Jo, we can make it without an activity director for a while," Colleen said.

When Vick arrived at the dancehall, there were six tables he needed to take down and fold up. He stacked them all against the wall for Sheila.

"Thank you," she said, placing the yoga mats down on the ground. "Can you also put out a few folding chairs? Some of the seniors have too hard of a time getting down on the ground, so I also offer chair yoga. Oh, and turn up the thermostat in here. We're doing hot yoga today."

Vick set out a few folding chairs, as his dad walked in wearing tight red sweatpants and a T-shirt that had the words 'life is good' printed on it.

"Hey, pop," Vick said, giving his dad a fist bump greeting. He went over to the thermostat and cranked it up to 90 degrees.

More residents filtered into the dancehall, taking their places by the mats and chairs.

"Good God! It's like an inferno in here!" Maybel grumbled, walking in.

"It's hot yoga." Arnie winked.

Maybel regretted her decision to take Sheila's yoga class. She found an empty mat and stood by it, wiping some sweat from the back of her neck.

"Alright everyone! Let's begin," Sheila called out, rolling her shoulders and neck around. "The first thing we'll do is stretch our necks. Follow along with my movements."

Maybel and the other residents rolled their necks around, and then their shoulders. Sheila raised her hands high in the air, and everyone mirrored her movements. She bent down and touched her toes, and so did her students. Sheila stood back up and twisted her torso from side to side with her arms stretched out. "Remember to breathe deep, in through the nose and out through the mouth."

This isn't so hard, Maybel thought, feeling her muscles loosen up. Breathing deep as Sheila instructed, Maybel felt her spine elongated. A drop of sweat trickled down the side of her face. She wiped it off and followed along with Sheila's next movement, bending one leg and extending the other one back.

"OK, now switch to the other leg," Sheila instructed the class in her most soothing tone of voice. Flute music with the sound of rushing water played in the background of the dancehall turned yoga studio. Before the class began, Sheila lit some incense. The smell of patchouli filled the air, and the dancehall rose to about 95 degrees.

After several more standing yoga poses, Sheila instructed everyone to either lie down on their mat or sit in their folding chair. Carefully, Maybel sat down on her mat, wondering how she was going to get back up. Once in a sitting position, she laid down. The heat made her want to take a nap. She raised her legs in the air and stretched some more, according to Sheila's instructions.

"I bet you're no stranger to this pose, huh Maybel?" Arnie laughed.

"Shut up!"

Sheila walked around the room, calling out more instructions. "For those of you on your mats, roll over on your stomach to prepare for downward dog pose."

Maybel heard Arnie's snickers. She looked to her other side and saw that Vera had fallen asleep. In the middle of the downward dog, Maybel heard a cry of pain. Looking around, revealed Arnie was not quite as nimble as she was. Arnie rolled over on his side, holding his back in agony.

"I think I pulled something!" he cried out to Sheila. She rushed to his side and helped him sit up.

"You probably over-extended yourself. Why don't you lay flat and see if that helps," Sheila said, trying to assist him in getting comfortable.

"That's what he gets for making fun of me," Maybel mumbled under her breath, with her rear end extended into the air.

Once the class concluded, Arnie excused himself so he could ice his back. Maybel, still in full investigation mode, made her way over to Sheila, after gingerly getting up off the floor.

Feeling dizzy from the heat, she said, "Great class. It's just what I needed. My back feels much looser."

"Wonderful! I'm so glad it helped." Sheila smiled.

Noticing Sheila held her car keys in her hand, Maybel asked, "So what are you off to do for the rest of the day?"

"I've got a run a few errands, and I need to go to the bank."

"What bank do you bank with? I've been thinking about changing banks," Maybel prodded, wondering if Sheila might be trying to cash in some Bearer bonds.

"SB Bank, the one that's on Fourth Street."

"Oh, good to know," Maybel said. "Well, I better get going. I promised Norma I'd attend her craft class today."

Once Maybel left the dancehall, she sent a text to Celeste that read: **Do you have time to drive over to the SB Bank on Fourth Street?**

Celeste texted back: **Why?**

Maybel texted: **I think Sheila is headed over there now, possibly to cash in the Bearer bonds she stole from Violet.**

Celeste asked: **And what do you expect me to do?**

Maybel texted: **Call the police**

Celeste texted: **Why don't you just call the police now?**

Maybel blew out a deep sigh and texted: **I'm not sure if she really is. We need to get the intel first. If I still drove, I'd do it myself.**

Celeste texted back: **Lucky for you, I just got ready to take a lunch break. I'll head over there now and keep an eye out for her.**

Maybel: **Thanks!**

Celeste logged off her computer, grabbed her purse, and headed out. While driving over to SB Bank, she wondered what she'd tell Brian if she discovered Sheila really cashed in the Bearer bonds. "Maybe I could tell him I set up a new bank account and ran into her… no, he'd never believe that." Celeste drew in a deep breath and wondered what Brian was up to.

Chapter Twenty-Eight

I'm Taking Home My Baby Bumblebee

Celeste found a parking spot right in front of the bank and waited for Sheila. Sitting in her car, wearing her dark sunglasses, she ate the sandwich she'd prepared for lunch. Several minutes later, Celeste grew tired of waiting. She contemplated leaving right before spotting Sheila walking into the bank, remembering what she looked like from meeting her at the luau.

Celeste hurried in after Sheila but kept her distance, darting behind a convenient pillar. She covertly watched Sheila approach the teller. Shelia pulled a big folder out of her bag and took some papers out of it. Celeste couldn't hear their conversation, but she looked on as the teller stared at something on her computer and shook her head at Sheila. Sheila placed her folder back in her bag and turned to leave.

After Sheila left, Celeste removed her sunglasses and approached the teller.

"Hello, how can I help you?" the teller quired.

"Does your bank allow its customers to cash in bearer bonds here?"

"No, I'm sorry. We don't do that anymore. You'd have to go back to the issuer of the bonds," the teller replied.

Celeste smiled. "Thank you."

Once back in her car, Celeste texted Maybel: **I think Sheila may have been trying to cash the Bearer bonds, but this bank doesn't do that anymore.**

Maybel texted: **Now what?**

Celeste texted: **She still has the folder she brought to the bank with her…**

Maybel texted: **Got it! Now I'm off to craft class.**

Several minutes later, Vick walked over to the room designated for the crafts. As he walked in, he heard Maybel say to Arnie, "You spilled yellow paint all over me, you dunce!"

Arnie retorted, "I'm rubber and you're glue."

"Really? That is so childish!" Maybel huffed, standing up to go clean paint off herself.

Norma rushed up to Vick. "Oh, I'm glad you're here. I'm going to need for you to cut some of these pinecones in half but not horizontally. I need them cut long ways vertically. They'll be easier to glue to the flower wreaths that way."

Vick thought about this. "That won't be easy. They might break into pieces in the process."

"Can you give it a try?" Norma urged.

Vick looked through his toolbox, taking out his hacksaw. He took the first pinecone out of the basket and tried cutting it in half, but just as he suspected, it crumbled.

"Oh, no." Norma scratched her head, trying to figure out an alternative.

"Let me try another one. I'll get one that's a lot bigger," Vick said, poking around the basket. He found the biggest pinecone. "This one is heavy! It should be sturdy enough…"

Watching Vick turn the pinecone upside down, Norma asked, "What is it? What are you looking at?"

He showed the bottom to Norma. Puzzled, she stared at it.

Maybel came over and asked, "What are we looking at?"

Arnie joined them. "What's going on, son?"

Maybel took the pinecone from Vick. "Is that a pipe in the middle of it?"

Vick nodded and took it back. "This is a lead pipe. Someone drilled a hole in this pinecone, vertically. Then they inserted a lead pipe into it. It's about six inches long, and my guess is it weighs about three pounds," he said, holding it in his hand.

"We should find out who drilled the vertical hole in it and have them help with this craft project, since you're not skilled enough to do it," Maybel suggested.

Vick gripped his tool tighter. "I can do it, Maybel! I don't need you to critique how I use my tools!"

"I wonder if someone was going to make this pinecone into a candle. Maybe that's why they drilled a hole in it. You could fill the pipe with wax and put a wick in it," Norma said.

"No," Maybel said. "That doesn't make sense because they drilled a hole at the bottom of the pinecone, and you can't turn it upside down and use it as a candle. It would fall over… and also, the pinecone would probably burn up."

"Who uses lead pipes anymore?" Arnie asked.

Vick said, "No one. They were outlawed back in the 80s. Everything is PVC now or sometimes copper."

"How do you know this?" Maybel asked.

"I'm a plumbing *expert*, Maybel." Vick examined it again.

"But you're not a licensed plumber," she retorted.

"That's not the point. I know a lot about plumbing, more than you do!" Vick said.

Arnie took the pinecone from Vick. "He learned everything he knows about plumbing from me. Wow, this pinecone is heavy," Arnie said, feeling the weight.

"Let's just set this one aside," Norma suggested. "Let's try cutting another one from the basket." She poked through all the pinecones and pulled another one out. "Here, this one should work."

Vick tried sawing it vertically, but it crumbled again.

"I guess we'll just have to make these bumblebees with whole pinecones. I hoped to slice them in half so we could glue them to the flower wreaths we made, but that plan is out the window." Norma continued instructing her craft class. Everyone picked out small pinecones for themselves, painted them yellow, and attached the black construction paper pieces to make them look like bumblebees.

When Maybel completed crafting hers, she took a good long look at it. With wonky black pipe cleaners for antennas and messy looking gold glitter, it seemed to her like another craft that a preschooler would make. She looked over at Arnie's, and his looked pretty good, but she would never tell him that.

"Well, if you'll excuse me ladies," Arnie said. "I'm going to go take a nap. I'm doing a stakeout tonight!"

Maybel frowned. "What are you staking out?"

"I'm going to sit out in the cemetery tonight and see if I can figure out what's causing that fog." Arnie looked out the window towards the cemetery.

"Happy ghost hunting," Norma said. "You won't catch me in the middle of a cemetery at night!"

"Me either," Vera added. "It's supposed to be really windy tonight. I'm going to curl up on my couch under my blanket and read a good book."

"Maybel, how about you?" Arnie asked.

"I think I'll pass. I have bigger fish to fry, and speaking of fish, I need to go feed Mr. Piddles. Please excuse me, everyone." Maybel walked back to her apartment.

Chapter Twenty-Nine

Stakeout

"I know, I know," Maybel said to a hungry meowing Mr. Piddles, setting his food dish down on the ground for him to eat. Feeling like she'd had enough socializing for the day, she chose not to eat in the dining room and heated a frozen dinner in her microwave. While watching tv, she finished the scarf she'd been knitting. Holding it in her hand, she admired her craftsmanship. She'd used shades of blue and green yarn and wove just a little bit of yellow through it for contrast.

Whipping wind rattled her window, and she thought about Arnie on his stakeout. She got up from the couch and walked over to her bureau, taking out a pair of binoculars. Peering out at the cemetery, she thought she saw someone sitting over by the tombstones. After refocusing the lenses, she spotted him. "He's out there alright, Mr. Piddles."

Remembering that old Bible verse about how, when you're kind to your enemy, it's like heaping burning coals on their head, she decided to take some of her own advice on forgiveness. "Get ready to feel the heat, Arnie."

Maybel went to her kitchenette and prepared something. She slipped on her coat, buttoned it up, and brought two items with her on her walk out to the cemetery.

Trudging along the dank ground, Maybel spotted Arnie sitting by himself in a lawn chair with his green Member's Only jacket zipped up. He must be freezing; she thought, approaching him. "Well, hello Mr. Ghost Chaser," she said with a smile. "Seen anything spooky?"

"Not yet," he answered. "But I'm not giving up!"

"I can't believe you are out here on such a chilly night."

"Ghosts always perform better at night." He blew into his hands and rubbed them together.

"You know, there's no shame in calling it quits. It's freezing out here tonight, and the wind makes it worse," she said, with the evening breeze rustling her silver hair.

"I'm not a quitter!"

"I brought a thermos of hot cocoa for you… and I just finished knitting this scarf. I thought these things would help keep you warm on your stakeout."

He eagerly grabbed the items "I love hot cocoa! Thank you," he said, wrapping the scarf around his neck and opened the thermos. "I could smell it before I even opened the thermos."

"I think that's the Chocolate Cosmos you were smelling."

"The chocolate what?"

"They're a rare type of flower. Someone brings them out to that grave over there," Maybel said, pointing. "The flowers smell like chocolate."

"Ah, I see. You want some?" he offered.

Maybel shook her head. "I can't bear to drink out of that thermos. It's too sentimental. It belonged to George. He took that to work with him for years."

"George is buried here, isn't he? My wife was buried right over there," Arnie said, pointing to the south, sipping his cocoa.

"I don't care what anyone says. I think this cemetery is so peaceful."

"Me too."

"Sometimes I lean away from my grief, and other times I lean into it and wallow in it… but like they say, you can't grieve if you didn't love, and love is always a good thing… even when it hurts… and that's what life is all about… love."

Arnie nodded. "What is life, anyway? We're all just these flesh and bones. The body gives out on us. The mind plays tricks on us. We've got to be more than just our bodies. We have to have souls, don't we?"

"I believe we do… there has to be life beyond this," Maybel replied.

"Yeah, if you plug 80 years into eternity, life here on earth is just a drop in the bucket."

"A heavenly bucket of love poured out on us," Maybel said, smiling.

"Despite the cold, it's a beautiful night. I can see the big dipper right there," Arnie said, pointing.

Maybel looked up at the twinkling sky. "God's love for us is written in those stars."

"Do you really think someone murdered Violet?"

"I do. I'm sure of it."

"Who do you think did it?"

Maybel paused before speaking. "I'm not sure, but I keep thinking of something George used to always say when we'd watch murder mysteries with me. He'd say, 'it's always the one you least suspect'."

"Do you need any help to find the murderer?" Arnie asked.

Maybel considered this for a few seconds. "Sheila has a folder full of papers, and I need to find out what's in the folder. They might be Violet's missing bearer bonds."

"Bearer bonds?" Arnie echoed. "They haven't issued those things for years. Doris and I used to have some, but I cashed those in a long time ago."

"I know. Her husband bought them years ago, and she hung onto them for sentimental reasons," Maybel explained.

"I'm great at sleight of hand. I can call Sheila and tell her I need help with my bad back," Arnie offered.

"I don't think that will work. She doesn't normally carry her purse around with her when she's working," Maybel said. "But wait a minute, you could do that as a distraction, and then we could have Vick search her place!"

"Wouldn't that be breaking and entering?"

Maybel thought about this. "We've got to run into her when she has her purse with her."

"Her place is just down the hall from mine," Arnie said. "I can keep an eye out for when she leaves with her bag."

"Maybe I could call her and ask if she could take me to a doctor's appointment."

"That would work. Then I can bump into you guys and work my magic!" Arnie said, wiggling his fingers. "Remember, the hand is quicker than the eye."

Maybel smiled. "I guess it's worth a try. I'll call her tomorrow morning, and I'll keep you posted. Now I'm going to go back to my place. It's too cold to stay out here." Maybel turned and took a few steps.

Arnie called out, "Maybel."

She turned around and looked at him.

"Thanks for the hot cocoa. It's delicious."

"Don't stay out here too long. You'll catch cold."

Chapter Thirty

Back to Basics

"**Y**es, that's right," Maybel said into her phone to Sheila the next morning. "I'm still having so much gas and I'm bloated. I think I should go to a gastrologist."

"That's probably a good idea," Sheila replied. "Just make sure they don't put you on any drugs. Natural cures are best."

"Yes, I agree. But could you give me a ride to the doctor this morning? I don't drive anymore, and my son had to work today so he can't take me."

"I guess I could do that. Let me grab my bag, and I'll meet you out in the parking lot."

"Sounds great!" Maybel said, signing off. She sent a text to Arnie that read: **The eagle has landed. We're heading out to the parking lot now.**

After reading the text, Arnie peeked out his window and, when he spied Sheila, he followed her out to the parking lot.

"Thank you again for taking me. I really appreciate it," Maybel said to Sheila when they met in the parking lot.

"No trouble at all. I am the healthcare facilitator, after all," Sheila said, flipping her long hair back and pulling her bag up over her shoulder.

"Oh, Sheila!" Arnie shouted, rushing up to them, faking a hobble. He hunched over in his pink and yellow plaid golf pants with a matching pink golf shirt. "There you are! I've been looking all over for you. I'm having a bit of a health issue."

"Is it urgent? I need to take Maybel to the gastrologist. Her gas has gotten worse." Sheila rubbed her stomach.

"I guess not, but–oh!!!!" Arnie keeled over, grabbing his lower back, performing even better than the night he played King Lear.

Using her finely honed acting skills she developed during her work on King Lear, Maybel exclaimed, "Oh God, Arnie! I hope you're OK!"

Sheila bent down to help him. "Goodness, you should probably ice your back. Don't use a heating pad. That will just draw blood to the area and cause more swelling. One of your muscles is probably inflamed."

Arnie flailed about, grabbing around. "Oh, sweet Jesus! The pain!"

Sheila placed her hand on Arnie's back. "Do you think you can make it back to your place on your own? I can swing by after I get back from taking Maybel to the doctor."

"Oh… oh… I don't know. The pain!" Arnie whaled and groaned. "Do you have your first aid kit with you? I need some painkillers."

Sheila opened her trunk. "Let me check."

Arnie whispered to Maybel, "The folder isn't in her bag, but I got her key." He placed Sheila's front door key in her hand. "We need to go with Plan B."

Maybel nodded.

When Sheila walked back over to them with some aspirin, Maybel said, "You know, Arnie seems so bad off I can call Celeste for a ride. I really think you need to tend to him."

Sheila hesitated for a second and said, "Well, if you're sure she can take you, then I can go back with Arnie and help him ice his back."

"Oh, I'm sure. You better do that right away," Maybel urged. In an effort to forestall Sheila from going back to her place too soon, she added, "Make sure to cleanse his chi, too!"

"Oh, that's a good idea!" Sheila said, grabbing Arnie's arm to help him along.

"Thank you, sweetheart! I appreciate the help." Arnie grunted while faking a limp.

With their ruse well under way, Maybel parted ways and hurried over to Sheila's. She looked around, making sure no one was watching her. Quickly unlocking Sheila's door, she slipped in. Looking around at Sheila's tiny apartment, she saw a lava lamp, beads hanging in a doorway, and a beanbag. "She really is a hippy," Maybel said. Flipping through her mail and a stack of papers sitting on her kitchen counter, she couldn't find a folder. She moved over to her desk and poked around there.

"Ah ha! Here it is!" she said, picking it up and reading through the first page of the document in the folder. "Oh, it's only her credit card bills… geez, she owes a lot of money." Maybel set it back down and looked through her desk drawers, finding no other folders.

She sent a text to Arnie that read: **I'm done. You can stop faking your back injury. I'm headed back to your place so we can get her key back in her purse.**

Several minutes later, Maybel knocked on Arnie's door with Sheila answering, purple healing crystals in hand. "Maybel, you're back from the doctor so soon?"

"Yeah, turns out I got my dates mixed up. My appointment is tomorrow," Maybel fibbed. "Oh, it looks like that icepack on Arnie's back is slipping. You should probably apply some pressure on it. You know, so it really helps his inflammation.

While Sheila tended to Arnie, Maybel snuck Sheila's key back in her purse. "Why don't I take over for you and I'll keep an eye on Arnie? I'm sure you have other residents you need to help today."

After Sheila grabbed her purse and left, Maybel poked her head into Arnie's bedroom and said, "The coast is clear. She's gone."

"Oh, thank God! I think I have freezer burn from this icepack, and she kept talking about how she could make a healing elixir for me from kale and spirulina. I'd rather eat grass."

"Speaking of eating, I'm going to go have lunch now. You better stay here for a while. You don't want Sheila to see you walking around so soon," Maybel said.

"Good idea," Arnie grunted, getting up from his bed. The little black book slipped out of his pocket, falling to the ground.

Pointing to the floor, Maybel said, "You dropped your little book."

Arnie bent down and picked it up. As he flipped through it, Maybel noticed he went white as a sheet. "Arnie, you look like you've seen a ghost."

"I think I have! Look at this." He held the book out to her.

Maybel shook her head. "I don't need to read about your BMs."

"No, no. It's not that. Read this journal entry." He handed her his book.

Reading it, she asked, "What is an LBM?"

"That stands for a loose bowel movement, but you're on the wrong page."

Maybel tossed the journal back to him. "Oh, geez! Do you wash your hands before you write in that book?"

"That's not the point. Look at this page." He pointed to it with a shaky finger.

She read aloud,

**"THE DEAD WILL HAVE NO REST
UNTIL YOU JOIN THEM."**

Maybel looked up at Arnie. "Why did you write that?"

"Maybel, I didn't write it! That is not my writing!"

"Well, if you didn't write it, who did?"

"That's a great question. I think it's ghost writing."

"Horse apples! You expect me to believe a ghost wrote this?" Maybel flipped the page. She read aloud again,

"THE HAND OF DEATH IS UPON YOU."

Arnie put his hands on his hips. "That sounds like a threat! And that's not my writing either."

"It's right next to your golf score. 18 holes, 75. Could one of your golf buddies have written it?"

Arnie shook his head. "I don't take it out to the golf course with me. I write in it when I get back."

"So, you left the book here at your place unattended? Someone could have gotten a hold of it and wrote in it as a joke."

"It's not funny, and who would do that?"

"Sheila was just here. Maybe she did it."

"No, it was in my pocket the whole time."

"Maybe you're not the only one who can do sleight of hand."

"I was lying on my back the whole time she was here. I don't think she could have gotten to it."

"Arnie, if this is some kind of dumb joke you're playing on me, I don't think it's funny. You know I don't believe in ghosts."

"Maybel, this isn't a joke. I didn't write those two journal entries."

Looking at the two journal entries and observing the writing looked distinctly different from Arnie's, she said, "We really need to get to the bottom of this…"

"I agree, but how?"

Maybel let out a deep breath. "I'm not sure yet."

***

Back in the dining room of Shady Sunset, the head server announced to Maybel's table, "Our specials for lunch today are vegetable soup and chicken casserole."

"I love vegetable soup," Vera said. "I'll have that, but I don't want the chicken casserole. I've eaten that before and it's too heavy, and it tasted like they made it with a rubber chicken. I'll take a turkey sandwich, please."

The server scribbled notes. He turned to Maybel. "And for you?"

"I'll just have the vegetable soup. I'm not very hungry."

Norma ordered the chicken casserole. "I don't care what you say, Vera. I think it's delicious."

With a twinge of sadness, Maybel said, "Violet loved the chicken casserole they serve."

The ladies nodded, and Maybel noticed Arnie entered the dining room. To the other ladies' surprise, she waved him over to their table. "Would you like to join us, Arnie?"

He took his seat and ordered his lunch.

Norma quired, "How is your investigation going, Maybel?"

"No luck so far." Maybel placed her napkin on her lap.

"You should probably just give it up," Norma urged. "You don't want to get hurt."

Maybel thought about this for a second. How odd that Norma would want her to stop searching for the murderer. She remembered Norma had been at both Violet and Vera's places and they were both missing jewelries. Norma, however, wasn't missing anything. Maybel looked at Norma and asked her, "Aren't you worried about your safety with a murderer on the loose? And what about your jewels? We all know there is a thief running around."

Norma bristled a bit. "First of all, through Colleen's wise counseling, I've realized I'm holding onto my riches too tightly, metaphorically speaking. I've placed way too much importance on things, and not people. And second, I keep my jewels safely hidden away. No one will find them! Most of the time, I don't even lock my door when I leave."

"Well, how nice for you," Maybel said, picking up her soup spoon.

Vera added, "Colleen gives the best advice. When I spoke to her about some issues I was having with my daughter, she pointed out that I might be a bit too quick-tempered. She explained to me the importance of holding your tongue. Words can be very hurtful, and you can't take them back. Always count to ten when you're stuck in the middle of an argument or table it all together for another day to give yourself time to cool off."

"I think we all need to be careful right now," Arnie warned. "Theft, murder, strange noises, mysterious fog out in the cemetery… something is going on!"

"Yes," Maybel said, looking at Norma. "And how odd it would be to not be concerned about it."

"This casserole is delicious!" Norma said, digging in. "By the way, Colleen asked me to host the square dance tomorrow afternoon since she still hasn't hired a new activities director."

"You know how to square dance?" Vera inquired.

"Of course," Norma answered. "I'm from Oklahoma. We all know how to square dance."

"Normally, I'd pass on something like that. It doesn't seem very dignified," Vera went on, "but at our last one-on-one, Colleen encouraged me to participate in more activities. She said it would help me with my grief, and physical exercise is good for depression."

Norma looked at Arnie and Maybel. "Will I see you two there?"

"I guess so," Maybel conceded.

Arnie nodded. "I'll be there with spurs on!"

Chapter Thirty-One

The Tears of a Widow

"**P**ut that cut-out of a horse over there," Norma barked at Vick, pointing to the corner of the dancehall. Piles of hay were stacked in the corner, and they'd hung some festive streamers from the ceiling. With all the tables and chairs out of the way, they hung a lasso from the ceiling fan. But many residents later thought looked a lot more like a noose than a lasso.

Vick said, "I also tested out the microphone to make sure it works."

"Oh, great! People will be here any minute." Norma covered what would be the punch and cookie table with a checkered tablecloth.

Right on cue, several residents walked into the dancehall. "Oh, Norma! This looks wonderful!" Vera said.

"Thank you. I've done some party planning back in my day." Norma smiled proudly.

"Well, it shows!" Colleen said. "Maybe I don't need to hire a new activities director after all, if you'd consider taking the job."

Feeling flattered, Norma replied, "Why I'd never considered going back to work again, but now that you say that, I just might think about it."

"Please do," Colleen said.

"Yee-haw!" Arnie shouted, wearing his most western-styled shirt and jeans. "I came prepared." He stuck out his foot, showing off his cowboy boots.

Norma checked out his boots. "Oh, how fun!"

"All the better to dance with you, my angel," Arnie replied, tipping his cowboy hat to her.

"Hey, where's Maybel?"

"She's running late," Arnie said, knowing Maybel's whereabouts. "She said to start without her."

Norma nodded and took the microphone. "Hello everyone! Thank you for coming to the square dance. Let's get partnered up."

Folks shuffled around, pairing up. Since the women outnumbered the men, some women danced with each other. Norma called out directions over the music. "Swing your partner round and round!"

Arnie hooked his arm through Vera's, dancing and swinging gaily in circles. He promenaded over to Ida and hooked his arm through hers. He clapped to the music and slapped his knee, stomping his feet.

Meanwhile, Maybel walked over to Norma's apartment. On a hunch, she tried her door and found it unlocked… just as Norma said. She quickly slipped in and looked around. After a thorough search of Norma's apartment turned up nothing, Maybel remembered something. Back when Norma lived at Regal Palms, she'd had a custom-made bookcase built. Within that bookcase, she had them build a hidden compartment where she stashed her jewels. She'd confided in Maybel once, saying if she were to die suddenly, make sure her family knew about it.

Maybel walked over to the bookcase and examined it carefully. She pulled a few books from the bookcase, looking behind them. Nothing. She ran her hand along every inch of the shelving panels, trying to find a catch. Then, she spotted it, a seam in the wood frame. She pushed on it, and out popped a little drawer full of jewelry. Maybel poked through the jewels but didn't find her pearls or Violet's diamond necklace. The secret compartment contained a ruby pendant, gold necklaces, a cameo ring and jade earrings. It appeared to be all of Norma's jewelry.

Satisfied Norma wasn't the thief, Maybel skipped the square dance to do something she'd been putting off for a long time. Slowly she made the pilgrimage out to the cemetery…

***

Walking along, Maybel searched for the marker for George's grave. Remembering the word *RESURRECTION* was on the curb straight out from where George's grave was, she found that and walked several yards into the grass area. Reading headstones along the way, she stopped and read one engraving aloud, "Until we meet again, may God hold you in the hollow of His hand." The ache of George's absence filled her heart. She walked on until she arrived at George's plot.

"Oh, George. I'm sorry it's taken me so long to come out here and visit you," Maybel spoke to George's grave, his bones beneath her feet. "I just knew how much it would hurt." Wiping the tears from her eyes, she set some flowers down that she'd picked from the back garden at Shady Sunset Retirement Home. "I miss you so much." Sobbing the sobs only grieving widows cry, she uttered, "I know your soul is not here. I know you're in heaven."

A flood of sadness poured out of her, and she told him, "Jeffrey is doing well. He's still working for the fire department. He takes good care of me. Oh, and he got married, but it ended in a disaster, and now he's in the middle of getting divorced." Wiping her eyes again, she went on, "Not everyone gets to have the kind of love we shared. I even wrote you a poem, George."

Maybel reached into her pocket, taking out a slip of paper. She unfolded the wrinkled paper and read it out loud to George:

"The moment you left, my heart split in two.
One side was filled with memories,
and the other side died with you.
I often lay awake at night when the world is
fast asleep
and take a walk down memory lane with tears
on my cheek.
Remembering you is easy, I do it every day.
But missing you is a heartache that never
goes away.
I hold you tightly in my heart, and there you
will remain.
You see, life has gone on without you,
but I will never be the same."

Loneliness surrounded Maybel's heart, making it beat with sorrow. Her eyesight blurred with tears, and she folded the poem, slipping it back into her pocket. Her other half was gone, but never forgotten. "I moved out of Regal Palms. That was so difficult. All our memories were there, but Jeffrey didn't think it was safe for me anymore. Now I'm here at Shady Sunset… right next door to you. I've made some new friends and reunited with some old friends. You remember Norma. She's here. This place isn't too bad, except for that Arnie Arnold. You remember that buffoon, don't you?

"You were always jealous of him, but you didn't need to be. You were the love of my life… no, you *are* the love of my life, George." Maybel's tears rolled down her cheeks.

"Anyway, they plan lots of activities here for us, so I should be able to stay busy. Jeffrey gave me a cat too, and I named him Mr. Piddles. He's a bit of a rascal, but he keeps me company until I can be with you again.

"And then there was Violet, a new friend of mine, but she died. We think someone murdered her. I'm trying to help the Sunshine Beach police solve the case. I've helped solve a few cases now, George. You'd be so proud of me. After I'm done visiting with you, I'm going to walk over to Violet's grave and take her some flowers, too. Maybe she said hello to you when she got up to the golden gates."

Maybel talked to George for quite a while. Leaning into her grief, the weight caused sobbing like she hadn't sobbed in a while. At the end of her visit with George, she felt lighter and closer to him somehow.

She carefully carried a batch of carnations over to Violet's headstone, paying close attention to the unlevel places in the grass so as not to trip. Maybel placed the pink flowers in the in-ground vase in front of Violet's headstone. "Don't you worry, Violet. We're going to find out who did this to you… but I know you are in a better place now… and you're with John and your son. I almost envy you…"

Overwhelmed with emotion, Maybel sat down on the cement bench, Violet's crying place. Under the shade of the great pine tree, she felt the cold cement of the bench on her sit points. Breathing deeply for a while allowed a peaceful calm to wash over her. Looking out at the cemetery, she saw bouquets of beautiful flowers scattered about.

With the cemetery being fenced in, she couldn't see or hear the outside world. The tranquility brought about a healing of sorts. In the distance, a statue of the Holy Mary glistened in the afternoon sunshine. Bright flowers bloomed all around the stone carving, and Maybel heard birds chirping. During the day, the cemetery didn't seem spooky at all. It was quite peaceful.

Wiping her eyes again, she prayed, "*God, please heal my broken heart and take good care of George and Violet and her family. And please, please help me find Violet's murderer. That dear woman deserves justice.*"

Happy memories of her times with George came flooding back to her. Staring at the cemetery land with green grass sprawled out for miles amidst a few rolling hills in the distance reminded her of the picnics she, George, and Jeffrey would have in the summer. George always complained that sitting on the grass in the park made him itchy. Maybel chuckled, picturing him scratching himself. Her mind wandered, and she thought about some residents at Shady Sunset thinking it was haunted. The cemetery at night felt l like an eerie Ghostland… was George just a ghost now? No, George was real, but she struggled to remember him. The sound of his voice… she closed her eyes, and she could hear his voice greeting her when he came through the door after a long day at work always setting his keys down on the counter instead of hanging them on the keyring holder liked she'd asked so many times. Maybel remembered something Colleen told her during their grief counseling; the past is gone, and the future is not promised. All we have is right now. Live in the moment.

Drawing in a deep breath, Maybel thought about right here, right now… this made her thankful for her comfortable little apartment, Mr. Piddles, her friends, her son Jeffrey, Celeste so dear to her like a daughter, her hobbies, her faith, and her many years with George.

A willowy wind blew wisps of hair across her face. Brushing them away, she sensed the Holy Spirit surrounding her. The breeze bent the pine tree branches back and forth. Pine needles fluttered about.

A prickly pinecone plopped down from the tree above, and with a loud thud, hit the cement bench, startling her. Maybel picked it up, feeling the heavy weight of it in her hand. "This thing is huge! It could have killed me!" She glanced up at the pine tree, and a light went on in her head. "I know what happened! Oh, thank you, God, for answering my prayer!"

Maybel stood up and looked around the cemetery. Most graves at the cemetery had flat, in-ground headstones, but some graves had tombstones that stood above ground. There, behind one of the larger tombstones, lay a tube from an oxygen tank. A few feet away from that, she found a wrapper. Maybel picked it up, examining it. She gasped when she saw what type of wrapper it was because she'd found a clue that helped her solve the mystery. The answer as to what happened to Violet snapped in her mind.

With evidence in hand, she said goodbye to George and Violet and hurried back to Shady Sunset to catch a killer.

Chapter Thirty-Two

Ghosts in the Attic

Colleen's overworked fingers jabbed at the keys on her keyboard. With T's crossed and I's dotted on a new resident's application, she completed one of her many tasks. Not having an assistant to input the information into Shady Sunset's database forced her to do it herself. Wearing too many hats for her measly salary, she often thought she deserved a raise. Looking down at the sleeve of her white cardigan and noticing a small hole, she *knew* she deserved a raise. While rolling the cuff back to hide it, Colleen heard a muffled voice outside her office. Poking her head out, she observed Maybel's frantic behavior. Colleen approached Maybel to find out what the matter could be.

"I'm looking for Vick," Maybel answered, a trifle flustered and panting from her haste. "I think I figured out how the killer murdered Violet!"

Concern gave way to Colleen's face. "Now Maybel, we've talked about this. I'm afraid you're having delusions of grandeur again. It's best not to meddle in this and leave the crime solving to the police. All this fuss and flurry is going to give you a nervous breakdown." Patting Maybel's shoulder, she urged, "I think we should do another counseling session. You're in luck because I just finished all my paperwork, and I have an hour before my next meeting. Why don't we go into my office and sit down?"

Frowning, Maybel consented. Once seated in Colleen's office, she fidgeted in her chair, tapping her orthopedic shoes on the tile.

"Maybel, I know how hard grief can be," Colleen began. "I've lost a loved one, too. I don't talk about it much, but I lost my sister years ago. I think about her almost every day… and when I remember that I forgot to think about her, I feel guilty that I'm not thinking about her."

Nodding, Maybel said, "I was just out at the cemetery visiting George. It was so difficult to go to his grave, but once I was there, I felt peace… like I know he's still with me somehow."

"That's good, Maybel. Stay with that feeling of peace. Running around here thinking there's a murderer on the loose isn't healthy. I think you're using that as a diversion tactic to keep from facing your grief."

Maybel took a deep breath and held it for a few seconds before letting it out; a technique Sheila taught her. "Are they having another cooking class today?"

Colleen shook her head. "No, but I'm glad you're getting more involved in the activities around here. It's good for you to stay active and be with your friends."

"It smells like someone is baking a chocolate soufflé," she said, sniffing the air. Maybel's eyes wandered over to the corner of Colleen's desk. A crystal vase brimming with rich burgundy flowers stared back at her. Chocolate Cosmos, she thought. She breathed in again, the scent unmistakable. Maybel's eyes traveled over to Colleen's.

Colleen leaned back in her chair and smiled. Running her slender hand through her short patent leather hair, she revealed the hole in her sweater. "Maybel, you look like you've seen a ghost."

"I don't believe in ghosts." Maybel's mouth went dry.

Colleen's smile turned grim. "Well, that's good. Some residents here have gotten really carried away with the idea that Shady Sunset is haunted."

"I think someone has deliberately been doing things to make us think this place is haunted," Maybel said.

Colleen cleared her throat. "And why would someone do that?"

Maybel sat straight up in her chair. "As a coverup."

Colleen adjusted the cuff of her sweater again. "A coverup?"

"Yes, like one of those diversion tactics you mentioned."

"A diversion tactic from what?" Colleen wondered.

"From all the thievery going on," Maybel held her gaze on Colleen before looking back at the Chocolate Cosmos flowers. "Those are Chocolate Cosmos, aren't they? They smell divine. Wherever did you get those? They're hard to find."

Colleen reached towards the vase and pulled one flower out, bringing it to her nose. Breathing deeply, she said, "They are divine, aren't they? I just love the smell."

"I noticed you have a hole in your sweater. I could knit that closed for you. It wouldn't look perfect, but it would keep it from unraveling. I know how much you like that sweater. You wear it all the time."

Colleen's cheeks flushed. "That won't be necessary, Maybel. I'll be getting a new one soon."

"You know… one of the graves out at the cemetery often has Chocolate Cosmos placed in the headstone vase," Maybel said.

Colleen ran her thumb and index finger along the velvety pedal of the cocoa scented flower. "What a coincidence."

"Is it?" Maybel asked, pulling at the thread between them.

Colleen leaned forward and put the flower back in the vase. "There's a florist around the corner from here. Sometimes he has them."

"What's the name of the florist? I'd love to get some." Maybel forced a smile, feeling her heart beating out of her chest.

"I think we should stay on topic. We were talking about your grief."

Carefully standing up, Maybel said, "I just remembered I'm late for dinner."

"But it's only 4 o'clock," Colleen replied.

"You know how us old people like to eat early. Now, if you'll excuse me, I've got to get going." Maybel briskly walked out of Colleen's office.

Rushing into the dining room, Maybel headed straight for the table Arnie and Vick were seated at. Breathless, she shouted, "Vick!"

Vick growled, "Maybel, I'm off the clock! Can't you see I'm having a late lunch?!"

"Yes, I can see that, but it's urgent. I believe I have the answer to this mystery! I think I know how the murderer killed Violet. I was out at the cemetery sitting on the cement bench under the pine tree and a huge, heavy pinecone fell from the tree, almost hitting me on the head!"

Snickering, Arnie said, "Too bad it didn't knock some sense into you."

"Cram it, Arnie!" Maybel looked back at Vick and continued, "remember the pinecone from craft class that had the lead pipe in it? I think the murderer put the lead pipe in the pinecone, climbed the pine tree, and waited for Violet to sit on the bench. Then they dropped the pinecone with the lead pipe in it on her head, knocking her out and causing that contusion Celeste and I saw on the back of Violet's head. After she fell on the ground, the murderer climbed down and disconnected her tank from her mask, replacing her tank with an empty tank. They were trying to make us think her tank ran out of oxygen and that she died of natural causes. But really, after she fell over from being hit with the pinecone, they held her down with their foot, causing her to suffocate!"

"That's a great theory, Maybel, but where did the murderer hide the second empty oxygen tank?" Vick asked.

"At first I thought maybe they had it tied to a tree branch, and it broke the branch," Maybel went on, "but while at the cemetery, I spotted something behind one of the tombstones. When I went to get a closer look, I found the tube from an oxygen tank and a wrapper for dry ice!"

"What does that prove?" Arnie asked.

"I think the murderer hid the oxygen tank out in the cemetery, behind a tombstone. They let the air out of a full tank… and the dry ice… well, if air was blowing out of the oxygen tank and hit the dry ice, it would cause those bursts of fog we saw!"

Arnie's eyes got big. "Good grief! But why would someone want to do that?"

"I don't know," Maybel said. "But I have an idea who did it, but until I have some hard evidence, I don't want to say who I think the murderer is. If we could find Violet's tank, the one the murderer switched out for the empty one, maybe it would have the murderer's fingerprints on it."

"I told you I searched Jo's place, and I didn't find an oxygen tank and neither did the police," Vick said.

"Vera said she kept hearing noises in the attic above her," in pursuit of her quarry, Maybel suggested, "I think we need to search the attic of this building. What's up there?"

Vick thought for a few seconds before speaking. "Not much… there are some electrical panels up there. There's a hatch that comes down with ladder stairs that lead up to the attic."

"I'm not sure we should go up there. It's probably haunted," Arnie said, standing up.

"Arnie, if you're too scared, you can just stay down here." Looking at his outfit, she said, "Good grief! Where did you get those bright blue pants?"

"The color is called electric blue," Arnie replied.

"They're brighter than my pants!"

"Stylish people aren't afraid of color, Maybel."

Maybel shook her head, turned to Vick and said, "Let's go." She scurried out of the dining room with Vick hot on her heels. Arnie dashed into the kitchen quickly, grabbed something and dashed back, following them.

Out of breath, they got to the end of the hall on the second floor, where the hatch to the attic was. Vick pulled on the rope and brought down the ladder stairs. "I'll go first," he said, taking the lead and climbing up.

Arnie said to Maybel, "I don't think you should go up the ladder stairs. You might fall off."

"Nonsense! I can do this. I'll just go slowly and hang on tight," she said.

"OK, I'll go last. In case you slip, I can catch you."

Maybel grabbed onto the sides of the ladder stairs, putting her right foot on the first rung. Carefully, she lifted her left foot to the next rung. She held on as tightly as she could, repeating this a few more times. "Arnie! Get your hand off my rear end!" she shouted.

"I'm helping you up," he said, grunting and climbing up behind her.

She ascended slowly. When she got to the top, Vick extended his hand and helped her into the dusty attic.

They waited for Arnie, and when he got to the top of the ladder, Vick carefully helped his dad get into the attic. The three of them stood there, looking around.

"There's not much to see up here," Vick said.

Maybel asked, "Is that garlic I smell?"

Arnie nodded. "Yeah, I brought some with me for protection."

"That's for vampires, not ghosts!"

"I thought you don't believe in ghosts." Arnie said.

"I don't, and I don't believe in vampires either." Maybel pointed at a large chest in the corner of the attic. "What's in that?"

"Let's go find out." Vick shined his flashlight in the corner of the dimly lit attic. "Be careful not to trip on the rafters," he warned.

Arnie flailed about, swinging his arms in the air. "Oh! What was that?"

"Spiderwebs," Maybel said. "There's nothing to be afraid of."

"I'm not afraid," Arnie insisted.

Vick tried to open the chest, but it was locked.

"Let's just break the lock, son," Arnie suggested.

Vick hit the lock with his flashlight, but no luck.

Guiding Vick aside, Arnie said, "Here, let me try." Arnie took his pocketknife out, extended the corkscrew feature and after a little finagling, he popped the lock. "Viola! I told you I can do all kinds of sleight of hand."

Maybel refused to admit it impressed her. The three of them looked into the chest. "Holy moly! There it is! The oxygen tank," Maybel said, stepping closer to the chest to get a better look.

"We'll be able to tell by the serial number on it if it's Violet's," Vick said.

Maybel nodded. "I'm sure it's hers!"

"What's all this other stuff?" Arnie asked, reaching into the depths of the chest moving things around.

"Look at this," Maybel said, pointing to a small projector. "I bet this is what the murderer used to project images onto the walls and windows to make everyone think they were seeing ghosts."

Vick held up a white chiffon gown. Upon inspecting it, he pulled out a deflated blow-up doll from inside the gown. "What in the world…"

Maybel stepped closer to examine it. "The murderer probably used this gown with an inflated doll to make it look like a ghost floating in the hallway. This must be what Vera saw… and look at this paint on the doll's face… and here's the bottle of fluorescent paint! This is why Vera said the ghost's face glowed in the dark."

Arnie added, "And maybe they used it out in the cemetery. This could have been what looked like the strange white filmy fog."

Looking through the chest, Maybel pulled out a bulky pouch and opened it. Her jaw dropped. "It's full of jewelry! My pearls!" She grabbed her necklace out of it and kissed them. "These were a birthday present from George!"

"Wow, look at all that loot!" Vick reached into the pouch and pulled out a diamond tennis bracelet.

"And here is some lavender perfume," Maybel said, pulling a small bottle out of the chest. "Vera said she smelled lavender in the hallway the night she thought she saw a ghost. Vera was so scared she thought it was the ghost of Beatrice Parkin's perfume she was smelling."

Vick took the bottle from Maybel and smelled it. "Someone really went to a lot of trouble to make everyone think this place is haunted."

"Wait, did you hear that?" Arnie asked.

They all turned around. The thrill of discovery gave way to horror. Maybel's pulse hammered.

There stood Colleen, the head of Shady Sunset's administration, and in her hand she held a loaded gun with a silencer.

Maybel gasped, putting her hands up. "Colleen! Oh, I was afraid it was you, but I just didn't want to believe it. Why did you do these things?"

"Not that I owe you any explanation, but there's no way to live on an administrator's salary in Southern California at an old folk's home. The pay is terrible."

"But why the dry ice?" Maybel asked, staring at the gun in Colleen's hand.

"I thought if I could get everyone talking about Shady Sunset being haunted, it would be easy to convince authorities that you guys are just a bunch of senile old folks losing your minds and your memories. You misplaced your jewelry, and you can't even remember where you put it." She laughed.

Maybel shook her head in disgust. "You took Violet's Bearer bonds, didn't you?"

"I did a counseling session with her in her place. She kept droning on about her sadness over the loss of her husband and son. I'm not really a licensed counselor, but I deserved to be paid for the time I spent listening to all of you complain about everything. She didn't need the money, anyway."

Maybel frowned. "But why did you have to kill her?"

Colleen kept the gun in her hand steady. "I didn't want to kill her. I just wanted the money, but I did her a favor, really. When I asked her if she was afraid to die, she said no. She couldn't wait to pass on and be with her husband and son. She knew I took her bonds. She figured it out after one of our counseling sessions at her apartment and confronted me. I denied it. She said she was going to go to the authorities and tell everyone… I couldn't have that, now, could I?"

"So, you're the one who took my pearls! At our counseling session at my place, you were there right before Arnie," Maybel said, piecing it together.

Colleen laughed. "I had a counseling session with Vera, too. When she got up to go to the bathroom, I found her stash of cash. I tried to rip Norma off, but I never could find where she kept her valuables, and she talks so much I just had to get out of there."

Disgust deepened the lines in Maybel's face. "We trusted you! You were counseling all of us on our grief, and meanwhile, you were stealing from us?!"

Colleen shrugged.

Arnie shook his head in disdain. "Physician, heal thyself! And I bet you're the one who wrote in my little black book trying to make me think a ghost did it!"

Colleen stood stoic. "And the hand of death really is upon you now, isn't it?"

"You can't kill all three of us," Vick said, his hands still in the air.

"Six bullets and a silencer. Plus, no one ever comes up here. It would be days before they find you, and I'll be long gone with everything by then." Colleen smiled smugly.

Maybel continued to pull a confession out of Colleen. "Ida saw you in the hallway. You put on the purple coat from the costume rack and walked down the hall with an oxygen tank. Violet always left her door unlocked. You waited until after she went to sleep and took one of her tanks and went down the hall with it… and you know about the side stairwell that leads out to the cemetery. That's how you went back and forth to create that fake fog without anyone seeing you."

"Oh, look at you figuring things out like the good amateur detective you are! You're pretty clever for an old lady.

Too bad you couldn't figure it out sooner!" Colleen raised her gun higher. "Violet never locked her door, and yes, I took one of her oxygen tanks. She was so senile she never even noticed one was missing. I wore the coat so that if anyone saw me, they'd mistake me for Violet."

With hands still in the air, Maybel said, "You came up here to hide the stuff you stole, and that's the noises everyone heard."

"Yes," Colleen said. "That's obvious now, isn't it?"

Maybel asked, "And the pinecone… you must have drilled a hole in it and put the pipe in it. But how did you do that? When Vick tried, the pinecones crumbled."

"Clearly, I'm better with the tools than Vick," Colleen said, giving a wicked wink.

"You climbed the tree and waited for Violet, and when she sat on the bench, you dropped the pinecone on her head," Maybel said.

"Well, I couldn't chloroform her. She always had that oxygen mask on. I'd have to have too much contact with her. I knocked her out first, and I climbed down from the tree, disconnected her oxygen tank, and held my foot on her back so she couldn't breathe while she lay face down in the dirt. Once she died, I switched out her full tank for the empty one I hid behind one of the tombstones. And the best part of all is, the pinecone with the lead pipe was just lying there by her body the whole time. No one suspected I used it as an assault weapon. It just sat there in plain sight, and I watched that stupid detective walk around it several times during his investigation," Collen admitted with a snarl.

"You're a horrible person! Don't you have any conscience?" Maybel asked.

"This place owes me," Colleen complained. "You can't even imagine what all I have to deal with, and for such little pay. But I never intended for anyone to get hurt."

Vick said, "I don't get paid well either, but I'd never resort to theft or murder. Why the hell didn't you get rid of the pinecone? Why did it end up in that basket?"

Colleen turned towards Vick. Pointing her gun at him, she cocked it. "I never thought that idiot Norma would do so many more crafts with those pinecones. I went back later and got it from under the pine tree, but to be careful, I picked up a few other pinecones along with the one with the lead pipe in it. I took them to the craft room, putting them in the basket with the others. That way, if anyone saw me with the pinecone, they'd just think I collected them for the crafts. I figured they'd all be thrown out, eventually."

"And that's why you had a lead pipe and tools under your sink!" Vick said, the light going on.

Sneering, Colleen asked, "Any last words before you die?" The gun stayed steady in her hand.

Arnie desperately did not want to see his son, the fruit of his loins, get shot. With a magician's sleight of hand, he reached into his pocket. In the blink of an eye, a fireball burst into the air, distracting Colleen for a few seconds. Vick took the cue and quickly picked up the oxygen tank, throwing the tank at Colleen's face as hard as he could, knocking her out.

"Oh, thank God!" Maybel exclaimed, taking her cell-phone out of her pocket to call 911.

Chapter Thirty-Three

Heavenly Souls

After being seated in the dining room and having given their statements to a police officer, Arnie asked Maybel, "We make a good team, don't we?"

Maybel flashed a warning look. "Don't get carried away, Arnie."

He nudged her side with his elbow. "Oh, come on, darling. You know we do. We just took down a swindler!"

"She isn't just a swindler; she's a murderer."

"Are you ever going to forgive me?"

Using her most innocent tone, Maybel asked, "And what would I need to forgive you for?"

"I think you know."

"In order for me to officially forgive you, I'd have to hear you say it."

Hanging his head down, he admitted, "I stole the Regal Palms HOA presidency from you."

"And how did you steal it from me?" Maybel set her eyes on him.

Arnie averted his eyes. "I may have leaked a little in the meeting."

"May have!?"

"OK, OK. I passed gas at the board meeting… and blamed it on you," Arnie confessed.

Pointing her finger at him, Maybel shouted, "I knew it! I knew you passed gas! You usurped my role as president!"

"Come on, it was a million years ago, and it was just a little toot."

"Just a little toot?! You crop dusted the entire homeowner's association board of Regal Palms and blamed it on me! Your silent but deadly release cost me my HOA presidency!"

"I really wanted the presidency because I didn't have anything else in my life at that time. I thought I could do a better job than you, but after I farted and saw the disgusted looks on everyone's faces, I panicked and blamed it on you."

Shaking her head, Maybel said, "What a lousy thing to do to me, and you also made a pass at me when I was a married woman."

"I'm sorry… my wife had just passed away, and I felt lost and lonely."

"I understand feeling lost and lonely. You're forgiven," she said, smiling.

"It must be fate that brought us together again," Arnie added.

"Is it? Or did you move in because you knew I lived here?"

Arnie paused before speaking, "Well, fate brought us together back at Regal Palms… and you being here may have swayed my decision to move in."

"Did you ever do any one-on-one counseling sessions with Colleen?" Maybel asked.

"No, I just stuck with the art therapy. I found that very soothing. Colleen commented once on how clever one of my drawings was. I must admit I fell for her flattery, and I thought I could actually draw, but now that we know what she was really up to, I suspect I can't really draw."

"Colleen asked me a strange question. She asked if I was afraid to die," Maybel said.

"Why is that strange? We're all afraid to die."

Thoughtfully, Maybel went on, "At first, I would have said yes. I'm afraid to die. But when I was out at George's grave, I kept thinking about it. I think that faith steals the power of the grave. I'm not afraid to die anymore, and I'm prepared to die."

"We're not dead yet, Maybel. We've still got a lot of living to do! And now that we've called a truce with each other… you never know what can happen. It's not too late for love." Arnie smiled.

"Arnie, George is, was, and will always be my one true love, but I'm happy to be friends with you. And truth be told, I'm also glad you're living here as well."

"Me too. I think this is the start of a beautiful friendship."

Detective Bahn approached them. "Good job everyone!"

Vick stood up. "It was mostly me. I'm the one that took down the murderer." He bumped his fist against Detective Bahn's.

Maybel rolled her eyes. She told Detective Bahn, "Celeste is on her way here. When I texted her about what happened, she said she wants to make sure I'm OK. Jeffrey is on his way, too. He said he's going to stay the night with me and make sure I'm not in shock."

Detective Bahn nodded. "Will you all excuse me for a moment?"

***

Stepping out of the dining room, Brian sent a text to Celeste that read: **When you get to Shady Sunset, meet me under the pine tree at the cemetery.**

Brian walked over to Heavenly Souls Cemetery and crafted something for Celeste he hoped would win her heart. Several minutes later, his eyes danced with delight watching her walk up. A smile took over his face, and his gaze rested on her.

She walked in the rays of light from the setting sun, glowing on the horizon. Her spring dress fluttered in the breeze. "Hello handsome," she greeted him. Standing with him under the shade of the pine tree, she asked, "Why did you want me to meet you out here?"

"I've been thinking…," he began.

With a laugh, Celeste said, "Uh oh."

"I thought about how I treated you the last time we were standing by this tree. I feel bad about it."

"You ignored me!"

Smiling, he said, "Ignoring you would be a tall order for any man to fill… but I think we should make a pact not to be rude to each other."

"I can agree to that. Should we pinkie swear by it?"

Brian pointed to the trunk of the pine tree. Carved inside a heart on the tree were their initials: **B + C**. Celeste ran her hand along the carving, feeling the grain, and her heart warmed from the gesture. "You know, you probably shouldn't have vandalized this tree."

"Ugh! You are the least romantic woman on the face of this planet. Most women would swoon over this."

She ginned at him. "I'm not most women. Don't you know that by now?"

"Maybe I didn't vandalize a pine tree. Maybe I grafted us into the tree of life."

Celeste tilted her head. "The tree of life?"

"Yes, this is where our love came alive."

"What?"

Brian took her hand in his. "The night you found Violet out here, that's the night our love came alive."

"You wouldn't even speak to me that night. You gave me the cold shoulder."

"But that's the night I knew I loved you." He ran his thumb along her knuckles.

"Giving me the silent treatment… standing next to a dead body?"

"Contrary to how callus you may think I am, it deeply affects me to see a dead body. I never forget them, and I never forget why I was called to this line of work. We, as human beings, are not to take another person's life. Life is a gift from God, and the victims of murder deserve justice. Looking down at Violet, I thought about how I wanted to live… and I knew I wanted to live life with you. So, these initials on this tree have grafted us together into the tree of life."

Celeste crinkled her brow. "But you were so mad you wouldn't even speak to me that night."

"That's not the point. I'm not talking about my words. I'm talking about my thoughts and desires. What do I have to do to get you to trust me? Buy us side-by-side plots here at Heavenly Souls?" He looked deep into her eyes, trying to connect. "I love you, Celeste…"

Celeste's dark eyes filled with tears. "A love that goes all the way to the grave?"

"And beyond… I feel like I've waited an eternity for you. I've never been a religious man, but I do believe there is someone up above." He smiled, wiping the salty tear rolling down her cheek. "May our relationship always be rooted in love."

"I see what you did there… tree of life… *rooted* in love…"

He grinned.

She stepped closer to him, and he put his hands around her waist. She looked at him and reached up. Surrendering in the shade of the sunset under the pine tree at the crying place, she told him, "I love you too, Brian."

And he kissed her.

When their lips parted, she winked and said, "I'm just glad you didn't bring a ladder out here with you."

Laughing, he kissed her again.

"Whatever happened with the mayor's case?" Celeste wondered.

"That's another thing I wanted to talk to you about." Brian paused and pulled in a deep breath. "On my way over here, I got a call from Officer Nelson, the first officer on the scene at the mayor's house and at Tube Solutions, when we got the call about the explosion. They found Hayward Hamilton dead in the warehouse of his company."

Celeste gasped. "Oh Brian! This isn't good."

"That's not all… I found the dirt on the mayor and brought it to the DA, but he refused to bring up any charges on the mayor… and the police chief told me to stand down and stop investigating the break in at the mayor's house."

Celeste's eyes got big.

"I found out that the environmental group demanded that Tube Solutions convert all their forklifts to electrical vehicles to be more environmentally friendly. The company got so much terrible publicity, Hamilton gave in and agreed, but when he went to the city to get permission for more power, he was denied. For fifteen electric forklifts, he would have needed more megawatt power than the entire city of Sunshine Beach uses."

"Is that how Hayward Hamilton met the mayor?"

Brian rubbed his chin. "I'd assume so. I had done some digging, and I found out they were in fact having an affair, and he is the man that broke into the mayor's garage… well, it wasn't a real break-in."

Celeste tilted her head to the side. "What about Michael Turnblast? Did you figure out how the explosion at Tube Solutions manufacturing plant happened?"

"OSHA ruled it an accident," Brian said. "But I know it wasn't. Hamilton paid off the OSHA investigator. I found the money trail, and I showed the proof to the police chief, and that's when he told me to drop the case… then Hamilton turned up dead today."

"Wow…" Brian's words hit Celeste like a lead balloon. She shifted her sinking feet. "You think Hayward Hamilton threatened to go public with the affair?"

"I'm not sure, but the mayor definitely took a bribe, and when I did a deep dive, I found out he's participated in some extortion and racketeering."

"Racketeering? You don't hear that very often anymore."

Brian took a deep breath. "But now I have a target on my back."

"We'll figure this out," Celeste assured him.

"There's nothing to figure out. The case is closed. The chief told me not to pursue it. You know he's friends with the mayor."

Celeste shook her head. "Politics."

"All politics are local… it's all that you scratch my back and I'll scratch your back shit."

Celeste's heartbeat quickened. "So, the mayor took a payola from Tube Solutions…"

"Yeah. Hamilton paid it to get the environmentalists off his back. If the city denied his request to go electric with all his company vehicles, then what could he do? The battle would be over."

"Oh, Brian, you really have a target on your back now. Just knowing the truth puts you in danger."

Grimly, Brian nodded.

The Epilogue

December 24, 2019
(Six months later)
The Most Wonderful Time of the Year

"**V**ick, push the star over a little to the left," Norma instructed, wearing the ugliest Christmas sweater she could find in her closet to be as festive as possible.

Vick, standing on a ladder in the Shady Sunset dancehall, pushed the gold star perched on top of the seven-foot Christmas tree in the instructed direction.

Norma clapped her hands. "Oh, perfect!"

"It's a nice tree," Vick commented, stepping down from the ladder and looking at the beautifully decorated balsam fir. "How many tables do you want me to set out for the party?"

"Eight is enough," Norma answered.

"Where should we put these garlands?" Vera asked Norma, the one in charge of organizing the Shady Sunset Christmas party.

Norma pointed to the stage instructing, "Over there. Line them along the edge of the stage in front of the nativity scene."

"These are lovely garlands. I like how the lights are already built into them, and the tips of the pine branches look like they are dusted with snow," Vera said, admiring the evergreen in her hands.

Norma's face lit up. "They are, aren't they! I thought they went nicely with the tiny tabletop trees I got for Maybel's cookie table."

Maybel volunteered to help Norma with the Christmas party by baking several types of cookies. She arranged them beautifully on silver platters, opting to wear a red and black checkered dress for the party instead of an ugly Christmas sweater. She prepared old-fashioned cut out sugar cookies and frosted them festively. Maybel rolled peanut butter balls and dipped them in melted chocolate and baked bar cookies and sliced them into square chunks. An elegant tablecloth of emerald green and a runner with Santa's reindeers trotting along in the snow, pulling his sleigh, covered the cookie table. Maybel also baked a cinnamon crunch bundt cake that used to be George's favorite and decorated the cake with edible holly leaves and berries made from molds filled with white chocolate and food coloring.

"Maybel, should I put some of these gold and silver pinecones on the cookie table?" Norma asked.

"I guess so…," Maybel said, feeling a twinge of sadness. "Quite frankly, I can't look at a pinecone anymore without thinking of Violet."

"I know what you mean," Norma said. "But she's with the angels now, singing in heaven's chorus."

Maybel nodded, wiping a tear from her eye. "Have you tried one of these?" Maybel asked, handing Norma a pretzel stick covered in dark chocolate and sprinkled with red and green candy pieces.

Norma crunched on the treat. "Delicious! Don't you think these snowflakes came out adorable?"

Earlier in the week, during one of their craft classes, they'd cut out snowflakes, and since every snowflake is different, the craft class cut out many shapes and sizes of snowflakes. Vick hung them at staggered heights from the ceiling per Norma's instructions, making the dancehall look like a lovely winter wonderland.

"This is going to be a grand party. I can't wait for everyone to get here!" Maybel said, fanning out napkins on the cookie table.

Norma tasked Arnie with wearing the Santa costume and passing out gifts to the residents attending the party. Arnie stuffed a pillow under his costume and practiced getting it to jiggle like a bowl full of jelly. His flask of brandy to spike the punch bowl full of eggnog fit perfectly in the pocket of his Santa suit. A tiny bouquet of mistletoe tied with a red velvet ribbon was tucked away in his other pocket in hopes of getting a kiss from Maybel.

The proprietor of Shady Sunset, upon hearing about the incidents involving Colleen, immediately discharged her. They hired Arlene Herrera as the new chief of administration, and everyone quite liked her. For her first order of business, Arlene hired an actual licensed counselor for the staff. She kept Sheila Anderson on board as the new age healthcare facilitator. Norma stayed on as the activities director because it turned out she was rather good at it, and it gave her a sense of purpose. Arlene also implemented a new menu in the dining room that everyone loved. All in all, everything at the Shady Sunset Retirement Home went back to normal.

Residents invited family and friends to the Christmas party. Maybel invited Jeffrey, Celeste, and Brian. She felt especially excited to see Celeste and Brian because it had been several months since she'd seen them.

With the party underway, all the classic Christmas songs played softly in the background. Some of the residents' grandchildren hopped up on the stage lined with gorgeous scarlet red poinsettia plants and danced around. Arnie passed out candy canes to them, wishing Vick would settle down and give him some grandkids. Some adults played holiday themed games Norma had organized.

With the Christmas celebration in full swing, Celeste and Brian arrived. Celeste, wearing a beautiful silver sparkly dress, felt thankful Brian tucked his shirt in for the party. "Hello you two!" Maybel greeted them and hurried to give hugs.

"This is for you," Celeste said, handing Maybel an elegantly wrapped gift. Opening it revealed a Sherlock Holmes style detective cap.

Maybel laughed at her new holiday treasure. "Oh, just what I wanted!"

"We decided you earned it," Brian said with an impish grin.

Celeste also handed Maybel a gift bag full of catnip and a few cat toys. "And this is for Mr. Piddles."

"Oh, he's going to love this!" Maybel smiled.

"I'm going to go get us some eggnog," Brian said, excusing himself after kissing Celeste on the cheek.

Once he was no longer in earshot, Maybel turned to Celeste and said, "You know what kind of bed he has, don't you?! I can tell something is different between the two of you. Your body language is different."

Celeste blushed, and looking down, she nodded. "I think I'm in love." She held out her left hand, showing Maybel the engagement ring Brian gave her. "It surprised me because early on he said he never wanted to get married again, but I guess he changed his mind."

"You changed his mind, dear," Maybel said, still smiling.

"He found my kryptonite," Celeste said. "He just kept sweet talking me into all of this, and I was powerless to his words. But he doesn't know that I know what his kryptonite is, and I just may have to use it on him someday." A sly smile snuck across her face.

"Are you two ever going to stop with this intellectual competition?" Maybel wondered.

"Yes," Celeste said. "When I win."

"It seems as though you already have. How is everything going with Brian's work?"

"Not good. They temporarily suspended him for not following procedure on a case, but he says it's a bunch of bull. He thinks someone set him up." Celeste lowered her voice to a whisper, "Remember how I told you someone on the force has it in for him?"

Maybel nodded, looking concerned.

"Well, after he the suspension, someone left a threatening note on his car."

"Oh, good heavens! That is very worrisome."

"Then someone left a threatening note on my car."

Maybel's eyes popped out. "Oh, dear!"

"Brian suggested he move in with me so he can protect me. Also, it saves him money since during his six-month suspension without pay. But he'll be back at work soon. His suspension is up next month. He's going to really need to watch his back."

Maybel wondered, "What has he been doing with his time off?"

"Surfing and he's done some handyman type work around my place," Celeste replied.

Maybel teased, "Is that what the young kids call it these days?"

Celeste giggled. "No, for real. He redid the staircase that leads up to the loft and put new tiles in the shower. He's also been researching what it would take for him to become a private detective."

"Oh, that's interesting! Maybe you two could go into business together. I can be one of your consultants." Maybel grinned.

"Only if you wear your Sherlock Holmes cap, but all joking aside, Brian said he's really enjoyed his time off. He's been able to relax for once without the stress of his job. And we're spending more time together. We even took a brief trip down the coast and stayed at a quaint little bed-and-breakfast."

"So, when is the wedding?"

"We're planning on getting married next year in 2020," Celeste replied.

"This is so exciting! Come on! Let's go tell Norma and Vera," Maybel said, guiding Celeste towards where the other ladies were.

"Congratulations!" Norma examined the ring on Celeste's finger. "This is lovely. Is it an antique ring?"

Celeste nodded. "Brian got it for me at the Velvet Sapphire. He knows that's my favorite store."

"That's a lovely ring, sweetie," Vera said, looking over Norma's shoulder.

"Ho, ho, ho!" Arnie sang out, approaching the ladies. They heard the pitter patter of his shiny black patent leather shoes walking up behind them. "Oh, I see you've been a very good girl," he said, looking at Celeste's ring.

"Or a very naughty girl," Brian said, handing her a cup of eggnog.

"Oh, stop!" Celeste scolded Brian and took the paper cup from him, feeling her cheeks flush.

He placed his arm around her and said, "We're gonna elope and go to Vegas and get married next year."

Maybel snapped, "Don't you dare! I have to attend this wedding."

"Wedding? Who's getting married?" Jeffrey asked, approaching the group wearing his most ugly Christmas sweater that had a big red pom pom ball for Rudolph's nose.

Celeste showed him her ring, to which he said, "Congratulations! Just whatever you do, don't get married on a boat."

"No way," Celeste said. "Veronica and Tom are getting married next year, too."

"Sounds like 2020 is going to be a great year!" Jeffrey said. "Unless something goes wrong…"

"What could possibly go wrong?" Maybel asked.

"Oh, don't be silly," Vera said. "Now, if you'll excuse me. It's time for TT and me to play Jingle Bells."

Everyone gathered around as Anthony Trutelli and Vera played a few Christmas carols. Vera looked smart in her forest green and burgundy plaid blazer with a poinsettia broach pinned to the lapel. Her piano playing accompanied Anthony's trumpet quite nicely. Celeste smiled as she watched, and when they played '*Oh Come, All Ye Faithful*', she got teary-eyed. She looked over at the manger scene they'd set up at the corner of the stage, and the joy of Christmas washed over her.

Brian whispered in her ear, "I know it's not Christmas yet, but I have a gift for you. I'm going to go out to the car and get it. I'll be right back."

Celeste, enjoying the party and munching on a snowball cookie, looked on as Maybel and Arnie interacted. He pulled something out of his Santa bag and handed it to her. When she unwrapped it, she discovered a lump of coal. Laughing, she playfully swatted at Arnie, and he hugged her. Celeste walked over to them and asked, "What's so funny, you two?"

"Oh, Arnie thought he'd give me a lump of coal this year. He thinks he's so funny."

"You were a bad girl this year," Arnie went on, "Let's see… you broke into at least two different resident's apartments, refused to listen to Colleen when she urged you not to interfere with police business, and you lied to Sheila by faking a doctor's appointment."

"You're one to talk. You faked a back injury!" Maybel replied, laughing.

"Touché," he said.

"Well, fella, I will admit you did a swell job of helping me distract her."

Arnie straightened out his beard. "Thank God you came over to my place to help me out of that mess!"

Celeste's eyes lit up, and she looked at Maybel, whispering, "You know what kind of bed he has, don't you?"

Maybel blushed. "Well, yes, but not because I was *in* it! Arnie and I have an agreement. He knows George was my one and only, but we're friends now."

"I'm glad to hear it. This is good for your personal development," Celeste said. "It looks like you're really fitting in here."

"It's not my first home, and it won't be my last home. My real home will be with my Father in heaven, but until then, this will do just fine."

Celeste smiled. "Arnie gave you a lump of coal, but what did you get him?"

"I knitted him some covers for his golf clubs. I used a bunch of garish colors, and he loved them. I was going to get him a ball warmer, but I found out he already had one."

"His balls get cold?"

Maybel laughed. "No, because he has a ball warmer for his golf balls."

"What happens if he hits a cold ball? I mean, why do his balls need to be warmed?"

"I guess a warm ball flies further and has more spin than a cold one. He can use all the help he can get."

"Oh, I see. What are you doing Christmas day?"

"Jeffrey invited me to his place, and he's cooking a prime rib! Oh! Before I forget. I have a gift for you, too," Maybel said, looking under the cookie table. She pulled back the low hanging cloth and grabbed a gift bag. Handing it to Celeste, she smiled and said, "I hope you like it."

Celeste took out the tissue paper from the bag and saw something green at the bottom of the bag. She reached it and felt it.

"I used my best Kelly-green chenille yarn to knit it," Maybel explained.

Celeste admired the beautiful sweater Maybel knit for her, holding it up to herself. "I love it! You really outdid yourself! Look at the stitching. It's exquisite."

"It has a V-neck. I thought that would be flattering to you. There's something else in the bag."

Celeste looked in it and pulled out a long, skinny jewelry box. Opening it, she exclaimed, "Oh, Maybel! You didn't! These are the pearls George gave you."

"Yes, they are… and I want you to have them. You know you're like the daughter I never had."

"Maybel, really, I shouldn't accept this. It's too generous."

"What am I going to do? Give them to Jeffrey?" Maybel chuckled. "Dear, you mean the world to me. One thing I love the most about our relationship is the pearls of wisdom we share with each other. So, I'm sharing my pearls with you. They will look beautiful on you! Besides, I never go anywhere anymore. Where am I going to wear them to?"

Teary-eyed, Celeste hugged Maybel. "Thank you! I'll wear them on Christmas with my new green sweater. Brian and I are going to cook a nice dinner and stay home for the holidays. Did you hear about that virus going around? We thought we'd play it safe and just lie low," Celeste said.

"I heard my name," Brian said, returning with his gift for Celeste. "Here, this is for you."

Celeste looked into the gift bag and found a set of oil paints and some small canvases. She looked at Brian. He said, "I know you like to draw, and you're so artistic. I thought maybe you'd like to start painting."

"How sweet!" Maybel said.

"I love art therapy," Arnie added. "There's something very soul satisfying about creating a work of art."

Brian went on, "When I shopped at the bookstore the other day, I saw these books called *Rent to Kill* and *A Harbor of Resentment*. The covers were hand painted instead of all those computer graphics and stock photos everyone uses."

Maybel remembered, "Oh, that's like how they made the original *Nancy Drew* and *Hardy Boys* book covers."

Celeste asked, "But who would buy a book with a hand painted cover design now? That would look like art and not a book cover. That's sort of old-fashioned, don't you think?"

"You never know what the future holds, baby!" Brian smiled, grinning from ear to ear.

To find out what's next for Celeste, Brian and the mayor, check out the 4ᵗʰ book in the Celeste Ravenna Mystery series titled:

PANDEMIC ALLEY

About the Author

Drew Dunmoore is a California native and enjoys visiting local amusement parks. Drew has worked in the financial services industry for twenty years but has been obsessed with murder mysteries for more than thirty years. This is Drew's fourth book, and God willing, there will be many more to come.

To find out more about the Celeste Ravenna Mystery Series, or to contact Drew, check out the following:

Follow Drew on Instagram: @drewdunmoore
www.dunmooredisports.com

Readers can reach Drew at ddunmoore@gmail.com

www.ingramcontent.com/pod-product-compliance
Lightning Source LLC
Chambersburg PA
CBHW051311300726
48976CB00002B/360